D0641020

The Gulf Scenario

Also by Richard Bulliet

The Tomb of the Twelfth Imam
Kicked to Death by a Camel

The Gulf Scenario

Richard Bulliet

A
Joan
Kahn
BOOK

St. Martin's Press
New York

THE GULF SCENARIO. Copyright © 1984 by Richard Bulliet. All rights reserved. Printed in the United States of America. No part of this book may be used or reproduced in any manner whatsoever without written permission except in the case of brief quotations embodied in critical articles or reviews. For information, address St. Martin's Press, 175 Fifth Avenue, New York, N.Y. 10010.

Copy editor: Leslie Sharpe

Library of Congress Cataloging in Publication Data

Bulliet, Richard W.
  The Gulf scenario.

  "A Joan Kahn book."
  I. Title.
PS3552.U44G8 1983   813'.54   83-13874
ISBN 0-312-35323-5

10 9 8 7 6 5 4 3 2

For my sister Nina

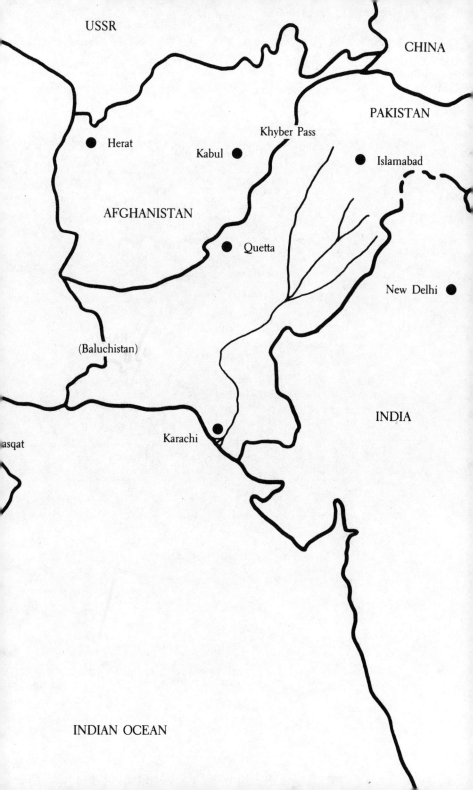

The Gulf
Scenario

1
ISLAMABAD:
THE THIRD WEEK IN JANUARY

Darkness had come to Pakistan's capital. In an austere private study poorly sealed against winter drafts, two men finished listening to the live broadcast over Voice of America of the new American president's inaugural address. Lieutenant General Mohammed Baber, Pakistan's third consecutive unelected president, leaned forward and turned off the radio. He was a round-faced, meticulously groomed man whose every white hair was perfectly aligned on his head and cut to precise length in his toothbrush mustache.

Pakistan's immediately preceding presidents had been generals as well. They had also been men of political ambition. Already in retirement at the time of his elevation, General Baber had not sought the office. The office had sought him. Unable to agree upon which of their number to honor with the country's highest office, the senior military commanders had settled upon their retired colleague partly because they perceived him to have no higher aspirations or concrete political views. He had never divulged to anyone his secret vision of Pakistan's future.

"Faiz, we are going to make Pakistan great. Praise be to God."

"Praise be to God," echoed the uniformed officer sharing the solitude of the general's study.

Brigadier Faiz was the brother of the general's wife, a fellow Punjabi, and the most highly decorated officer in Pakistan's army. Younger than General Baber by ten years, Faiz, too, was seeing new duty after retirement. On the general's instructions, he had left Pakistan's army to take the position of deputy chief of staff of the tiny army of the United Arab Emirates in the Persian Gulf. His nominal superior was an Arab from the ruling family of Ra's al-Khaima, one of the four oil-poor ministates in the seven-member confederation, but the one that supplied most of the native-born manpower in an army largely comprised of foreigners. For all practical purposes, Brigadier Faiz wielded the powers of a supreme commander—except that his entire force was far weaker than even one brigade of the highly trained army he had devoted his career to.

General Baber scrutinized the long, waxed mustaches and heavily lined, leathery face of his brother-in-law and saw there nothing but loyalty and devotion to duty. "You will be only the fourth person in the entire world to hear the details of this plan. I have named it 'Operation Tanzim.' In English you would say 'Operation Reordering.'" The general always spoke English with members of his family. Despite his ferocious Pakistani patriotism, he regarded the language of his country's former imperial masters as the superior tongue of civilized discourse. "We are going to create a new world order, a new *nizam*, and we begin tomorrow."

The brigadier's dour expression showed no change.

"In America, Faiz, the first hundred days of a president's term are considered a period of honeymoon when mistakes are made and lessons are learned. We shall take advantage of this. Our target date is the end of Ramadan. When all Muslims are celebrating the end of our month of fasting, we shall present them with a special gift, Operation Tanzim. We have one hundred and thirty-five days to prepare before June the fifth."

In his own inaugural address the year before, General Baber had not spoken of national renewal, as his American counterpart just had, nor of the grim problems facing his poor and overpopulated country, locked between a hostile India to the east and a dangerous Russian army occupying Afghanistan to the west. He had spoken rather of greatness, the greatness of Islam, the greatness of the role Pakistan was destined to play in reviving the power of the faith. He was privately pleased, though not surprised, to find that the few foreign journalists who commented on the speech compared his breadth of vision to that of de Gaulle. But the vast distance between the stark reality of Pakistan's poverty and the general's evocation of greatness had struck domestic commentators differently. The speech had not been a political success. But General Baber was above politics.

"We are a poor country, Faiz, but greatness is our destiny. We alone have been ordained to lead the Muslim world; it is in our power to do so. Our army is the largest and the finest; our people are warriors; we have been tested in battle. We are ready. But we must look beyond our petty wars with India. Through Operation Tanzim, my dear Faiz, we shall gain, in one single stroke, planned in the utmost secrecy, total control of the oil wealth of the Gulf, the wealth that God has bestowed on the lands of Islam for the good of all Muslims, and not just for a few decadent Arab families to enjoy. That oil is ours. We shall take it. And you, Faiz, shall command Operation Tanzim."

The brigadier finally spoke. "I am the fourth to know this plan. Who are the others?"

"The three who devised it. I am one. A brilliant American strategist is another. And I will let you try to guess what country the third is from."

2
CAMBRIDGE:
THE FIRST WEEK IN FEBRUARY

Deep chill had set in again after a late January thaw. The Charles River was once more frozen, but irregular plates of jammed ice marred its snowy surface. High overhead at three AM a bright winter moon transformed the icy crags into a miniature mountain range with deeply shadowed canyons and broad, smooth glaciers. It was a transformation that came easily to the mind of the man seated in frozen solitude next to his attaché case on a park bench, gazing at the river. Carl Webster's mind was accustomed to transforming things, to reducing great and complex matters to small, understandable proportions. In recent months only two problems had defied its analytical powers: his wife Roseanne and a nagging flaw in GULFSCENE III.

Behind Webster's back, beyond deserted Memorial Drive, loomed the dark mass of Eliot House, its Harvard civility conveyed by the Georgian silhouette of its roofline while the industry of its undergraduate occupants was revealed by the occasional study window still illumined at that early-morning hour. Further behind him, exactly a mile and a quarter away along a line drawn from the park bench through the middle of the Eliot House facade, another lit window marked Carl Webster's bedroom, where his wife murmured sleepily to her lover over the telephone.

Carl thought about ruling the world. He thought about his immigrant father and uncle. He thought about the cold. He thought again about ruling the world. He thought about his wife.

Carl could fathom his wife's desire to take a lover. He realized that as he had become ever more solidly immured in his work over the previous year, he had become as unreachable as a man in prison. Roseanne Webster—lean, taut, and striking looking at age thirty-eight—logically would turn elsewhere for affection and have no trouble attracting a roving and appreciative faculty eye either at Harvard or MIT. Carl Webster came close to worshiping logical thought processes, as close as he came to worshiping anything, and he could respect Roseanne's acting in accordance with them as he might the devotions of a pious friend.

What he could not understand was her openness, in fact, her delight, in telling him she was having an affair and then her refusal to tell him who her lover was. It displayed a taunting contrariness, a meanness of spirit, that was unlike her; he had always known her to be considerate and even warm beneath her hard exterior. He considered for the hundredth time the possibility that she might be having an affair with one of his close colleagues and that her attitude was a reflection of her lover's opinion of him, but none of the men he worked with in the Harvard-MIT Strategic Research Group, the HMSRG, were up to Roseanne's standards.

He sighed, looked out at the river, and thought about ruling the world. It had been two weeks since he first began sitting alone by the river whenever the night was crisp and cold. He reminded himself of a computer that had to be kept in an air-conditioned room in order to prevent malfunction. He took off a glove and pressed the tiny light button on his digital watch. It was seven minutes after three on the morning of the fourteenth day after the presidential inauguration. It was time to go home. The flaw in GULFSCENE III would have to await another night's contemplation, but its resolution could not be put off indefinitely. He must solve it within four months or die, for disaster loomed in the first week of June.

As usual he had a choice of walking toward Anderson Bridge

and then up through Harvard Square or toward Weekes Bridge
and then up Plimpton Street to Harvard Yard. The time it took
to reach his apartment was the same either way. Tonight he
chose the path toward Weekes Bridge, the one on which he
could see the dark outlines of two men strolling along the river-
bank. As he passed from the circle of streetlight illumining his
customary bench, Carl too became a dark, unidentifiable silhouette. Presently his shape met and fused with the other two.
It did not separate again. Carl Webster had disappeared.

Roseanne Webster had glossy black hair pulled back tightly in
a bun from her fine-boned face. Her glasses were dramatically
oversized with black plastic rims, her skin delicate and pale,
with hollows in the cheeks and a hint of fine creases at the
corners of the eyes. She wore a high-necked black dress with
white trim and sat on a plain couch covered with very expensive
white fabric to receive her police interviewer.

Her interrogator was dressed in the kind of tasteless, func-
tional clothing that decades of movies and television series had
taught people to expect of policemen. Pete Grandeville liked to
dress that way. It made people feel at ease around him because
they could either identify with him as another poor working
stiff, stereotype him as a TV cop, or look down on him as an
unsophisticated clod. Any way they liked was okay with Pete as
long as they answered his questions.

Pete Grandeville was fussy about his name, which he pronounced with the emphasis on the last syllable—"veal"—but
he was not above thinking the way cops were supposed to think.
Right now he was looking at a haughty-looking, expensive
woman with superb legs and thinking what a kick it would be to
cause the ice to melt. But that would be after he had cracked
the case wide open, of course, and shown her that there was at
least one French Canadian from North Cambridge who had a
touch of class and a Harvard-caliber brain.

Unfortunately, the case at hand did not support his fantasy very well. Carl Webster had only disappeared; so what Pete was supposed to do was get the husband back, which ran counter to the idea of consoling the grieving widow after apprehending her husband's killer. Perhaps the situation would improve and Webster would turn out to be dead after all. You never could tell. He hadn't been heard from at home or at work for two days, and the routine check of hospitals and morgues had drawn a blank.

"What I need, Mrs. Webster," said the short, swarthy detective, "are the names of people who might be able to tell me what your husband was doing before he disappeared and what sort of mood he was in."

"Then you must speak to his colleagues in the Strategic Research Group."

"Of course. I've already made arrangements to go over there. What I had in mind were other people—friends, social acquaintances, people he saw outside of work."

"My husband didn't see anyone outside of work."

Grandeville noted both the finality of the statement and the past tense. The elegant wife seemed well on the way to thinking herself a widow, and the thought didn't seem to be bothering her a bit.

"Carl was completely absorbed in his work with the Group. If he saw anyone else regularly, I didn't know about it; and it would be unlike him to conceal something. He was a very open man in some ways."

"But not all ways?"

"Not all ways." Roseanne Webster removed a speck of lint from the oval glass top of the coffee table. Her fingernail polish looked fresh.

"You told me that your husband went out at one-thirty in the morning and didn't come home, and that he normally would have been home by three-thirty. Was this every night?"

"Only during good weather and only for the last two weeks. We had two nights last week when it snowed. Those nights he stayed home."

"And while he was out he just sat on a park bench and thought? In the cold?"

"That's what he told me. I have no reason to disbelieve him. I told you which bench it was, the one under the streetlight midway between the bridges."

Grandeville looked at the piece of lined yellow paper on his clipboard. "Yes, I have that down." He tried a bit of dark, curly French magnetism and looked her directly in the eye. "Could he have been visiting another woman on these nights out?"

The iceberg floated serenely past. "No. He would have told me. He wasn't interested."

"What about any fights with you or with these colleagues of his who you say were his only human contacts?"

"No fights. Carl was very easy to get along with as long as you didn't mind being ignored and accepted the fact that he was a strategic genius."

"Did you mind being ignored?"

"Yes."

"Did you do anything about it?"

"Nothing that concerns my husband's disappearance."

"No, I don't suppose Roseanne does know exactly what Carl does for us," said Professor Morris Gratz in response to the Cambridge police detective's question. In late middle age but still trying to look too young and boyish for his role as director of the prestigious Harvard-MIT Strategic Research Group, Gratz tossed papers and books hectically about his desk in a mock-frenzied search for matches to light his cigarette. "Carl is a brilliant strategist and an uncanny games player. He has a remarkable knack for seeing things differently from other people and then being able to convince them of the logic of his point of view. From the Group's standpoint, this makes him extremely valuable as a scenario writer."

Grandeville waited for the sallow, young-old political scientist to continue and then decided he needed prompting. "In my vocabulary a scenario is a movie script or an educated guess about what might happen in the future."

"The latter. We're not in the movie business. More specifically, the Strategic Research Group conducts crisis simulation games as one of its primary activities. The crisis is a hypothetical future occurrence. Players impersonating government officials and so on respond to the crisis. Then we study the response and reach conclusions as to the capacity of the government or the military to respond to crises of that sort."

"Like civilian war games?"

"Exactly. More sophisticated in some respects because all sorts of political and diplomatic variables are involved, but essentially we simulate a real crisis in the same way wars are simulated at advanced levels of military officer training."

"And Carl Webster's role in this is what?"

"He writes scenarios, as I told you. He's not the only one, but he's our best. No one is supposed to know until the game begins just what sort of crisis they will be confronting, even though they may have a general idea. It's like the real world in that respect. The problem is that most strategists think along predictable lines, and you can guess in most cases what is going to be coming up next. Carl Webster always comes up with the unexpected. That's his genius."

Grandeville saw the dark cloud of a lecture on crisis-simulation games forming on the horizon and moved to dissipate it. "Thank you, Professor Gratz, I think I get the picture just fine. Now let's get to why Carl Webster might have disappeared and where he might be. Has he had any friction with members of the group here that you know of?"

"No. Carl never has friction with anyone. Quite frankly, he

doesn't even come around here that often. This house we're in is very nicely painted on the outside to look colonial, and it's been redesigned on the inside to look ultramodern; but as you have no doubt noticed, it's really a very small building. It's one of those old places Harvard buys, decorates nicely and holds on to until it decides to put up some monstrous new building, then bulldozes into kindling in half an hour. But I know you want to stick to the point. The point is that Carl shares an office with two other people when he's around, but he usually works at home or in the library or wherever he happens to be. He carries his work around with him in an attaché case."

"Then you haven't seen much of him lately?"

"No. In fact, very little."

"What does his disappearance do to your activities? How long can you do without him?"

Gratz fiddled uncomfortably with a silver letter opener he had unearthed from beneath the disordered clumps of paper on his desk. "That's quite hard to say. I don't know precisely what he was working on. Of course, in a way, I'm not supposed to. But I'm more in the dark than usual."

Grandeville sensed that the reason for this lapse of knowledge was something that the professor did not want to talk about. "Is there anyone who would know more specifically what he was doing?"

"You could try his office mates," replied Gratz vaguely as he tracked his eyes over an empty expanse of mustard-colored wall. "Selma Dorfman and Ted Bonny. Neither of them is in today."

The names were duly noted on the yellow pad. "Fine. Now, one last thing, and then I'll get out of your hair. I'm sure you've seen enough TV for me to cover this in one question. Do you know or have any reason to suspect that Webster's disappearance might be connected with drug use, homosexual activity, involvement with a woman, excessive gambling, mental breakdown, personal vendetta"—Gratz's head shook steadily and slowly as the list proceeded—"loansharking, criminal activity past or present, or depression leading to suicide?"

"No."

"I didn't think so. It's never that easy with people everybody describes as normal. If any of those things was obviously indicated, they wouldn't seem normal, would they. Well, I'll be back. Let me know if you think of anything helpful." The professor showed no inclination to see the policeman out, but Grandeville was accustomed to slight snubs from the Cambridge academics he was employed to protect. At the door he gave his best dramatic pause and looked back to ask, "Any idea why Webster would have taken to sitting by the river in the middle of the night over the last couple of weeks?"

Gratz's expression conveyed no particular emotion. "I've always been under the impression he doesn't like cold weather."

"So his wife says. So long. Thanks for your time." Grandeville let himself out through the shiny white office door and then through the ornamental Victorian front door that opened onto Bow Street.

The walk to Weld Hall—a hulking late nineteenth-century brick dormitory in Harvard Yard in the basement of which the campus police had their headquarters—was short. But Pete Grandeville was in no rush. He loathed talking to Tom O'Malley and willingly put it off as long as possible, in this instance until it became a more attractive alternative than surveying the colorless array of obscure German novels and French neo-Marxist tomes in the window of Schoenhoff's bookstore. Pete considered himself an intellectual diamond in the rough and fancied he could hold his own in conversation with the Cambridge intelligentsia, but sometimes he became distinctly aware that he was at best a medium-quality industrial diamond.

This still put him a long jump ahead of Tom O'Malley, though. The two men had gone through Cambridge High School together, perpetually at odds over everything from girlfriends to what constituted fair play in street hockey. Never far from the surface had been the long-standing North Cambridge animosity between Irish Catholic and French Canadian, and neither man was inclined by nature to try to rise above it. It sometimes irritated Pete that his beefy Irish nemesis, who had never advanced the least claim to erudition, and only the slightest to basic literacy, was with the university police force while his own career had been with the less highly regarded—in Harvard circles—Cambridge city police. At other times he remembered that he had both better pay and more interesting work.

"How are ya, Frenchie!" bellowed O'Malley in a brassy voice as soon as the stocky detective appeared in the doorway. "Come on in. What's your business?"

"Carl Webster. What have you got?"

"I got nothin'. What you got?"

"Harvard University is not a separate state, Tom, and you are not the head of the state police. We work together, we get things done. Okay? Then we don't bother each other so much. Now, what have you got?"

"What happens on university property is the business of the President and Fellows, not of the city council," responded O'Malley with continued belligerence.

"His wife says he was by the river last she knew. That's not university property."

"Yeah, but that's under the Metropolitan District Commission park police. Have you talked to them about horning in?"

"Holy Mother of God!"

"I knew you was gonna say that. You always say that." The Harvard cop lifted his defensive-tackle bulk from his black wooden armchair with the Harvard seal and came around the desk to clap a massive forearm around Grandeville's shoulder. "I'm gonna give you a break, Frenchie. I'm not gonna cause you no trouble for a change. But this doesn't mean I'm necessarily gonna be a nice guy the next time you guys come here demanding a dope bust because of some flower pot you see in some dumb-ass freshman's windowbox."

"Don't do me no favors. Just tell me what you got on Webster."

O'Malley returned to the desk and squared up a few sheets of paper with sausage fingers. His voice droned bureaucratically. "Dr. Carl Webster, BA 1964, PhD 1968, five foot ten, hundred and eighty pounds, blond hair in a crewcut, no scars, slight limp from a poorly healed Achilles tendon. Didn't you have one of them once after the Somerville game our junior year? You was too small to play football."

"And you were too dumb. If the guy had done his exercises right, his foot would have been okay. He sounds soft and lazy like—"

"—a Harvard cop. Very funny. You've said it before." O'Malley continued to read. "There's nothin' here of any special interest. Nothin' from the health service except the foot. He's here as a senior research associate so he doesn't have any teaching or administrative duties. Pays his faculty club bill. There's a note here saying his name used to be Kovacs; I don't know how that got here."

"You're not helping me, Tom. What have you got that's interesting?"

"You begging me?" The big man's eyes gleamed. "Okay, I got three things. First, the guy who covers Weekes Bridge to ask the muggers for their ID cards says that three men crossed toward the Business School a little bit after three AM the night Webster disappeared. One man looked drunk and was being helped. He looked like he limped, too. At least, that's what Rodney said after he found out Webster had a limp. Second, a senior in Eliot House saw two guys meet a third guy on the path by the river right around three o'clock. He thought they were robbing the guy and was going to call the cops, but then the three went away together."

"Was the one guy being forced to go along?"

"The senior don't know. Even with the leaves gone you can't see too much through those sycamores along the Drive. Third, I had a visit yesterday from Dr. Theodore Bonny of the HMSRG."

"That's Webster's office mate. Why did he come in here? Did you call him in?"

"No, I never heard of him. Maybe he's just a good citizen. Who knows?"

"What did Bonny say?"

"He wanted that if we should run across some papers called GULFSCENE III, like in a briefcase, while we're looking for Webster, we should give 'em to him because they're his."

"He thought you were looking for Webster?"

"Yeah."

"Are you?"

"No. That's your job."

"Did you tell Dr. Bonny that?"

"Yeah. Then he said again how important the papers were. I think he wanted to get me interested in finding Webster."

"So are you interested in finding Webster?"

"No. That's still your job. If Webster wants to disappear, God bless him."

When Grandeville finally tracked Theodore Bonny to his den, an unmarked rathole office barely large enough for a desk and bookcase in one of the great gray MIT engineering buildings, he was met by a well-prepared recitation of all matters germane to Carl Webster's disappearance—at least in the opinion of Ted Bonny. The scrawny bald man began speaking with crisp precision as soon as Pete introduced himself and sat down on an almost invisible visitor's chair crammed between the tidy desk and a dirt-streaked window.

"You will be wanting to know everything I can tell you about Carl Webster's disappearance." He didn't wait for Pete's nodded assent. "I last saw Carl shortly after lunch five days ago in our office on Bow Street. We spoke for five minutes about GULF-SCENE III. He did not seem unusually depressed or emo-tionally disturbed. On the night he was last seen, two days ago, I was at home with my wife. I know of no reason for him to commit suicide or cause himself to disappear. I know of no enemies or personal embarrassments that would explain murder or kidnapping. He is always agreeable when he is with me. We talk about work." Grandeville had no difficulty believing the last remark. "His working relations with colleagues are good, but he has had disagreements over GULFSCENE III with Professor Gratz. If you speak to Dr. Dorfman, you will find that she does not like him. I have never asked her why and cannot speculate. It is important to me that I receive back the papers that he carries in his briefcase. They are the property of the Group, and they may contain classified information that should not be seen by people without clearance."

"What kind of clearance?"

"Top secret. Our work is with national security, so we all must have access to such materials."

"Webster was using classified materials for GULFSCENE III?"

Bonny paused. "I don't know. He could have been. That is all I am saying."

"But you have no particular reason to believe that he was."

Bonny's silence was an answer.

"Didn't you tell Lieutenant O'Malley of the Harvard police that the GULFSCENE III papers were yours? Now you say they belong to the Group."

"Lieutenant O'Malley was not being attentive. I spoke to him on behalf of the Group."

"At Professor Gratz's suggestion?"

"I know more about the importance of the papers than Dr. Gratz. I felt I should act promptly to keep the papers from being read by unauthorized parties."

Grandeville got the sudden feeling that he didn't want to talk to Dr. Bonny any longer. But there would be other days.

The remaining name on the list of interview subjects was Dr. Selma Dorfman, who turned out to be a cheery, round-cheeked, thirtyish person, running to overweight in a splendidly buxom fashion, and wearing her blond hair in an unsuccessful attempt at a lion's mane. Grandeville found her at home in a triple-decker frame house on Shepard Street, but she insisted that they hold their talk over coffee and unneeded cheesecake in a nearby restaurant on Massachusetts Avenue.

Since Pete had not been expecting to leave the tense intellectual environment of Harvard all day, he was delighted to encounter someone who was both relaxed and willing to tell him interesting things. And it was still only three in the afternoon. After running through his opening set of questions, he started back over the names of those he had already checked off on his clipboard.

"Dr. Dorfman, how would you characterize Carl Webster's relationship with your office mate, Dr. Bonny?"

"Asymmetrical. Carl ignored Ted; Ted envied Carl. You will want to know what I mean by envy. Carl was brilliant, at least in the sense of having a knack for seeing things differently. Ted is extremely good with numbers and computers, but he has never had an original idea in his life. He envied that quality in Carl."

"How much?"

Dr. Dorfman savored her last bit of cheesecake and considered the question. "Three good ideas are enough to make a successful academic career: one for the PhD thesis, a good second one to get tenure on, and a third to prove you aren't a flash in the pan and qualify you as a sanctified elder. I can think offhand of six ideas of that order of magnitude that Carl has come up with over the last three years. Ted is still working on his first. He borrowed one from his professor for his doctoral thesis, and he would have given anything to be able to borrow a second one from Carl."

"So why didn't he?"

"Because with Carl you never knew what he was thinking until he finished with it. He kept all of his papers at home or with him in an attaché case."

"Why did he do that?"

"He thought his ideas were being stolen."

"Were they? Or was he just suspicious?"

"They probably were. It's hard to prove, you know."

Grandeville felt there was something missing from the picture being presented, but he couldn't put his finger on it.

"What about Professor Gratz? Did he and Webster get on well?"

"Very well. Up until GULFSCENE III." Dorfman grinned engagingly. "Now you ask me about GULFSCENE III and I tell you. Okay?"

"Sounds good."

"If you got the introduction for tourists from Gratz, you have some idea what a scenario is and what crisis-simulation gaming is all about." Grandeville nodded. "Okay. Carl's current interest is in oil supplies in the Persian Gulf—or Arab Gulf, take your pick. He wrote GULFSCENE I, which simulated a Soviet military attack on the oilfields. It played in real time—"

"Real time?"

"It went at the same rate that real events would go. No

skipped time; no shortened time. Forget it. It doesn't make any difference."

"How did it come out?"

"U.S. military forces were still too weak after years of Reagan's upgrading to hold off the Russians, so there was an all-out nuclear exchange after seventy-two hours. In other words, we were all blown up. It's interesting work, as you can see. Now for GULFSCENE II. This envisioned an attack on the oilfields by regional forces, in this case Israelis with Kurdish and Iranian collaborators. Its outcome was less satisfactory from an analytical point of view, but it was a beautifully logical and convincing scenario."

"Was the world blown up?"

"Yes and no. Part of it was; part of it wasn't. What you really want to know about is GULFSCENE III, though. This is where Carl and Dr. Gratz parted company. Gratz didn't want Carl to pursue the Gulfscene series any further. Carl insisted and even maintained that the basic idea for a third scenario had been given to him by someone in Washington, but he refused to keep Gratz informed as to the direction his work was headed."

"Why didn't Gratz want him to proceed?"

"Diminishing returns. The object of the series was to measure American strategic responses to challenges to our energy supply. Gratz felt that any further scenario would just be playing games, if you'll pardon the expression, with few new insights likely to emerge."

"So why did Webster continue?"

"He disagreed. He said that the new idea represented a new breakthrough in thinking about the Gulf that prior strategic planners had never taken into account. He insisted that Gratz permit him to develop a game."

"Was Webster's time so valuable that Gratz couldn't let him follow out his ideas?"

"No, but the crisis simulation itself is a big, expensive undertaking. A game of this sort might have fifty people involved, split between the A team, the B team, and the Control team; and it might go on for a week. But more than that, our money sources in Washington don't go in for frivolity. Gratz keeps the bucks rolling in by making us look lean and mean in dollars and cents terms. He's afraid that GULFSCENE III will make the Strategic Research Group look foolish and jeopardize future funding. That's why he's so annoyed that Carl hasn't told him what exactly GULFSCENE III is about. He thinks Carl made up the story about the basic idea coming out of Washington."

"Annoyed isn't a very strong word. How bad were their relations?"

"Annoyed is the right word. I gather Carl threatened at one time to quit if he didn't get to work on GULFSCENE III, but he won the battle months ago, and Gratz has to live with it and defend it against any flak that might arise from Washington. There's no anger or hatred involved, or anything like that."

"What about classified information? Dr. Bonny seems to feel that Webster may have been carrying some around with him."

"It's possible. Nothing's supposed to leave the locked files overnight, but Ted and I have both known of instances when Carl cheated on that rule. His work style almost required it, and he was too valuable to the Group to be held to the rule."

Grandeville looked at his watch and decided to wind up the interview while there was still time to pick up his dry cleaning on the way home. "Perhaps you can tell me something about Dr. Webster's relations with his wife."

"Indeed, I can," replied Dr. Dorfman matter-of-factly. "Carl ignored Roseanne to an intolerable degree. It was his worst fault. In fact, it made it difficult for me to work in a friendly way with Carl. I know Roseanne well, and I always had to suppress my feelings of resentment when I dealt with Carl."

Grandeville recalled Dr. Bonny's remark that Selma Dorfman disliked Webster and decided that her effort at suppression was probably less effective than she thought it was. "Would you believe it possible that Mrs. Webster, or possibly some friend of Mrs. Webster, thought her life would be easier if her husband weren't around?"

Selma Dorfman laughed heartily. "Nothing is more improbable than that Roseanne Webster's lover killed her husband, if that's what you're trying to ask."

"Does she have a lover?"

"You should ask her."

"I did."

"What did she say?"

"My question was indirect. She avoided a direct answer."

3
CAMBRIDGE:
THE SECOND WEEK IN FEBRUARY

Roseanne Webster pulled her arm from under her lover's head and rolled onto her side without waking. It was cold on her bare skin. She pulled the down comforter up over her exposed shoulder and neck. In her dream she was ascending alone in an elevator to a floor in a strange and immense hotel at which she already knew the elevator would not stop. She wasn't worried because she knew that she could find the correct elevator when she reached the floor at which the elevator actually would stop by passing to the hotel's other wing along a mazelike hallway. Without passage of time the transit was made, and she was alone in a different elevator. But somehow this one too was wrong. She realized that she was only wearing a slip, a creamy satin one with a lace bodice. She had forgotten her dress someplace. She would have to find her room quickly before people saw her undressed. There was a bad smell. Suddenly she realized that she was not in the right hotel at all and that she would have to walk through a lobby full of people when the elevator finally stopped. The smell was worse. She coughed. There was someone else in the elevator, and she coughed too. It seemed impossible to breathe.

"Hey, Frenchie, wake up!" Pete Grandeville held the telephone away from his ear in order to turn the harsh voice into small, harmless squawking. The digital clock-radio said it was 5:36. Not at all the time to expect a social call from Tom O'Malley. His muzzy morning thought process overlooked the fact that he had never received or hoped to receive a social call from Tom O'Malley. "Ya awake yet, Frenchie?" Pete had incautiously let the receiver drift back toward his ear.

"I'm awake," he said in a low blur.

"Good. Carl Webster's apartment has burnt up, and we got two dead bodies in the bedroom."

"Holy Mother of God!"

"I knew you was gonna say that. You always say that."

"Where're you calling from?" Grandeville was out of bed and scrabbling about for some clothes. When he heard the reply, he dropped the receiver back in place without saying good-bye. Holy Mother of God, he said to himself.

Bitter cold air shocked the last bit of sleep from Pete's system as he pushed open the front door of the North Cambridge frame house he lived in with his mother and clomped onto the porch and down the steps. Signs of dawn were not yet showing in the overcast sky; its dark gray was the same as the sooty snow heaps lining the sidewalks and driveways. Pete slid behind the steering wheel of his Toyota. The seat was cold, the wheel was cold, the engine was cold. He wondered how many people he was waking up as he kept the starting motor whining and groaning in an effort to bring life to the engine.

At last the miracle of internal combustion occurred, and he crunched onto the street, took a right down Rindge Avenue, and another right onto Mass. Ave. He passed a fire truck returning to its garage as he neared the address of Webster's apartment house. Tom O'Malley, even more a giant in parka and fur hat, was waiting for him on the curb.

"What took ya so long?"

"I stopped to have breakfast and read the paper," answered Pete mechanically as he scanned the exterior of the six-story brick building. Either the cold had discouraged gaping tenants from standing in the street, or there had been no general rout from neighboring apartments. The few onlookers were bundled-up and looked disappointed that there was nothing to see but three blackened, empty window frames on the third floor.

"How come you got called here before I did?" Pete wished he had put on boots.

"It's our building. Assistant fire chief called both police forces after he decided the fire had been set. I got a good man on duty who remembers what business we've been looking into recently, and you don't. What can I say? My man called me, and yours didn't."

"What's going on inside?"

"Go look if you want to. You won't find much. The apartment's completely trashed."

"Bodies?"

"Your people already took them. No identification yet. They were burnt pretty bad."

"Webster and his wife?"

"Nope."

"How do you know?"

"Two women." The deep shadows created by the street lights turned the Harvard cop's smile into a leer. "They never got out of bed. Naked, too." Grandville was staring at a pile of black debris lying in the snow where it had been thrown from the windows. "You caught on yet, Frenchie, or should I give you some more time?"

"Why hadn't they gotten out of bed?"

"The chief said the accelerant—some stuff I never heard of—gives off this heavy smoke. He thinks they suffocated before they woke up. The windows were closed. Goddamn well shouldn't have been sleeping naked in this weather. The smoke set off the detector in the corridor so fast that the trucks got here before the fire had got to the rest of the building."

"So why should he wait three days, Tom? Tell me that?"

"What can I tell you? Professors are creeps. Gimpy research

associate ain't got no friends, finds out his wife is so bored she's started making it with another woman, holes up somewhere to think about it for a few days, goes bananas and burns up the wife and the girlfriend."

"Maybe, maybe. I think I'll go home and get some breakfast. It's cold out here. You notice that? The report from arson and identification won't be ready until noon anyway."

Grandeville ducked his small frame back into the Toyota. Through the closed window he heard Tom O'Malley say, "You could thank me for calling you." Pete made a firm but ambiguous gesture with his gloved hand.

Morris Gratz looked with growing horror at the inventory of classified materials missing from the combination-locked file cabinet in Carl Webster's office. Trembling fingers wandered through his thinning hair. The foundations of his world were starting to slip. Leakage of information: a charge that career men in the intelligence community were constantly laying at the door of academic strategists like himself. One unrefuted allegation of poor security could make itself felt in diminished access to government agencies, reductions in financial support, and eventually loss of status in the university.

Gratz had labored hard to build the kind of reputation for being an insider that his ivory tower liberal colleagues in philosophy and biology so vociferously condemned. Every strident charge of being too cozy with the military-industrial complex or the intelligence community warmed a secret inner chamber of his heart. A reputation for being too well connected was one of the tools by which such connections were forged. If the pacifists hated you, the military and intelligence establishments could only conclude that you were their kind of guy. But if one of the people you were responsible for decided to hand secrets around, the open doors could shut so fast that the breeze might blow you out of your job.

By the look of things, Carl Webster's manner of dealing with classified documents threatened to be not just a leak, but an arterial hemorrhage. The seriousness of the wound was still not clear, but it was a grisly mess to look upon. Appraisals of Indian, Pakistani, and Israeli nuclear capabilities; intelligence surveys of clandestine organizations and activities in every oil-soaked country of the Gulf; estimates of force arrays on the southern border of the USSR and in the Indian Ocean—Gratz ticked off a total of eight files that had last been signed for by Webster and were now missing. To be sure, there was nothing that was not legitimately tied to his work on the Gulf, but with Carl himself missing, safe recovery of the files became an urgent necessity.

Gratz punched an intercom button. "Peggy, would you get me Selma right away on the phone? And call Roseanne Webster. Ask her when she'll be home so I can come over for a visit. Don't make it sound official. Just tell her I want to sympathize about Carl. Also, call Ted Bonny and ask him if he can come see me at three this afternoon." He checked his watch. It was twelve-thirty.

On release of the button the refined Bostonian intonation of his secretary crackled back at him. "Mr. Grandeville, the police detective, is here to see you again, Dr. Gratz. Should I wait to call Selma until you're finished?"

The Group director was momentarily petrified. Against all conceivable logic, he was suddenly gripped by the conviction that Washington had somehow already found out about the papers. He forced a deep breath and spoke again into the intercom. "Tell him to come right in, Peggy. Hold the call to Selma."

By the time Pete Grandeville had been cleared into the inner office by Peggy Inman and taken a seat on a bright red plastic stacking chair, Gratz had lit a cigarette, nonchalantly hoisted his feet onto the corner of his desk, and casually slipped the document inventory into its top drawer.

This man is not well, thought Pete. Facial pallor that had not been present two days before had removed all trace of the boyishness that had impressed the detective on his first visit. The ebbing gray perimeter of coarse, curly hair didn't look premature today; its color matched the director's complexion and reinforced the haunted look around his eyes.

"I can save you some of your phone calls," said Pete in a friendly but solemn fashion. To his surprise, the professor's hand began to shake so badly that the ash fell off his cigarette. "Are you feeling all right, Dr. Gratz?"

"What have you found?" asked the director in a croaking voice brimming with resignation.

"Not Carl Webster," answered Pete in an effort to lighten the atmosphere. "You really don't look well. Are you sure you're okay?" Gratz nodded. Pete wondered if he already knew what he was about to tell him. "I have very bad news, but perhaps you've already heard." Gratz returned a dead man's stare. "Selma Dorfman and Roseanne Webster were both killed last night in a fire that burned out the Webster apartment."

"A fire?" Dr. Gratz didn't seem to be grasping the information.

"Yes. Late at night. Theirs was the only apartment affected. Death was by smoke inhalation, but the bodies were only positively identified an hour ago. I came to ask you whom we should contact—what family members." That was only part of Pete's reason for the visit, but the rest could wait until he had time to observe the director's reaction.

"Next of kin," murmured Gratz vaguely. There was a long pause. "Of course, Peggy will have it in the files." He looked like a drowning man floundering about for a life belt. "I don't know what to say. Selma and Roseanne—I—they . . ." His voice trailed off.

"Would you know if Mrs. Webster and Dr. Dorfman were, uh, special friends, Dr. Gratz?" Grandville's tone was studiously neutral.

"Selma?" Gratz was recalling that he was accustomed to rely upon Selma to tell him what Carl was up to when Carl was being uncommunicative. "She may have been good friends with Roseanne. This is so hard to take in—all of a sudden." He was finding composure in talking. "Selma always seemed to know exactly what Carl was doing. I suppose she must have been good friends with them both, now that I think of it."

Grandeville was satisfied that the director was ignorant of any deeper relationship and changed the subject. "I couldn't help hearing you ask your secretary to make an appointment for you to see Mrs. Webster. May I ask what it was you were going to see her about?"

Gratz looked annoyed, which had the pleasing effect of returning some color to his face. "I don't see what business that is of yours."

"The fire department has determined that the fire was deliberately set, Dr. Gratz."

"Set? Arson?" The director again struggled to comprehend an unexpected situation.

"And homicide. We go on the assumption, naturally, that the arsonist knew the women were in the apartment when he set the fire."

"Are you certain that it was just Webster's apartment that was intended?"

"It was the only apartment affected. Flammable liquid was squirted under the door. The entrance lock to the building wasn't forced, and no other tenant buzzed to let someone in at that hour. So the arsonist probably had a key to the building."

"Or Roseanne could have let him in." Gratz was falling in with the detective's train of thought.

"In that case, liquid would most likely have been poured inside the apartment instead of under the door. The firemen found the door locked." He didn't add that the two women had been asleep in bed.

The light of a sudden idea flushed a bit more of the gray from Gratz's cheeks. "Could it have been Carl?" He quickly recalled his words. "No, of course not. Carl is as gentle as a lamb. He could never have done such a ghastly thing."

"We have to consider the possibility that he did do it, however, Dr. Gratz. For that reason I have to tell you that any contact you might have with Carl Webster must be brought to police attention. I'm afraid we're no longer dealing simply with a missing person."

Gratz looked properly sober. "I'll do whatever I can to help, of course, Mr. Grenville." He shifted the accent of Pete's name from the second to the first syllable. "But I can't believe that Carl Webster would do such a thing."

The remainder of the conversation covered what Gratz knew of the personal life of Selma Dorfman, which was little indeed. Throughout the desultory sequence of perfunctory questions and uninformed answers the director's mind was making calculations of the changed circumstances presented by the burning of the apartment. He was fully aware both from Selma Dorfman and from Carl Webster himself that Carl did much of his work and kept most of his papers at home. The question was whether the missing reports had been in the apartment at the time of the fire and whether they were still there either intact or incinerated. He waited for the detective to finish his litany of questions and beg his leave before asking him the crucial question, as if it was an afterthought.

"By the way, Mr. Grenville, how much damage was there to the Webster apartment? You said Roseanne and Selma were killed by smoke. Was there also a great deal of flame?"

"A fair amount—easily flammable stuff like curtains, uphol-

stery, papers, clothes, some furniture. No basic structural damage."

"Desk? File cabinets?"

Pete Grandeville smiled inwardly. So the learned professor
was as interested in the papers that Carl Webster carried around
with him as his subordinate, Dr. Bonny. "If we find anything
labeled GULFSCENE III, I'll let you know. Or anything else
that belongs to your Group. Don't hold your breath waiting,
though. Between the fire and the water, there's an awful lot of
damage."

Outside in the cold, damp air Pete considered the results of
his interview. Three things stood out. First, Gratz knew nothing
about the connection between Selma Dorfman and Roseanne
Webster—and Pete was willing to bet that no one else did, either, given the strong, controlled personalities that both women
had so recently displayed. Second, he was more interested in
Carl Webster's papers than in Webster himself. And third, there
was some unknown factor involved that was causing a good deal
of apprehension. In time, Pete was certain he would find out
what that factor was, but for now it was enough to know that it
was there.

Peggy Inman, Morris Gratz's secretary, was fat, proper, a vo-
racious consumer and retailer of the gossip that titillated her
propriety, and the one person without whom the Strategic Research Group could not carry on its activities. She possessed the
grasp of administrative detail that the director lacked and the
intelligent concern for her fellow human beings that everyone
else connected with the Group seemed to be short on. Her
Episcopalian charity moved her mightily to grieve for the two
dead women as soon as Dr. Gratz informed her of their terrible
end, but it did not blind her to the recollection that Roseanne
Webster had been a cold and distant woman and Selma Dorf-

man an aggressive, bottom-rung academic striving to climb the magic ladder of scholarly preferment at whatever cost. As for Carl Webster, Peggy had always been fond of him, rather in the way she was fond of her cats at home. She still harbored the private conviction that he was just a big, yellow-haired, unaltered male who had gone off on his own for a while but would eventually return, thin and subdued, and never give a hint as to where he had been.

Ted Bonny also reminded her of a cat, a disagreeable neutered Burmese she had once had that hissed and yowled at any other cat intruding on its territory but always ended up slinking away and hiding under the bed. It was very much out of character, in her mind, to hear his normally flat, mechanical voice raised in unmistakable anger filtering through the door of Dr. Gratz's office. She took off her round, silver-rimmed spectacles and concentrated on eavesdropping. She had always considered the practice a legitimate, indeed, a necessary, part of her job; but it was a source of great enjoyment for her as well.

The substance of the shouting, or at least of Theodore Bonny's shouting, since she couldn't hear Gratz's side of the conversation, was that the researcher was unwilling to take the blame for mishandling secret documents. Not even if it was necessary to save the Group's support in Washington. Peggy sympathized, in principle, with his point of view; but she had always been scrupulously loyal to Morris Gratz. If he felt that Ted should take the blame for something—she assumed it had to do with Carl Webster—he was probably right. The Group enjoyed too much respect inside and outside the university to risk putting it in jeopardy.

Inside the office, Gratz was quietly making the same point to an irate Bonny. He was trying to sell the idea that if Bonny would accept responsibility for controlling access to the documents missing from the filing cabinet in his office, any damage stemming from their mishandling, or even their loss, might still be limited. Unfortunately, as far as Gratz was concerned, the diminutive researcher wasn't buying. In fact, the mouse had become very much a lion.

"God damn you, Morrie!" he shouted. "I'll quit before I get you off the goddamn hook. You haven't done anything for years but draw a goddamn salary and show us off to your friends in Washington. Why should I help you now? What have you done for me lately?"

"Now, calm down, Ted. You're exaggerating this whole business. All I'm saying is that it would be nice for it to appear that we had tight control of that file cabinet. There are various ways we can do that, but with Selma gone, you're the only one in the office, so you have to go along with the story."

"I'm not going along with any story, Morrie. This has got to come out just the way it happened."

"Even if the entire Group loses its funding?"

"Maybe we deserve to lose our funding," replied Bonny morosely. Gratz was shocked to the core of his being, but he stoically controlled his expression. Bonny's voice had suddenly gone from gratingly shrill to so quiet that it could barely be heard. "I think Carl's disappearance is more complicated than it looks."

"What's that?"

"I said, I think there's more going on with Carl's disappearance than we've been willing to admit."

"What do you mean by that?" The director's tone was guarded.

Dr. Bonny appeared to contemplate the inner noise of some cerebral calculation before he replied. "Carl asked me if I could make up some one-time-use random number pads for him," he said at length. Gratz looked blank. "He said he was developing a new way of playing chess, and he needed unduplicatable pairs of random number pads. So I had a dozen run up by the computer."

"Cipher pads?"

"He said it was for a game. You know how he was always thinking about games. It didn't occur to me until after he disappeared that they might be used for cipher pads. I was hoping they would turn up somewhere and I could get them back without anyone knowing about it."

"If he's found with them and the missing documents together, it will be assumed that he was spying." Gratz was talking mostly to himself while he looked out the window onto Bow Street. A few flakes of snow were eddying down from the gray sky.

"That's not all, Morrie. I've been telephoning some of the people Carl's been in touch with over GULFSCENE III. They're gone too."

"What do you mean, gone?"

"Well, there's an Indian physicist named Lal Chatterjee who's here as a visiting professor. His department says he left for New Delhi the day before Carl disappeared because of a family emergency. Then there are two Pakistani political scientists who are here as research fellows, Makhdum Khan and Said Mukhtar. They both returned to Pakistan yesterday according to the administrative assistant at the International Studies Center. They had announced their plans to leave a couple of weeks ago. No explanation given."

"Who else?"

"No one so far, but Carl had a lot more informants that I haven't tried to get in touch with yet. It's too bad Selma's gone. She always knew a lot more about Carl's work than I did." There was nothing in his voice to indicate that he would miss his incinerated office mate in any other way.

"Does it all make sense to you, Ted?" asked Gratz hopefully.

"Sense? Not really. It's just that so much is happening at the same time, there has to be some connection. Hasn't there?" The two men's eyes met, found nothing, and wandered on, one pair to the book-lined wall opposite the door and the other to the snow falling past the window.

"I'll have to call Washington," said Gratz finally. He touched the intercom button. "Peggy, get me Lincoln Hoskins in Washington." He looked at Bonny and thought that his colleague looked shrunken and lined in a way he had never seen before. "Will you be in your office here, Ted, or are you going back to MIT?"

Bonny accepted the dismissal and rose to leave. "I'll have to get back. My car's in the lot down there, and I want to get it out before this snow gets bad."

Phone wedged on her shoulder, Peggy Inman eyed him as he passed without a word through the reception room and out into the entrance hall, pulling on his black wool overcoat as he walked. The last minutes of the conversation had escaped her, but she could tell by the stoop of his skinny shoulders that the wind had left his sails. "Professor Morris Gratz calling from Cambridge, will you hold please?" she said officiously into the phone.

"Hello, Link? This is Morrie." Gratz waited for the slight click that told him that Peggy had quit listening in. "I have some distrubing news."

Selma Dorfman's Shepard Street apartment was small and meticulously kept. A simple sitting room with a few pieces of modern wood furniture tucked among an extravagant array of potted plants, a recently redone efficiency kitchen, a bedroom-study combination with a single bed. In the latter room were a large desk and two walls of suspended bookcases filled partially with books and partially with thick sheaves of paper clasped in various types of temporary binders.

Pete Grandeville pulled a few at random from the shelves and leafed through them. They seemed to be unpublished reports on a variety of subjects, but one was filled with computer printout. The detective couldn't put his finger upon just what he had expected to find in the apartment, but nothing suggestive leaped to the eye. The desk and dresser were equally uninformative. Acting upon the recollection of his one conversation with the apartment's dead tenant, he returned to the kitchen alcove and looked in the refrigerator. A third of a ready-made lemon meringue pie lay on the middle shelf. He found a fork and finished it while continuing to look around.

Having satisfied himself after half an hour of unfocused searching that nothing further was to be gained, Grandeville locked the apartment, let himself out of the building and scuffed through the half-inch of rapidly accumulating snow down the street to his parked car. As he drove away past the house, he noticed through the snow a chunky figure standing on the porch. He mused that soon Selma Dorfman's family would be permitted to clear out the tidy apartment, and a new tenant would move in who would obliterate forever the memory of the woman who had once lived there.

Having gotten into the building with comparative ease, it took Peggy Inman several minutes and some chipping of the paint on the wooden door frame to get into Selma's apartment. While not a practiced burglar, she was a woman of infinite resource. She rapidly found what Pete Grandeville had not thought to look for.

Five days after his disappearance from the banks of the Charles River and two days after the death by fire of his wife and his research colleague, Carl Webster was identified through his passport number as a passenger on Pakistan International Airways flight #132 from Montreal to Karachi, with intermediate stops in London, Cairo, and Dubai. The plane had departed Canada less than twenty-four hours after he had last been seen in Cambridge, or more than two days before the fire in his apartment.

The news from Canadian Immigration and Naturalization cast a gloomy shadow on Pete Grandeville's day. He left Cambridge police headquarters for an early lunch, and trudged through the already dirty new snow in Central Square to a bar where he could sit in the dark with a beer and a hamburger and think.

Wasted time and effort were all that came to mind. Carl Webster had left the country, but he had committed no crime, skipped out on no debts, abandoned no children, and, most important, had not set fire to his Cambridge apartment. While still a missing person in the sense that his precise whereabouts were unknown, his being missing was no longer a police matter. Case closed. But the svelte, elegant wife whom Pete had once envisioned forcing her favors upon him for bringing to book her husband's imaginary killer—Pete shook his head at the thought that Roseanne Webster's favors had actually gone to Selma Dorfman—had died with her lover at the hand of an unknown arsonist. Case opened, and an ugly one at that.

Pete was unhappy. Although he had not progressed very far in penetrating the mystery of Carl Webster, he had enjoyed confronting the Harvard-MIT elite in their ivory tower retreats. Plain people who think a lot of themselves, thought Pete, as he invariably did after such encounters with the academic world. Yet there had been something intriguing about the conversations he had had; and while he would still have to badger Gratz and Bonny and probably others to develop leads regarding the fire, without Carl Webster in the picture the mysterious element seemed lacking.

He toyed irresolutely with his beer glass, tracing lines of water on the formica tabletop from the ring that had formed at its base. A few more inquiries can't take too much time, he thought. It would at least clear the air to find out how Webster had gotten from Boston to Montreal and whether he had obtained a visa for Pakistan. A few phone calls would do it. The thought of making phone calls prompted a further idea that led him a minute later to the pay phone by the men's room, where he placed a call to Tom O'Malley.

The two policemen met in a pool hall around the corner from the bar. Midday was a slow time, and there was no one else in the room but the man who clocked them in and gave them the balls, and a pair of black youths who punctuated the quiet with alternating self-praise of their unique talents with a cue. Grandeville was down three games of nine ball at a dollar a game before he and O'Malley had completed the exchange of bitter pleasantries that characterized their relationship. O'Malley was stoic about the souring of his theory of a timid professor transformed into a crazed murderer by a lesbian threat to his manhood.

"I don't give a shit whether he killed his wife or not. His wife was not an employee of Harvard University. If she wasn't killed by her husband, I don't care who killed her—as long as it wasn't an employee of Harvard University. Setting fire to the apartment is something else." He pocketed the nine ball for a fourth win and reformed the balls into a diamond while Pete fished another dollar from his wallet. So far O'Malley had expressed no curiosity as to why Pete had insisted on meeting personally to tell him something he could have conveyed with less possibility of friction by phone. He liked to play pool with a loser. It was its own justification.

"I want to ask you a personal favor, Tom," Grandeville said as he broke the balls.

O'Malley watched the four ball career around the table, carom off the seven and into the side pocket. "Since when do we do each other favors, Frenchie?" he replied. The rhetorical question was a genuine disinvitation to pursue the matter.

"I'll owe you one, Tom."

"Get one of your own boys to do it. I don't run errands." The big Irishman chalked his cue and ran out the rack.

"I can't. This is personal." There was a flicker of interest in the Irishman's eyes. "I have a hunch, and I want to know if it's right." The flicker vanished. "I want you to make an informal check on all the Pakistanis at Harvard. I just want to know if anyone has done anything unusual lately."

"Call the foreign students office."

"This isn't an official request." Pete felt heat rising in his voice. "I just want to know."

O'Malley straightened up from the table and stared at him coldly. "Fuck off, Frenchie." He turned to put his cue in the wall rack.

"Dumb Mick," muttered Grandeville at the massive back of his fellow law enforcement officer. "I already done you a favor!" he shouted after him. "I coulda won every game!"

4
DUBAI:
THE FOURTH WEEK IN FEBRUARY

Major Hamza Rahim reached for his upper lip to tease the waxed extremity of his splendid mustache, then stopped his hand in mid-action. He diverted it instead to his ear and administered a perfunctory poke. Twiddling a mustache that was no longer there not only looked foolish, it was the kind of habit he must learn to suppress. An unskilled construction worker breaking rock for the giant Jebel Ali industrial complex, a pet project of the emir of Dubai, should not display the mannerisms of a Pakistani army officer. It was not that the Japanese engineers who were overseeing the project would ever notice the lapse in behavior. It was all they could do to make themselves understood in English to their Pakistani crew. Nor were the common members of the work gang likely to comment on it if they noticed. However, his own men, who made up a third of the sixty-worker crew, deserved a better example from their commander. Most of them had sacrificed mustaches, too.

Major Hamza swung his pick and wistfully recalled his mustache. And his uniform with the coveted red beret of the Special Services Group. And his family village near Rawalpindi in the Punjab. And hills, and trees, and cool weather. And the color green. He stopped there. The next step would be women.

It had all been a mistake, of course. Volunteers for lengthy, out-of-uniform, secret assignment: the verbal request circulated to officers of the elite commando unit had been universally interpreted in the SSG as an invitation to be sent to Afghanistan as unofficial Pakistani reinforcement of the still active anti-Soviet resistance. Since Pakistan acknowledged no support for the guerrillas, volunteers would obviously have to be severed from their normal unit affiliation; but for Major Hamza and his troop, whom he volunteered first and told later, it was a chance to fight the Russians. Major Hamza wanted to fight Russians— or anyone else, for that matter.

But all had gone wrong. The destination wasn't Afghanistan. It was Dubai. And there was no fighting, only backbreaking work in as dully flat and unappealing a desert as Major Hamza had ever seen in his native land.

After two weeks of orientation about life and work in the Gulf, which most of his men knew about anyway from friends who had gone there to make money, Major Hamza's troop had been given money to pay their fees and travel costs and told to apply for work on the Jebel Ali construction project at one of the labor exchanges licensed to hire Pakistanis for employment in the Gulf area. Since, by secret arrangement, all applications for that particular project were culled out for screening by a government functionary, there had been no difficulty in ensuring that the labor crew sent to work for the Japanese contractor included Major Hamza's entire unit—with Major Hamza as foreman.

Ironically, Major Hamza's had been the only dejected face in the crowd of new workers that tunneled out of the PIA jet into the futuristic white, diamond-shaped corridors of Dubai International Airport. For the others, the contrast between the immaculate white spaciousness of the superbly air-conditioned terminal and the teeming, steaming crush of their departure from Karachi airport, where the lazy overhead fans were more a mockery than a relief, spelled only one thing: money. Only Major Hamza knew that a genuine military assignment in a Gulf country would have paid substantially more.

With every village and neighborhood in Pakistan feeding at least one son into the pool of nearly a million workers on contract to employers in Saudi Arabia, Kuwait, Bahrain, the United Arab Emirates (of which Dubai was one), Qatar, or

Oman, it was impossible to grow up ignorant of the vast piles of money in the hands of the Gulf Arabs. When an uneducated and unskilled laborer in Abu Dhabi (another of the United Arab Emirates) could make more than a middle-level bureaucrat with a bachelor's degree in a Pakistani government ministry, the knock of opportunity resounded throughout the land. And when the bureaucrat's driver could drive in Saudi Arabia for two years and clear enough money to dress his wife in a finer chemise and *shalwar* than the bureaucrat's wife, the knock of opportunity seemed to some to threaten the entire social order.

To these realities of Pakistani life in the 1980s Major Hamza's men were far from indifferent. For the most part from Punjabi and Pathan families with long traditions of producing some of the world's fiercest and proudest soldiers, the major's men were additionally proud of being part of the Special Services Group, the elite antiterrorist and commando force that Pakistan had patterned on Britain's Special Air Service. At fighting, killing, and surviving in the wilds on snakes and toads, they were without peer east of Jerusalem; and their loyalty to their God, their country, and their commander was absolute.

Nevertheless, while well remunerated by Pakistani standards, elite soldiers trained to kill silently in twelve different ways still did not pull down a quarter of the pay of a Pakistani gardener or driver working in Dubai, not to mention a skilled craftsman. Consequently, what disappointment Major Hamza's men may have felt on not being sent to fight the Russians was more than compensated for by the high civilian wages they were earning in their assumed roles as laborers. And even their commander admitted that the air conditioning in the ramshackle corrugated-iron huts they were given to live in at the desert work site was an improvement over their home barracks in torrid Hyderabad, and the imported European food prepared by Pakistani cooks a better feed than their accustomed mess. So the ache for combat, adventure, and promotion brought suffering only to the unit commander, who had not even his mustache to console him.

A fortnight after their arrival his ache was suddenly intensified by the sight of two military staff cars unloading a party of officers in front of the small fenced compound where the Japanese engineers and supervisors lived a separate and comfortable life, well insulated from their foreign employees. Major Hamza felt a terrible yearning as he leaned on his pick and squinted at the distant flash of epaulets and brass and the commanding gestures of a swagger stick. Apparently the construction engineers were pointing out to the visitors the emerging features of the colossal complex.

Then a beatific vision took form. One of the cars, with a single officer inside, restarted and drove in the major's direction. He momentarily imagined that the car was coming to rescue him from his purgatory and instinctively prepared to snap to attention. Then he deliberately relaxed his militarily disciplined muscles. By the time the car actually did pull to a dusty stop right next to him, he looked like any other turbaned Pakistani leaning on his pick. When the driver's window rolled down, revealing the coarsely weathered and mustachioed face of an officer wearing brigadier's insignia, Major Hamza could scarcely believe it.

"Major Hamza Rahim?" came a voice that carried command strength even though it was little above a whisper.

"Sir!" responded the major, struggling with his urge to salute.

"I have only a moment because I shall say that I only stopped to ask you directions." The language was Punjabi. "Tomorrow you will feign a severe pain in your lower right abdomen. You will be sent to hospital, and I shall see you there. Be convincing!" The window rolled up. The car bumped away down the rutted construction road. Major Hamza's heart was pounding as if he had been given an order to attack a Russian tank with his bare hands.

At breakfast time the men sharing his hut were appalled to find the major writhing in pain on his bunk and unable to straighten his body when helped to stand. Within an hour he had been examined by a Filipino doctor and placed aboard a helicopter for the sixty-mile trip to a hospital on the Creek, a winding estuary in the heart of Dubai city where old-fashioned merchants and modern financiers alike had offices in gleaming glass and concrete towers overlooking the water. Moaning and occasionally sobbing, he was deposited in an ultramodern hospital room where an Egyptian orderly helped him into a hospital gown. A doctor arrived, shooed the orderly away, and shut the door.

"You may relax, Major," said the doctor in a cultured English accent. "I am Doctor Ahmed. Brigadier Faiz will be here momentarily. After you speak with him, I will return and pronounce you cured of severe abdominal cramps. Right now I need to do a blood count to ascertain for the record that you do not have appendicitis." Hearing the name of one of the most famous officers in the Pakistani army so startled the major that he scarcely was aware of the doctor grabbing his ear and inflicting a small wound. After extracting a few drops of blood, Dr. Ahmed directed his patient to squeeze a bit of cotton on the earlobe. "Needless to say, if you have bad health, your employers will ship you back to Karachi. We don't want that. So this is the only time we can use this means of contact." With that the doctor spun around and opened the door. He stepped back to allow the brigadier to enter and quietly departed.

"Stay seated, Major," ordered the solemn-faced, ramrod-straight officer. The major was struck dumb at being addressed by so glorious a personage. "My name is Brigadier Faiz. I am your commanding officer. Ignore the United Arab Emirates uniform I am wearing. Our loyalty to our country does not evaporate just because we are on duty in another country's army. You received no briefing about your mission before you came here because we are working in utmost secrecy and can take no chances with intelligence lapses. This will be your only briefing here, at least for the time being, so listen carefully.

"Our nation has three great enemies: the Russians in Afghanistan, the Indians, and poverty. The first two enemies you have been trained to know and, if necessary, to fight. The third is the one that has caused you to be posted to Dubai.

"The long and the short of our mission is to prevent the cutting of the golden artery that keeps Pakistan's economy alive. The money coming into Pakistan from our workers here in the Gulf is vital to our survival. It is our largest source of foreign exchange. As a consequence, it is in our national interest to guarantee that the money flow from the Gulf never be interrupted, whether by war or revolution or economic crisis. We *must* have these funds.

"Yet when we look at the countries here in the Gulf, what do we see? We see weakness! Tiny powerless countries. The seven emirates of the U.A.E. combined have only one-twentieth the number of Pakistanis that live in the city of Karachi alone. And who do we see ruling over these lands of gold? We see rulers without will or public support and mercenary armies without the training and leadership needed to use the weapons the Arabs' oil money has bought. Here we see the richest and the weakest place in the entire world. The Gulf is nothing but a bunch of clucking hens waiting to have their throats cut and be eaten. And if that happens, we in Pakistan shall suffer from it as much as the Arabs.

"You might think, of course, that with people like myself serving in the army of the Emirates we are already in a position to safeguard our interest. In a sense, this is true, because we have planned carefully our role in the armies of these weak Arab countries. As you may know, almost half the army of

Oman is composed of Baluch tribesmen from Pakistan, and we have officers, training missions, and advisers throughout the Gulf. In addition, we furnish most of the clerks used to maintain logistic functions and a good number of air force pilots. But we still have a serious lack of capability. Until now we have had no strike force of undisputed loyalty capable of acting entirely outside the local military command structure.

"That is why you are here. That is your role. When and if a crisis occurs, it is you who will receive the order to act. You are few; you are secret; you are our best. If necessary, you should have sufficient power to seize control of the government for a brief period, particularly in view of the capacity of those of us regularly in service here to delay or prevent organized military opposition.

"We do not know what might happen or when, but you will secretly exhort your men to be ready at all times for the word of command. If nothing happens in a year's time, you will be rotated back to Pakistan. Your service here will be regarded as a duty of great merit. We are proud of you."

Throughout the brigadier's harangue, which had swung dramatically from heights of emotion to briefing officer matter-of-factness to conspiratorial whisper, Major Hamza had sat transfixed on the bed with his hairy legs and thighs sticking out from under his hospital gown. Several times he had unconsciously stroked his upper lip as the brigadier's vision of patriotic service took root in his mind. For moments after the famed senior officer had finished, Major Hamza made no response. Suddenly he returned from his mesmerized state and said simply, "We don't have any weapons."

Brigadier Faiz laughed heartily as if a joke of rare worth had been told. "You're a fine officer, my boy, even with your pants off. You're right. You and your men couldn't fight your way out of your compound in your present condition." Major Hamza bristled. Fighting their way out of the compound would be child's play, but taking over the country with twenty unarmed men was a different matter. "Remember what I said about our penetration of the logistics arm. We have already stockpiled weapons and ammunition deleted from the supply lists of the U.A.E. army. Vehicles we can get at a moment's notice; many of our men are drivers. Don't worry. When you receive the command to take action, you can be transformed into a superbly armed force in less than two hours."

"That command will come from you, sir?"

"I am your commanding officer. If the chain of command is altered, you will be notified."

"May I ask one further question, sir?" The brigadier looked receptive. "Am I the first?"

"You are the first. The decision to create this capacity was taken only recently. There will soon be counterpart forces concealed in Qatar, Kuwait, Bahrain, and Abu Dhabi. Oman and Saudi Arabia are too large to be handled in the same fashion. Do you have any other questions?" The major was silent. "Good. It's better not to. Now I must leave. But this final word of caution, although I don't think I really need to say it to an officer of the SSG. This is a mission requiring the utmost secrecy and absolute discipline in maintaining concealment. The wealth and weakness of the Gulf states is known to every government in the world. It would be simple-minded to believe that they have not implanted some of their own intelligence officers. But we don't believe that anyone else can achieve an on-call secret commando capability. No one else has the penetration of the local military that we have or as sizable a contract labor force to conceal their men. But you must be always on your guard and always prepared to take action."

With that and an exchange of salutes, the brigadier departed and the doctor returned. An hour later a slightly dazed but enormously proud Major Hamza climbed into the cab of a white Subaru pickup for the ride back to Jebel Ali.

At the end of his hospital duty at four o'clock, Dr. Ahmed telephoned a second secretary in the political section at the British embassy in Abu Dhabi and intimated that it would be well worth his time to drive the two and a half hours from Abu Dhabi to Dubai and take him out to dinner. The second secretary had had sufficient prior dealings with Dr. Ahmed to accept the date.

The doctor never appeared. In a freak accident the driver of a two and a half ton U.A.E. army truck lost control and sideswiped the doctor's car into an overpass abutment under construction. The truck driver, also a Pakistani, was unhurt and was the first to reach the doctor in the wreckage. He truthfully announced to the second person to reach the scene that the doctor had died in his arms. He did not add that death had been by strangulation.

5
ISLAMABAD:
THE FIRST WEEK IN MARCH

Still under four weeks. His confinement had as yet been neither uncomfortable nor burdensomely long. But it was confinement, nevertheless, and Carl Webster was growing impatient. Bahador was the name of the First Interrogator—the label Carl had assigned to such a hypothetical personality in conceiving GULFSCENE III—and he was turning out to be a bit of a dullard. Carl was eager to get on to the Second Interrogator. However, he knew that the time thus far elapsed since his abduction from the bank of the Charles River was still within the range of statistical probability calculated in the scenario. There was still ample time to take control of affairs before the first week in June.

He assumed that he was being held somewhere in Islamabad, Pakistan's capital and place of residence of General Baber, the nation's current military ruler. He had the upstairs of a small, fairly new house to himself: two bedrooms with lofty ceilings, numerous built-in cupboard closets, and large but spartan bathrooms. The landing onto which the bedrooms opened was equipped with a noisy refrigerator, which was kept stocked with potable water, and a table where his breakfast was served every morning. A guard wearing a uniform without insignia was stationed at the bottom of the stairs. There was also a glassed door out onto the flat roof of the front part of the house, but the door was locked. Carl saw no reason to court trouble by forcing it. Through the windows he could see trees and parts of other buildings that looked like residences. A large, gray jaylike bird with blue wings periodically sunned itself on the roof, but Carl had never made a study of birds so it told him nothing about his whereabouts. Nor, for that matter, did the mangoes he was served at breakfast or the multicolored felt tea cozy confirm that he was in Pakistan. Both could be found on sale in Harvard Square.

Yet he was reasonably sure of where he was because it was where he had intended himself to be. The abduction had been a necessary although thoroughly unpleasant means of getting there; but since he had been disoriented or rendered unconscious by injections during much of the transit, he could not be absolutely sure where he had ended up.

The First Interrogator, naturally, had told him nothing. His job was to extract a personal history and scrutinize it for inconsistencies. Carl had cooperated and now regretted that he had said so much about himself since it had given the First Interrogator more to chew on than he was mentally capable of masticating.

His impressions from childhood and his family relations had been a particular mistake to bring up since the First Interrogator, despite his civilian clothes, was obviously a man with military training, no doubt an intelligence officer, and certainly too provincial in his background and uninformed about American life to understand the fine points of Carl's story. But Carl himself never tired of contemplating his autobiography, and out of boredom and a misplaced feeling of helpfulness he had told the poor stolid Bahador more than he would ever have divulged to a psychotherapist. More than once the chubby brown man's eyes had drooped shut as Carl detailed at length the rancorous family arguing that had filled his teenage years and profoundly shaped his character. . . .

It had begun late in 1956 with the arrival in the Websters' orderly middle-class universe of Andras Lajos Kovacs, his father's younger brother from Hungary.

What Carl had understood of his family background up to that point was that his father had brought him to the United

States in the aftermath of World War II. Carl was then three. His father told him years later that his mother had died during the war, but Carl grew up believing the sweet, homely woman his father married in America to be his mother. Try as he might, he could never bring to consciousness any recollection of his real mother or his early childhood in Europe.

The woman Carl's father married was Katharine Webster, the young but already spinsterish daughter of a foursquare Indiana industrialist who had given the middle-aged, immigrant, mechanical engineer a job and quickly realized that he had gained an employee of extraordinary competence. When his new son-in-law informed him in 1948, after the Communist takeover of Hungary, that he wished to cut his ties with his fallen homeland and adopt Webster as his family name, Ames Webster had been profoundly flattered and patriotically moved at the same time. Less than a year later Anton Kovacs, now Anthony Webster, became president of The Webster Hobbing Machine Company. From his board chairmanship, Ames Webster looked with pride and satisfaction upon the happy transition he had accomplished from his generation to the next, guaranteeing that Webster Hobbing would be as conservative and well managed in the future as it had been under his own father, who had passed away in 1923. Shortly thereafter, Ames Webster, too, died a happy man.

Thus, at the age of ten, Carl Webster was living the privileged life the scion of a successful and highly respected industrialist was entitled to live. Home was large and exceedingly clean, the furniture antique. The neighborhood was in the newer part of town, but in a subdivision that retained large lots and respectable old elms. The country club was the better—in social terms if not in the quality of its greenskeeping—of the two in town. The car was a black Cadillac.

All of this meant nothing to Carl at that age, of course, since there was nothing in the portion of the public school system that he was exposed to to suggest that other children lived markedly different sorts of lives. All of his teachers called him precocious, and he basked in their attention and agreed with their evaluation once he had looked up the meaning of the word. His precocity was particularly evident in mathematics and puzzle solving. In matters physical, however, he was quite the opposite.

Passive, unathletic, and bookish, Carl was never popular. One particular phrase from the ten-year-olds' vocabulary of his childhood stuck in his memory and in later years symbolized for him his early schooldays. It was the phrase "fairy farmer," an appelation resulting from an unconscious combination of two objects of middle-class distaste: farmers, whose hick manners reminded people too strongly of their own rural roots; and fairies, the legendary sexual perverts who were rumored to lurk in the evil parts of big cities where their very presence posed a threat to the Republic. Its confusion of meaning did nothing to deaden its sting, however; and jeered at on the playground with this and other stigmatizing expressions, Carl buried himself increasingly in his studies. By the time his uncle Andras appeared on the scene, he had become a truly outstanding student, the best in his teachers' memory.

With the coming of Uncle Andras, however, Carl's idyllic home life started to blur, like a familiar picture he could no longer see quite right because he had put on the wrong pair of glasses. For Uncle Andras was a socialist, perhaps even a Communist. To be sure, during the preceding spring he had fled Soviet tanks rolling into Budapest and escaped Hungary through Austria, but by deep conviction he was a person of the left.

His appearance in the Webster household had come as the result of heated arguments, surreptitiously overheard by Carl, between Anthony Webster and his normally docile and soft-spoken wife. Carl's father had been adamantly opposed to giving even a temporary home to his brother, whose existence had never before been hinted at in Carl's presence; but his mother had been even more insistent, to the point of tears, that Anthony take his brother in, both as an act of family charity, in which she deeply believed, and as a patriotic gesture of support for the oppressed peoples behind the Iron Curtain.

Katharine Webster had won, and Andras Kovacs arrived with a single suitcase late in November to commence what would prove to be five years of residence in the guest room with the pink-flowered wallpaper. Despite twelve years difference in age, Uncle Andras looked very much like his older brother. Both were blond and lean, reflecting, Carl learned, the family's remote German origins. They had hard grayish eyes, deeply sunk, lips that looked as though they had been carefully outlined by a makeup artist, and long-fingered, large-knuckled hands. Carl himself had inherited only the blondness, taking his rounder, less sharply defined features, his blue eyes, and his small, stubby hands and feet from some other eddy of the gene pool.

Father and uncle were also alike in talent and temperament. At first Anthony Webster had sternly insisted that Andras work at a different company to avoid unspecified accusations of favoritism, but Katherine Webster had soon cajoled her husband into putting him to work at Webster Hobbing. Thereafter she took quiet pleasure in reminding him that Andras was both a superior draftsman and an energetic and reliable employee. Such mollifying reminders did little to postpone or deflect the storm that was gathering little by little in the conversations between the two brothers, conversations that were always carried out in English because of his father's refusal to revert to Hungarian.

At first, Carl understood the bone of contention to be political and economic theory. Anthony Webster was a Republican businessman who had succeeded in his adopted country by dint of hard work and native ability. Andras Kovacs believed passionately and humanistically in a benevolent welfare state in which equality took precedence over aggressive individual achievement. While he did not claim that the country he had recently fled was in any way a model for this ideal, his ability to argue eloquently for his vision improved steadily with his English. Katherine Webster, who usually declined participation in the brothers' debates out of a general aversion to family disharmony, honored and respected her husband's views but sympathized in the natural charity of her Methodist heart with Andras's utopia, or at least with his ardent espousal of it, which made his gray eyes glisten with emotion.

Uncle Andras's ardor also impressed the quietly listening teenager. The arguments of his father and uncle were not always within his range of understanding, but his mother's soothing explanations, in response to his questions, always seemed to tend toward Uncle Andras's side. Slowly, Carl became secretly attached to his uncle and critical of his father. He was at pains to conceal his changing affections from both men since he feared their arguing, but on possessions he thought his father would never look at he took to writing his name as Carl Kovacs. And he began to read books on political thought to enable him to understand more of what he overheard after dinner when he was supposed to be doing his homework.

As Carl proceeded brilliantly through high school, his grasp of political thought improved steadily, but the household debates became rarer and their conclusion more often than not an exchange of heated words, now usually Hungarian, followed by Uncle Andras's stomping retreat to his pink cell. Carl resolved to teach himself Hungarian as a further secret gesture of support for his uncle and defiance of his father's obstinate conservatism. Implementing this resolve was not easy since books on Hungarian were far from numerous in the city library; but Uncle Andras had ferreted out the few other Hungarians in town, whose existence his father chose not to acknowledge, and Carl persuaded one of them, a baker, to tutor him without telling the family.

So it was that in his senior year of high school Carl discovered for the first time what his uncle really thought of his father. By indirect statement, always in Hungarian, Uncle Andras made it very clear that Anthony Webster, when he was Anton Kovacs, had cooperated in some sort of shameful fashion with the Nazi occupation forces during World War II. Moreover, there was often a threatening overtone that Uncle Andras could make serious trouble for his brother if circumstances warranted it.

Carl spent the summer after his high school graduation and prior to his departure for Harvard in deep and private contemplation. He barely communicated with family and friends and spent most of his time reading. Political theory had lost its savor with his new perception that it had probably never been more than a disguise for a deeper animosity between his father and uncle. With adolescent cynicism he concluded that politics were probably always a disguise for baser sentiments. He read instead about World War II, first in general and then in as much detail as he could find. His morbid fantasy was that his father had been a death camp guard and his mother a condemned Jew; but in July his uncle happened to mention, during one of the rare lapses of the brothers' apparent agreement that conversation about Anton Kovacs's first wife in Hungary would be insulting to the present Mrs. Webster, that he had been very fond of Carl's real mother and deeply depressed when she had accidentally died in a fall from a crowded streetcar.

By that time Carl had already been captivated by the military side of the world conflict, however, and he pressed his reading into matters of strategy and tactics as far as he could. The concrete reality of people living and dying because of other people's right or wrong decisions gripped him with a fascination that he realized was a compensation for the hollowness and superficiality that he now associated with political and economic theorizing.

Away from home as a freshman, Carl boldly decided to sign his name Kovacs and ask that it be changed in the freshman dean's office, even at the risk of his father finding out. He was no longer the uncritical admirer of Uncle Andras that he had previously been, for the scent of blackmail that he had picked up from his rudimentary Hungarian eavesdropping had been strengthened by further observation that his father kept paying Uncle Andras's bills despite their open hostility. But his disgust at what he imagined his father's past to have been went unabated.

At Christmas he went home to see his family. No one was in the house but his father. Katharine Webster and Andras Kovacs had departed a month previously for California after telling his father that they had only concealed their love affair and delayed their elopement until Carl was in college so as not to shatter his home environment.

The news *was* shattering, and not just to Carl. Anthony Webster became morose and uncommunicative, turning over the active management of Webster Hobbing to the vice-president in charge of sales. On the first day of spring he shot himself.

The unexpected loss of a second parent in one year did not affect Carl as much as the first had; it only reinforced his feeling that his mother had needlessly and cruelly inflicted great pain upon them both, father and son. He refused to look at her at the funeral or to answer her letters. He likewise rebuffed Uncle Andras's occasional efforts to maintain contact. He notified the freshman dean's office that his name was again Webster. Three years later when he tried to make contact with his mother concerning the sale of Webster Hobbing, which he and she jointly controlled, to a larger firm, the company attorney informed him that Mrs. Kovacs's attorney was under specific instructions to divulge her address to no one. Further inquiries among his parents' friends yielded only the uncertain information that Andras

Kovacs had left California and gone to work for the government.

Every time Carl thought back over the five years of living with Uncle Andras and their catastrophic end, he marveled at his own ambivalence toward it all. On the one hand, he could view the story as a tragedy, though this was more an intellectual exercise than an emotional one. True, he had lost his entire family. Yet his father had been an unfeeling mossback with a soiled if not criminal past. And his uncle, despite his intelligence and forcefulness, had turned out to be the kind of opportunist and moocher who saw no contradiction between grand moral discourse and discreet blackmail. As for his stepmother: a woman, with a woman's weakness.

On the nontragic side, Carl had become on his twenty-first birthday, by the terms of his father's will, a one-quarter owner of Webster Hobbing. Almost immediately he had been notified by the company attorney of his stepmother's desire to accept a bid for the company, and the transaction had left him a man of means. This, in turn, had made it possible for him to pursue his own interests without worrying about long-term career goals and to marry a svelte, well-polished daughter of the upper class—with a great pair of legs.

Yet a third approach, and to Carl's way of thinking a crucial one, was to see his personal history as a profound educational experience. Political ideology, patriotism, filial piety, love of woman, capitalist enterprise, social conscience, family charity, religious faith: not a single great adolescent dream had survived. Unattached to society by material needs, Carl was equally unfettered by ideals. All he trusted in and all he admired was his own mental capability and the limits to which it could be pushed.

Such was the story of his life as Carl Webster told it to Bahador. And why in the hell it had not been interesting enough to keep the First Interrogator awake was beyond Carl's understanding. In fact, he was again for the umpteenth time feeling deeply insulted by the recollection of Bahador's torpor when a lighter tread on the staircase leading to his penthouse prison gave his spirits a lift. The Second Interrogator had arrived.

"Good afternoon," said the middle-aged, orange sari-clad woman when she reached the landing at the top of the stairs. "You are Dr. Webster? I am Dr. Singh." She seated herself at the breakfast table and raised to her eyes a pair of wire-rimmed glasses hanging from a fine gold chain around her neck. She took her time inserting the bows into the gray hair at her temples and adjusting the fit on her large hooked nose. She took even longer looking for the papers she wanted in her briefcase and getting them aligned on the table to her satisfaction. Carl was still standing at the door of the front bedroom. A familiar heavy clump of steps drew his eye back to the staircase. It was the ill-shaven servant who had served his breakfast, carrying a tray of tea things.

"Won't you have tea with me?" said Dr. Singh. Her voice was deep and melodious. She poured two cups but did not wait for Carl to sit down. "The papers you brought with you when you came—"

"I was physically seized and brought here in a drugged condition."

"But not against your will?" She lifted her eyebrows expressively. "You choose your words carefully, Dr. Webster. As I was saying, the papers that were in your possession when you came into our possession are extremely interesting and have been thoroughly evaluated by our experts. The dissemination of these documents must be very disturbing to your government. As for the long report labeled GULFSCENE III, the study of its seriousness and feasibility is still being conducted. I have only been permitted to read the preamble myself, but it is very provocative. You seem to envision a radical change in the entire world balance of power."

Carl slipped into the chair opposite the Second Interrogator. "That is a highly probable result if events occur in precisely the correct fashion."

Dr. Singh did not react to the comment. "The reason I am here is to carry out a psychological evaluation. There are people of much higher rank than I who would like to speak with you, but they do not wish to waste their time—you'll pardon the terms—upon a lunatic, a criminal, or a spy."

"I quite understand. I can only—"

"There is one paramount question that has been raised by your conduct thus far," continued the psychologist in a sterner voice.

"What is that?"

"If you are willing to betray your own country by giving secret documents to a foreign government, why should we believe that you would not betray us as well?"

Carl felt a professional gaze examining his face for reaction. What he thought of to say was that loyalty was not a concept that meant much to him, but he realized that the answer would do him little good and stifled it in his throat. He took a sip of tea instead.

"I'm going to give you an injection before we begin our conversation, Dr. Webster. It will help us both if it enhances my assurance of the fullness of your answers." The Second Interrogator produced a syringe and ampule from her case and reached across the table for Carl's bare forearm. "I would have preferred a lie detector, but you may be flattered to know that my colleagues judged that you would have a high ability to deceive it." The needle stung a prominent blue vein. "Now, I want you to start counting backward from one hundred. When you get to one, I will begin to ask you questions about your childhood."

6
WASHINGTON:
THE FIRST WEEK IN APRIL

Lincoln Joseph Hoskins had not picked a good time, economically, to come in from the cold. As CIA station chief, he had been a hidden power in two Central American countries, but he had not put down as firm roots in Washington as others of his rank and seniority in the agency. So when the time had finally come for permanent reassignment to D.C., he had been forced onto a brutally inflated housing market. Sweating it out in the tropics, he had often imagined a genteel row house in Georgetown or a refurbished farm in Virginia horse country, the types of places American spies in the thrillers he was addicted to reading called home. In reality, both were out of his price range. He had been lucky to find an unprepossessing three-bedroom house with a semifinished basement and the unfulfilled promise of a garden in Fairfax, Virginia.

The commute wasn't too bad, and the local high school was comparatively free of subversive educational notions; but the romantic side of his nature, which he was professionally at pains to discipline, longed for a walnut-paneled study with a high ceiling, a plaster floral medallion dangling an antique chandelier, and an inlaid mahogany desk. If world-shaking intrigues were to be hatched under his direction, that was the kind of room they should incubate in.

In Link Hoskins's career, whenever reality and romanticism had clashed, reality had won. Twice he had written tentative proposals to overthrow undesirable governments; twice his proposals had been rejected. In neither instance had the continuation in power of the undesirable dictator hindered the pursuit of U.S. policy. It had been his job, however, at that time, to raise such possibilities, just as it was now his job to review and quash the overly adventurous schemes of his subordinates.

Mistakes avoided counted for more than coups successfully carried out in Hoskins's job, but it was to visit an old friend in the intelligence community rather than an agency troubleshooter that Morris Gratz flew down from Cambridge. In addition to a camaraderie going back to college years, the two men shared a zeal for coming on younger and spryer than their years. The short trip from Dulles was Link's chance to show off his new second-hand Porche, and Morris Gratz responded enthusiastically to the wind rushing past his head. Only to themselves did both men admit that March was too early in the season to take a car's top off in Washington.

Ensconced in the piney warmth of Hoskins's basement study and supplied with tumblers of whiskey to restore their circulation, they finally got around to serious matters.

"The damage control report is as follows, Morrie. You're not in the clear, but things could be a lot worse. Fortunately, whatever papers your man had he took with him when he left the country. Nothing classified could be identified in his apartment. Best possibility, from your standpoint, is that he's now in the Soviet Union telling all. We assume, naturally, that the KGB has scores of their ethnic Tajik and Uzbek agents planted among the Afghan refugees in Pakistan. Since the border is essentially open to anyone who knows the right paths, it's a crossing point that's harder to trace than any in Europe. If that's where Mr. Webster has gone or been taken, we classify him as a spy or defector and reckon that, with his clearance, he could have stolen the papers regardless of your security procedures. This makes you a turkey for hiring a spy, but the onus really falls on security for clearing him."

"I would have sworn he wasn't a spy, Link."

"Morrie, you wouldn't know how to spot a spy if he had a

hammer and sickle tattooed on his forehead. Face it, you guys just don't have any hands-on experience in this sort of thing. That's what gets my pals in the Agency so pissed off when we loan you the family jewels and they disappear. But in this case, you may be right. Some Agency specialist with impeccable credentials has personally vouched for Webster."

Gratz's face brightened. "That's great!"

"Maybe, but not for you. If Webster wasn't a spy, he was a fuckoff; and they can roast your ass for hiring a fuckoff and giving him the run of the national archives."

"But if he's just a fuckoff, where is he and why did he take the documents?"

"Those are questions you had better start thinking of answers to because the way we spring leaks around here, I wouldn't be surprised if some congressman gets wind of this before long. As for the Agency position, the security team in Cambridge will keep on working to find out what really happened, and our boys in Pakistan will see if they can get a lead on him there."

"But you know, Link, it just doesn't make sense for him to have gone to Pakistan." Gratz revolved his whiskey glass before the light like a jeweler appraising a stone. "I mean, we know he probably went there: the visa, the passport, and all that. He probably even went there with those two Pak research-types who left Harvard at the same time. But what good is it going to do Pakistan to have those documents? Even groups trying to boot General Baber out of the presidential palace don't have any use for that information, except maybe to sell it to the Russians. And then there's the torching of Carl's apartment. How does that fit in?"

"Damned if I know!" replied Hoskins vehemently. "This whole thing isn't my headache. Remember? I'm just telling you friend to friend how things look and what's being said. What's being said is that if Webster isn't in Moscow, he's probably in Pakistan. And if he's in Pakistan, somebody had better figure

out real quick what he's doing there before some asshole colum-
nist breaks the story of a mysterious intelligence leak to a
friendly nation. What I'm driving at, Morrie, what I'm recom-
mending, is an active defense. Instead of hiding in your office
waiting for your lease to run out, you should come forward and
volunteer your team to analyze what Webster is up to. And put
yourself up front. If you come up with something, fine. If not,
you still get good marks for effort and conduct, and maybe you
won't get sacked."

Gratz drained the last inch of amber in his glass with the
sound of the word "sacked" echoing in his head. From childhood he had had a morbid fear of breaking a tooth on a cherry
pit, and now that fear returned, as he sensed that he was being
asked to bite a bullet.

"That's good advice, Link," he said reflectively after a long
silence. "That's good advice."

The veteran agent gave him a broad grin, a shake of his
floppy brown forelock, and a firm clutch on the elbow. In
Hoskins's dreamworld it was his distinctive superspy tribute to a
friend or enemy who was about to be wasted.

In recognition of the fact that the vanished documents were
primarily of a military character, Arlington Hall, the headquarters of the Defense Intelligence Agency, had been designated
the meeting site for a board of inquiry investigating the circumstances of Carl Webster's disappearance. Board member Rufus
Snipe would have much preferred one of the comfortably appointed conference rooms in the State Department close to his
office in Intelligence and Research, but the often-abused spirit
of intelligence community cooperation dictated a trek across the
Potomac, barracks drabness, and uncomfortable army straight-
backed chairs instead.

For board member Walker Rankin of CIA, the surroundings
were less objectionable than the company. By his estimation,

Rufus Snipe was a token black who had risen far on the basis of that and an easy personality rather than on actual ability; and Colonel Edward Seymour, the board's chairman, was a lead-footed plodder who didn't believe that anything of importance existed that couldn't be circled and counted on a satellite photograph.

In truth, all three had been tapped for the job by their respective agencies because they were senior enough to know what to do and the importance of doing it, while at the same time being expendable from their regular duties for as long as the inquiry might take, or even longer.

Their first substantive discussion was over the disposition of the furniture. Snipe fancied making a square of the two rectangular tables and distributing chairs around it. Rankin had no opinion. Colonel Seymour favored the board sitting behind one table with himself in the center, Rankin on his right as the more senior board member, and Snipe on his left. He visualized the "witnesses" sitting at the second table facing the board across six feet of open space. The board deferred to its chairman and disposed itself to await the arrival of the gentlemen from Cambridge.

"It's a court martial," whispered Ted Bonny in Morris Gratz's ear as they entered the room. The apprehension that had been welling up within him during the taxi ride from the air-shuttle terminal at National Airport threatened to constrict his vocal cords.

His boss strode confidently to the occupied table. "Hi! Morrie Gratz." He gave a firm hand to the man whose uniform haircut betrayed a military calling. He was more gentle with Rankin's Charleston-bred wrist. "Walker, nice to see you again."

"Dr. Gratz, this is Colonel Edward Seymour," drawled Rankin.

Gratz nodded again at the steelhead and then at the light aquiline-nosed black beside him. "Morrie Gratz."

"Rufus Snipe, INR." They shook hands. "Very pleased to meet you."

Gratz looked back toward Ted Bonny who was still quaking just inside the door. "This is my associate, Dr. Theodore Bonny." More handshaking ensued during which Gratz pulled chairs from behind the second table and drew them up to the board's table. "Do we need this third chair?"

"Bring it, Morrie," said Rankin. "An FBI fellow's going to join us after we get done telling secrets."

After the group was finally seated, Colonel Seymour stood unnecessarily to convene the session. He intoned an official statement defining the board's mandate and then listed as agenda items the reports of Drs. Gratz and Bonny and of Special Agent Storm. Next came a pause for comment or correction.

"Well, let's get on with it," said Rufus Snipe. "We don't want to spend all day over here."

Colonel Seymour opened his mouth to speak but was beaten to the draw.

"I agree," said Gratz positively. "Dr. Bonny, who has worked very closely with Carl Webster, can summarize what we've been able to find out from our end. But before I give over to him, I want to say one or two things for the record. First, this is the first imputation of security malfunction ever to be directed at HMSRG. By comparison with any other research organization we have an excellent record. Second, Carl Webster was not and still cannot be considered a security risk by any of the normal criteria. What he has done, or is doing, we are beginning to piece together, as you will see; but why he is doing it is still a mystery. I'm not saying this, you understand, to try to divest myself as the Group's director of responsibility for this breach of security. But we must try to see it in perspective and learn from it so we can all avoid future mistakes." Gratz took note of the averted glances of the board members and put his hand on Bonny's shoulder. "Ted, why don't you take it from here?"

Like an instant-on electronic device, his scrawny accomplice efficiently dealt a stapled packet of papers to each board member. As they leafed through it, he catalogued its contents: "Part A lists the name, position, specialties, citizenship, and current address of each of the associates of Webster whom I've interviewed over the last two weeks. Part B is part of a background piece Webster did for GULFSCENE III. Parts C and D are the summary evaluations of GULFSCENE I and GULFSCENE II. Part E is Webster's letter to Dr. Gratz outlining his plan for a third Gulf scenario. And part F lists people yet to be interviewed."

"Was there a response to this letter to Dr. Gratz, Dr. Bonny?" asked Rufus Snipe.

"Yes, there was," interjected Gratz, "but I didn't think it was germane."

"A routine approval?"

"Actually, it was a denial of permission to proceed. But I later reversed that decision and gave him the go-ahead orally."

"Would you mind telling us why you changed your mind, Dr. Gratz?"

"I don't believe it's germane to our inquiry, but essentially I was persuaded by Carl's arguments for a third scenario once he gave me his full thought on the matter."

Walker Rankin's lazy right eyebrow lifted. "You mean he told you just what GULFSCENE III was all about? Then why are we wasting our time guessing at it?"

"Look fellas, it's silly to waste time on this. Webster's full thought was that if I didn't let him work on it, he'd quit. It was a persuasive argument. So I let him work on it."

All three board members made notes on the yellow pads before them. "You may proceed, Dr. Bonny," said Colonel Seymour.

The machine restarted. "Carl Webster's working procedure was to write think pieces on various elements of a problem. He would research a topic, come up with some ideas, put it down in a few pages, and tuck it away. Sometimes he had a specialist check a piece out; sometimes he didn't. The scenario as finally written in a form to be given to the players would only be a couple of dozen pages long, but a full scenario file might be a hundred pages or more. A scenario writer always has to be able to justify strategically not just the opening situation but the pre-planned interjections of new information or events made by the control team in the course of play.

"What I have been able to do is trace five of the problem areas Carl worked on in building up GULFSCENE III: Indian and Pakistani nuclear strength and delivery capability, decision-making procedures for defense policy formulation by those same two countries, the military capacities of the armies of some of the Gulf states, the history of Soviet-Indian relations, and in-stances of utilization of the Moscow-Washington hotline. My preliminary conclusion is that GULFSCENE III envisioned an Indo-Soviet squeeze of Pakistan that would necessitate a deci-sion to commit the Rapid Deployment Force to Pakistan rather than the Gulf. It's not the only possibility that can be made to fit the data, but it makes sense to me." Bonny abruptly stopped speaking and looked at the board.

"Why that's just horseshit, Mr. Bonny," drawled Walker Rankin. "I can think off the top of my head of at least a half-dozen other possibilities, and there isn't a one of them that the government of the Soviet Union or the government of Pakistan either one would cross the room to read if they were chalked on the blackboard. Frankly, I don't think this GULFSCENE III has a damn thing to do with Carl Webster going over. He's just a rotten little punk traitor."

"Then who burnt up his wife?" asked Rufus Snipe quietly.

"Gentlemen," said Colonel Seymour, "we have to hear Special Agent Storm before lunch, and it is now eleven-thirty. I think we should shelve this discussion until after we eat and call Storm in right now. After lunch we'll go through Dr. Bonny's list of informants one by one and have him tell us in detail what each of them had to say."

The answering sighs of resignation were still in the air when Seymour returned from sticking his head into the corridor and calling the name of David Storm. Hard on his heels through the open door came a trim young man with wavy yellow hair and eyes like faded blueberry stains on a white tablecloth. The colonel motioned him to the empty chair that Morris Gratz had placed at the end of the table and identified, in order of seniority, the four other men.

"The board chairman has read your preliminary report, Mr. Storm, but it would be helpful if you would summarize the status of your investigation for these other gentlemen. We'll try not to keep you very long."

"Thank you, Colonel. The report is in several sections, some of which are more detailed than others." The slowness of Storm's speech bordered on the pathological. "Strictly criminal matters not involving federal law are the province of the local police and are touched on only as they relate to the matters of concern to the Bureau. Those matters are the following: By what agency did Dr. Carl Webster's transfer across state lines take place? What violations of national security laws took place, and who was responsible? Were agents of a foreign government involved and in what way? What federal laws has Dr. Webster violated?"

"We only have half an hour, Mr. Storm," interjected Rufus Snipe politely. "If you would give us some answers, we could try to dope out the questions for ourselves."

"Yes, sir." The agent turned over several sheets of paper from the pile before him. "It appears to us quite certain that Carl Webster disappeared in the company of two Pakistani nationals named Said Mukhtar and Makhdum Khan. We have been unable to check the background of either man because we do not wish to alert the Pakistani government, but ostensibly both of them were postdoctoral researchers in international affairs with no previous experience in the United States.

"Makhdum Khan rented a car under his own name and parked it on the night of Webster's disappearance in the parking lot of the Harvard Business School, where it was ticketed for illegal parking. The lot is near the end of the foot bridge across the Charles River, where Webster was last seen by a Harvard university patrolman in the company of two men. We cannot ascertain the degree of coercion, if any, used by the Pakistanis in taking Webster away; but we assume that it was not an altogether preplanned, voluntary action.

"The three then drove to Montreal where they boarded a Pakistan International Airways flight to London, Cairo, Dubai, and Karachi. The airline reports that all three passengers deplaned in Karachi, but we haven't been able to check their progress from there. The rented car was properly checked in in Montreal. The plane tickets had been purchased through a travel service in Boston two weeks earlier. The agent has identified the purchaser from a photograph as Said Mukhtar. The two Pakistanis had announced their projected departure to Harvard administrative staff at approximately the same time that the tickets were purchased. They gave no specific reason for their action. We assume, therefore, that the decision to kidnap Webster was taken at approximately the time of the presidential inauguration.

"Dr. Gratz," the agent eyed the named member of his audience, "has supplied a list of missing documents and in-and-out logs pertaining to their use. Whether these constitute a complete record is uncertain since Dr. Bonny has stated that there were occasions when the security file in the office he shared with Dr. Webster was left unlocked or documents were taken out without signature. None of the documents we presume to have been in Webster's possession was supposed to have been out of the office at that time.

"Now for the likelihood that Webster took the documents with him." Walker Rankin rested his eyes against a thumb and forefinger while Ted Bonny constructed a chain of paperclips from an ashtray full of them placed fortuitously near his seat. "We've gone through his apartment with the help of a burn-and-char specialist and have not turned up a single sheet of identifiable classified paper. We also searched the apartment of Selma Dorfman, who was killed with Mrs. Webster, and found nothing beyond evidence that the door had been forced before we arrived. Given the testimony that Webster had his attaché case with him when last seen, we assume he took everything with him.

"Finally, who set fire to the Webster apartment? We have no finding. Our guess is that it was an unidentified party associated either with Webster or the Pakistanis. I will be happy to answer any questions."

"Perhaps, Colonel Seymour, in the interest of time we should thank Mr. Storm and break for lunch now." The colonel warmly seconded Walker Rankin's suggestion and with military efficiency evacuated all persons from the room in under a minute.

"Never heard anybody talk so slow," said Rufus Snipe to his CIA counterpart as they clacked their way down the resonant corridor. "Makes you wonder what kind of people they're recruiting these days."

"I liked that padded holster around his ankle," replied Rankin. "But he should either wear his cuffs longer or not cross his legs so far."

At fifty-five, Arch Thornton, CIA Chief of Field Operations and Lincoln Hoskins's superior two giant steps up the CIA organizational ladder, was only five years senior to Link. He owned a Georgetown row house with a walnut-paneled study in the center of which stood an antique globe, three feet in diameter, cradled in a wooden stand consisting of three carved damsels with upraised arms entwined. Only twice before had Link been invited into Arch Thornton's inner sanctum, and now, as on those previous occasions, he was so struck in the gut with envy that it took a major effort of will to attend to his master's voice. Even so, half his mind was occupied in making a list of individual items that he coveted.

Through the windows looking onto the sunny, enclosed back garden he could see bright green new leaves on carefully maintained shrubbery. A marble cherub bearing an urn on his chubby shoulder surmounted a birdbath at the garden's center. Link charitably decided that Thornton could keep his birdbath. The date was April third, two months to the day since Carl Webster's disappearance.

"The reason we made you our point man on this, Link, is that while you're officially uninvolved, you're close enough to Morrie Gratz to keep track of what's going on and nudge things in the right direction. So correct me if I'm wrong, but I don't see much coming out of everybody's effort to date other than the lid being kept on. But thank God for small favors on that one."

"The problem, Arch," replied Hoskins, hoisting his Wallabees onto a soft, highly covetable, leather hassock, "is that Webster, or somebody, cleaned up pretty thoroughly in Cambridge; and Pakistan is a place that we really don't cover all that well, at least on the domestic side." Link's first name relationship with his superior was a survival of close working relations at lower-grade levels in earlier years. "The board of inquiry has written a report saying nothing important happened, but it's on hold until Seymour has run out of minor agenda items. Morrie is still in a sweat about being found guilty of something and losing his contracts. He's even relocated down here temporarily to keep his finger on our pulse. Then there's the FBI. They're being stiff on jurisdiction. Since this is foreign, they want us to take the responsibility for everything. So when you come right down to it, all we've really done is keep the goddamn Congress from finding out about the snafu and feeding it to the press. But I submit that that is no mean feat."

"I wish Congress was our only source of leaks," mused Thornton. The knowledge that a Soviet mole was lurking somewhere in the highest echelon of the executive branch of the government was constantly on his mind. "Anyhow, that's not your problem. What I really want from you is your considered opinion on the matter of what we should do with Carl Webster." The slightest spread of Thornton's thin-lipped mouth disclosed his relish in taking his colleague by surprise.

"We've got him?" asked Hoskins carefully as if sniffing around a trap.

"That's one possibility," chuckled Thornton. "Don't worry, I won't play games with you, Link. The fact is, we know where he is. He's in Islamabad in an abandoned hostel that used to be part of a U.S.-Pak educational exchange program. Not only that, but it's almost within sight of our embassy. They tried the trick of putting him so close under our nose that we couldn't see him, and it almost worked. If one of the embassy boys hadn't noticed the Pakistani foreign minister stopping at the building in an unofficial car, we would probably still be in the dark." At the words "foreign minister" Thornton raised his bristly gray eyebrows suggestively. "We got positive photo identification of Webster standing at an upstairs window a week ago. According to surveillance, he's confined to the upper floor of the hostel with a pair of guards and a servant living downstairs. The guard uniforms are military, but no unit insignia have been made out yet. They stay inside out of sight."

"What do you make of it?"

"What do *you* make of it? The guards are either keeping him in or keeping us out. Which is it?"

"Maybe it's both," answered Link sagely.

"Well, if we don't want to make a demarche to the Pakistani government over it—and I don't think we do since we don't know what their interest is—we have three options: go get him, kill him, or ignore him. Do you think he's a serious enough problem for us to waste some Pak goodwill by springing him?"

Link sensed that his response would weigh heavily in the final decision, and possibly in his own career future. "Is it my call?" Thornton dipped his head affirmatively. Link stared down at the stately green Chinese carpet and mulled the matter over. "You know, Morrie Gratz has a mechanical chihuahua he keeps with him named Ted Bonny. Every time Morrie wants to know something, he says 'speak' and Bonny delivers a little recorded message. Morrie has assigned him to piece together just what Webster was thinking about for his GULFSCENE III scenario. So far he has come up with a dozen possibilities, none of which has sounded plausible. But one thing I have gotten out of listening to him is the idea that Pakistan is a lot more important to our interests in the Persian Gulf than we're accustomed to thinking. It's big, poor, close by, and Muslim; and it has a hell of a good army. In other words, I think we've got too much at stake to assume that Webster is unimportant. I think we had better go get him."

Fifteen minutes later, as he was picking his way down the uneven brick sidewalk toward his car and pondering the rightness of his decision, it occurred to Link to wonder why Arch Thornton couldn't have brought the matter up at Langley during working hours. Did he feel that his home was the only secure place to talk? And could Webster be important enough to take such a precaution?

In the gloomy borrowed apartment off Connecticut Avenue that was serving temporarily as the emergency southern office of the Strategic Research Group, Ted Bonny was nervously trying to cope with the unprecedented advent of an original idea. He tugged at a tuft of hair growing from his protruding Adam's apple and paced quickly from the front sitting room to the back bedroom. Stepping out onto the back porch, he compulsively checked every sock and article of underwear hanging from an improvised line for dampness. From a third-floor back window of the building directly opposite, a frowsy woman's head appeared. It was a belligerent, alcoholic whore who was both the bane of the neighborhood's respectable residents and their secret party attraction whenever they led guests to their back windows to listen to her screaming obscenities at the top of her lungs to her clients.

"Can't you get a woman to do that for you, you little twerp?" she yelled raucously.

Bonny leaped six inches in the air and scuttled back into the apartment. Suddenly and miraculously, his mind was clear, as if a stuck record needle inside it had been jarred from its worn groove. Of course Pakistan could seize the Gulf! Surprise and careful planning . . . the best army in the area and the poorest economy. It wouldn't be easy, but they could do it.

7
IN TRANSIT:
THE SECOND WEEK IN APRIL

TO: GENERAL MAXIM TEJIRIAN, KGB, MOSCOW
FROM: GHOSTWRITER, WASHINGTON
INVESTIGATION OF CIA SECURITY LEAK IS BEGIN-
NING. SUBJECT: CARL WEBSTER, STRATEGIC ANA-
LYST, DISAPPEARED FEBRUARY 3. AUTHOR OF REPORT
NAMED GULFSCENE III. THOUGHT TO BE IN MOSCOW OR
ISLAMABAD. RUMOR OF POSSIBLE TIE-IN WITH UN-
SPECIFIED MAJOR EVENT IN GULF.

8
CAMBRIDGE:
THE SECOND WEEK IN APRIL

Selma Dorfman's mother wrote with the clear round letters of an elementary schoolteacher:

Dear Mr. Grandeville,

In going through Selma's things that we brought back from her apartment my husband found the enclosed papers. Since they were written by Mr. Webster, he thought that we should bring them to your attention. We don't know what to think of Mr. Webster or whether he was in some way responsible for our Selma's death, but if these help in any way to find out who set fire to that building, it will do a great deal to set our minds at ease. I am also sending a note to Professor Gratz telling him that I've sent these to you.

Mr. Dorfman and I want to thank you for being so kind and understanding. It meant a great deal to us, and we shall always be grateful.

Yours sincerely,
(Mrs.) Sarah Dorfman

Pete Grandeville set the letter aside and perused the four stapled enclosures. Each was headed with Carl Webster's name and a date, none more than a year old. All were xeroxed from messy longhand originals and had the appearance of rough drafts. The handwriting of the text did not match that of the headings and dates. He did not have to read far to discover that none pertained to the GULFSCENE series of scenarios.

With the intervention of Special Agent David Storm and a

dead end in the search for the arsonist, Pete's interest in the Webster case, both official and extracurricular, had receded. He still occasionally brought to mind the deceased Roseanne Webster, whom he would always remember as real class, but his initial urge to snoop around on his own had been cooled by the absence of things to sniff at.

One thing he had done, however, was put together a xeroxed file of Carl Webster's published articles and unpublished papers circulated within the Strategic Research Group. It was to that he now turned, after a few minutes' consideration of the fresh material brought by the day's mail. An hour later he put the file away and considered again Selma Dorfman's cache of Webster's writings. A surge of mental sap was quickly reinvigorating his dormant interest.

By her own testimony, Selma Dorfman had found it difficult to be civil to Carl Webster because of his neglect of his wife. This was made all the more understandable by the revelation of her own sexual involvement with the same woman. For his part, Carl Webster had been described as secretive about his ideas and worried about unnamed parties stealing them. Moreover, he was reported to have kept all important papers on his person or at home.

If, therefore, Selma Dorfman kept copies of longhand drafts of papers by Webster in her apartment, and those same papers were not included in what was supposed to be a complete file of his available work, how had they come into her possession? Experience had taught Pete that the academic world was peopled by proud and devious human beings who did not behave normally, but surely it was beyond credibility that a pudgy female PhD with a yen for cheesecake would seduce a colleague's wife just to get access to his unpublished work.

On further reflection, he decided it was more than credible and thanked the BVM that he had never become a part of John Harvard's world. It was odd that the slow-talking FBI golden boy hadn't hit on the Webster papers during his own search of Selma Dorfman's belongings, but Pete remembered that he himself had done little more in her apartment than eat her last piece of pie.

The FBI had come up with the suspicion that the apartment had been forcibly entered, however. The molding opposite the lock was dented and chipped to the point where a knife or credit card might have been inserted to force back the bolt, but there had been no paint chips on the floor and no proof that the damage hadn't been done before Dorfman's death.

The discovery of the chipped molding hadn't sat well with Pete. He had missed seeing it during his own visit, and it had been humiliating to admit to its presence once Storm had pointed it out. The cheap, hollow door installed during some spasm of modernization fit its frame so poorly that very little damage had been required to gain entry, but the damage was unmistakably there.

Now, two months later, he would have his chance to get even with the FBI. Pete picked up the phone and cradled it on his shoulder while he fished in the cluttered center drawer of his desk for the special telephone number Storm had given him to use. His rummaging slowed. He put down the phone and extracted instead from the drawer a piece of lined yellow paper. An idea had begun to bubble in his mind. Staring at his desktop but focusing on nothing, he slowly wrote the name Gratz on the paper and crossed it out. He wouldn't have kept it secret, he thought. He then wrote the name Bonny and likewise crossed it out. "He wouldn't have either," he murmured aloud. Finally he wrote a third name and looked at it long and hard. He underlined it and then underlined it again.

Peggy Inman was a morning person. Her small, tidy house in Belmont received good morning light through an east-facing bay window. She lived on the uphill side of the street and every year gave thanks to her Puritan God when the last of the ice melted away from her steep driveway. April the tenth was still too early to be certain that God was done punishing Boston, but for the time being, at least, her driveway was clear for the Cambridge police detective's small red Toyota to park in.

Peggy shooed her cats back from the door and greeted him with a characteristic jollity that usually stuck with her until about two in the afternoon. Pete Grandeville had called the previous evening and asked to see her at home, but she had put him off till seven-thirty AM, at which time, she had promised, she would not only be happy to talk to him but would have some homemade coffee cake and fresh coffee ready to make up for forcing him to go to work so early.

Accordingly, the first segment of the interview consisted of Peggy chattering away about crocuses and cats while Pete enjoyed a few minutes of bliss and recalled what life had been like before his mother decided that frozen waffles were a suitable replacement for all breakfast pastries. But after dabbing the last crumbs from the plate he finally had to put the question.

"Ha!" shouted Peggy exuberantly. "You finally figured it out! I knew someone would, and I'm glad it's you. That Storm fellow from the FBI rubs me the wrong way with that slow way of talking. Have you noticed his eyes? Almost lavender. They make him look like a Nazi youth leader. And that silly gun! It looks like a goiter around his ankle. You'd think he would learn not to cross his legs."

"Miss Inman—" began Pete.

"Oh, I know. You don't have to remind me. Of course I have Selma's copy of GULFSCENE III. I'll get it for you."

Pete stood up to follow her to the sunny living room, but she was back before he got to the door.

"Here it is. I just had it in the drawer of my telephone table." She handed him a half-inch thick manila envelope. "I read it. It's excellent. Probably the most original piece of work ever done for the Group." She hefted her bulky chest in a sigh. "Such a pity it didn't work out."

Pete thought about the incinerated corpses of Roseanne Webster and Selma Dorfman. "Why did you steal it, Miss Inman?"

"Well, Selma certainly had no right to it! It was Group work. I hardly consider what I did stealing." She gave Pete a small, prissy smile. "Of course, I did use gloves and clean up the paint chips on the floor. If I had been just a little bit quicker, I would have been in and out before you arrived to look at the apartment, and you probably would never have known I'd broken in." Peggy Inman's tone was that of an inveterate reader of mysteries. "Now, if you ask me how I knew Selma had a copy of GULFSCENE III, that was just common sense. The rumor that Selma was gay was all over among the graduate assistants who work at the Group, but I was sure that Roseanne wasn't normally that way because she always dressed so obviously to appeal to men. And then, of course, I also knew that Selma was terrifically ambitious. That was just the way she was. I've seen a lot of it around Cambridge, and with that kind of ambition you often get a little unscrupulousness mixed in. Finally, I knew that both Professor Gratz and Ted Bonny normally asked Selma whenever they wanted to know about Carl's work. Knowing Carl's work habits, there was only one conclusion I could draw."

Pete was still standing, weighing the envelope on his fingertips. He wondered if anyone had ever won a court case using absence of criminal spirit as a defense. Peggy was pouring a third cup of coffee in his cup. He sat down and looked at the steam rising. "Why didn't you give this to me or Professor Gratz?"

"Well, I thought of both of those things, of course. But I decided against giving it to you because it would surely have made things worse for Professor Gratz. There was already this question of security, and showing Selma to be untrustworthy right after the problem with Carl would have been bad. As it's turned out, you know, Professor Gratz has been able to keep his channels to Washington open by helping them figure out what GULFSCENE III is about, which he couldn't do if everyone actually knew what it was about. So obviously I did the right thing there.

"As to why I didn't give it to Professor Gratz himself, that was because he wouldn't have known how to handle it. I know exactly what he would have done. He would have lied about it and claimed it was a file copy from Carl's office that had been overlooked. No one in Washington would have believed him, given what they already knew about Carl's work habits and the disagreement the two of them had had over doing GULF-SCENE III in the first place. Besides, it would have left the Group with nothing more to talk to Washington about. Now if I had thought he would keep the copy as our secret, I would have given it to him. In fact, I was planning to as soon as he and Ted needed a big breakthrough in their work for Washington."

"Did Miss Dorfman have anything else by Webster? Or any classified documents?"

"She had a few things of Carl's that weren't related to the Gulf scenarios. I debated about taking those, but they were all together on a shelf, and I didn't want to leave too large a space or take a chance on disturbing something by moving a bookend to close one up. I doubt there were any documents, but I really don't know. I didn't search the whole apartment. I just looked in the most obvious place."

"Which was?"

"Next to Carl's published papers, of course. They were all in alphabetical order by author. Poor Selma had a very orderly mind." There was a sudden sharp ringing sound. "There goes my alarm." Peggy reached for a brown plastic kitchen timer and twisted the dial to silence it. "I have to leave now, but I certainly thank you for coming by. This has been great fun. I kept wondering when somebody would catch on."

Pete rose like a student dismissed from class. "There will be questions of laws violated, Miss Inman—" he began.

"It's Peggy. I know. You don't have to tell me. Withholding evidence blah, blah, blah." She led the way through the living room to the front door. "Pish and tush, Mr. Grandeville. My family has lived in Belmont for seven generations. I don't intend to skip town." She held the door open for Pete as he pulled on his checked wool jacket.

"By the way, you said GULFSCENE III was so interesting. What is it about?"

"You'll have to read it for yourself. Basically, it's a plan for India and Pakistan to capture control of all the oil in the Persian Gulf without us or the Soviet Union being able to stop them. Read it. You'll enjoy it."

Having bid his hostess good-bye, Pete drew in a deep breath of chilly air. For the first time in weeks, he didn't feel like a policeman.

The drive back to Cambridge was spent trying to decide whether to go home and read GULFSCENE III in private or go directly to the office and telephone David Storm. At the Fresh Pond traffic circle he had still not made up his mind. It took him three times around the circle to choose, but he finally headed off along the Pond as the quickest route to police headquarters. A quick look in the rearview mirror suddenly cut short his musing. The unfamiliar beige Dodge that had been behind him when he entered the traffic circle was still there, despite the three full circuits. A slight knot of apprehension formed in Pete's chest. To test his suspicion he sped up and changed lanes. The Dodge followed. Pete couldn't make out the driver's face.

Looking ahead as he neared Huron Avenue, Pete could see that he was going to be packed into a line of cars at the long red light. He reached for his radiophone as he slowed to stop. His finger on the call button, he looked in the mirror and saw the Dodge come to a halt close behind him and the driver's door open. Only when he saw who it was, did he relax and put down the phone. As the driver of the Dodge walked up, Pete rolled down the window to talk. Suddenly the man's hand came up and a small red hole made by a twenty-two caliber bullet appeared on Pete's forehead. Reaching across the policeman's slumping back as the line of cars began to move, the killer picked up the manila envelope from the seat beside him. He stooped for a moment as the oncoming cars roared past and replaced the silencer-equipped gun in the holster at his ankle. Then he ran back to the Dodge, swung it into the unblocked lane, and drove away.

Peggy Inman returned home at five-thirty. She parked her car in the garage and entered her house through the breezeway to the kitchen. Her last living sight was of her calico cat picking its way among the coffee cups and breakfast plates on the yellow oilcloth cover of her kitchen table. The last sound she ever heard was a slight whoosh of air as a lead pipe descended on the back of her skull.

9
DHAHRAN:
THE SECOND WEEK IN APRIL

In Dhahran, Saudi Arabia, petroleum engineer Virgil Foltz eyed the light caramel color of the watery distillate that dripped from his experimental rig. Color was a better indicator than smell, and he was looking for a deeper brown. The Rausch bottle filled. Virgil closed the cock on the stainless-steel apparatus, carefully sealed the bottle, and held it up to the light. It'll burn, but that's about all it'll do, he thought.

With a disappointed shrug he put the bottle in the cardboard carton beside him and grabbed another of the heavy, resealable, fruit juice bottles that had made the German manufacturer's name, Rausch, a household word among ARAMCO's drunks. Like many other basements beneath the air-conditioned, suburban bungaloes of the ARAMCO residential compound, Virgil's was equipped for brewing, fermenting, distilling—and quick concealment in the event of a raid by the Saudi religious police. An after-hours covert product of the company welding shop, the stainless steel still had cost Virgil over a thousand dollars, and he was dispirited by the discovery that while his "white" was a reasonable substitute for gin and vodka, his "brown" came out more like a bad Scotch than like the bourbon he had dreamed of producing.

"Just the wrong goddamn wood chips," he muttered as he took a swig from a Rausch bottle of ersatz Schlitz and watched the fresh Rausch bottle fill. He wondered whether his son would be stopped by the Saudi customs inspectors if he brought twenty pounds of hickory wood chips with him when he came back from college for the summer.

"Virgil!" sounded his wife Billie's call from the kitchen. "Virgil! I'm going to Bible study group at Susan Murphy's. Okay?"

"Okay, dear," called back her husband automatically. Presently he heard the front door latch. Friday's half gone, he thought, time for some serious drinking. He settled his lanky but potbellied body into a green and white aluminum lawn chair situated within arm's reach of the still and gazed at the concrete ceiling. Ten years in Arabia and nothing to show for it but money. He poured three fingers of a clear fluid from an open Rausch bottle. It burned all the way down.

Life in Arabia had not always been thus for Virgil and Billie Foltz. The thirty-year-old engineer who had gotten off the plane at Dhahran airport ten years earlier had been clear of head, taut of stomach, and ambitious to play his part in the great adventure of finding oil in the flat sand wastes of Saudi Arabia's Eastern Province. Billie had been a real soldier about swapping life in Bartlesville, Oklahoma, for life in Arabia and had suffered a private sense of deflation in discovering that the two places were not that much different. There had been a fence around the compound then: Americans on the inside with trim lawns nurtured on chemically sweetened sand; Arabs on the outside in the native town of Khobar or looking studious on the modern campus of the University of Petroleum and Mining. Little Eddie Foltz had gone to an American-style school with American teachers and had eaten Skippy peanut butter bought in an American-style supermarket.

In the early years Virgil had often helicoptered into the sands where expanding production capacity called for laying miles of pipe and installing innumerable valves and meters. The routine had had an adventurous side, what with sandstorms, showboat pilots dropping down on temporary runways, and even an encounter or two with genuine Arab nomads, already then a vanishing species highly susceptible to the Saudi plague of gold poisoning. But Virgil had worked for advancement. And he advanced—to a desk job in ARAMCO headquarters.

Being at home more often had opened Virgil's eyes. His farm-bred, clear-eyed, tolerably pretty wife, he discovered, had become a lush. After ninth grade, company policy had required that Eddie be sent abroad for schooling, and Billie had filled the vacuum at home by knocking down a few "white" and tonics every morning with her female cronies. What she did in the afternoon on the days she was not shopping the Khobar market for bedouin jewelry Virgil didn't ask. He had collected enough offers of periodic home companionship from other bored wives to catch on that the best way to avoid heartache was to stay dumb.

On the job there wasn't much to cheer about either. After the Saudi government bought the assets of ARAMCO in the late seventies, the old spirit of American enterprise started to run down. Saudization, which Virgil and all of his co-workers regarded as a ludicrous sham, was the guiding principle of company policy. Henceforth, promotions would go to the Saudi workers exclusively, and the American company men were to undertake the training of thousands more Arabs who would eventually move into their teachers' jobs. For Americans at ARAMCO, the future was effectively canceled. So why the hell not get drunk?

The American suburban atmosphere that had once made Dhahran a haven of comfort in a primitive country distrustful of foreigners and socially shackled by the dictates of religious law had become a stifling, demoralized cyst cut off from the boom-time feel of Jidda and Riyadh and poisoned by its own introspection. Paternalistic feelings toward backward natives gave way to hatred and fear. Pride in training Arabs to work efficiently in technical jobs was replaced by the drunkenly and monotonously reiterated conviction that the Saudis would never be smart enough or industrious enough to run the company for themselves.

All of this Virgil Foltz ruminated on. After all, there was little else to think about in his sunbelt ghetto surrounded by desert and oppressed by Saudi legal restrictions on public entertainment and mixed-sex activities. That is why Virgil consciously set about becoming a drunk. Illegal boozing was the most enjoyable way of flouting Saudi morality. An understanding with the regular police made the risk of a raid and a possible public whipping or stay in jail slim. The more unpredictable religious police added the necessary pinch of danger. It was a good hobby, almost a patriotic act.

Ironically, Billie discovered Jesus and swore off sinning about the same time that Virgil first got the knack of adding the right amount of yeast and sugar to imported nonalcoholic Schlitz— decanted in the inevitable Rausch bottle—to change the unpalatable stuff into ersatz beer. Billie didn't criticize Virgil's new preoccupation because she and Virgil hadn't been tuned to the same station for some time. It did mean that Virgil drank alone, however. Drank and pondered the world's two major problems: how to find a filtering agent that would make his distillate taste like bourbon and how long the kingdom of Saudi Arabia would survive.

10
BAHRAIN:
THE SECOND WEEK IN APRIL

Two hundred and thirty miles west of Dhahran on a feature-less sandy plain, Riyadh, the capital city of Saudi Arabia, propagates shiny new facets of office tower and princely palace at breathtaking speed like a complex crystal taking form in a mineral solution. The secret formula: oil revenues from the Eastern Province fields, electricity generated by associated gas from the same fields, and desalinated water distilled from the Gulf through use of still more gas. Dhahran is the vital pump that keeps the capital's and the kingdom's life-support system operating.

Thirty miles east of Dhahran, across a shallow eight-mile channel of Gulf water, is a second capital city: Manama, the seat of rule of the emir of Bahrain. The same geologic formations that enable Dhahran to support Riyadh make Bahrain an independent, if not so well-favored, organism. Manama's buildings are not Sixth Avenue skyscrapers; rather, they look somewhat drab and tired. But their fresh water comes from the island's own wells. Its streets are not embellished with marvelously engineered flyovers and interchanges; the occasional lazy roundabout is sufficient for the usual flow of traffic. But the BAPCO gasoline that keeps the traffic flowing comes from nearly exhausted wells less than twenty miles away on the southern part of the island, and the comparative absence of exotic sports cars and limousines is compensated for by frequent views of luxuriant date groves and roadside tropical gardens.

Yet for thousands of Saudi Arabia's inhabitants, differences of wealth, style, and aesthetic impact pale beside Bahrain's primary allure: in Bahrain a Saudi can sin against his nation's puritanical code. He can ogle a woman in a bikini at a mixed swimming pool. He can buy alcohol and drink it. He can see unveiled women on the street and driving cars. In short, he can breathe. No place as close offers as much.

To non-Saudis, Bahrain has other things to offer. To a grizzled old Texan named Felix sitting at the dimly lit bar of the Ramada Inn in Stetson, stitched boots, and jeans, it is his entire world, and a make-believe one at that.

"The only goddamn free country left in the world! Been here eighteen years. No matter what happens, you can do what you want in Bahrain. Am I telling you the truth? Bet your sweet ass I am! Saudi, Kooowait . . . no way they can compare with Bahrain. Ol' Uncle Sam get mixed up with that Khomeini? No trouble for me here in Bahrain. I shipped Betamaxes across to Iran by dhow, and then I sold 'em dirty movies so's they'd have something to watch. What I say is to hell with anybody who wants to fuck up this free country! Back December of '81? Remember them boys who tried a coup? I was the one who told the police! Heard 'em talking about it in a bar. I thought, they're the kinds of sons of bitches who fuck up free countries. Went right down and told Captain Aubrey who they was. Don't believe me? Ask the captain. You fixing to have another beer, son?"

"A Budweiser and a Tanqueray and tonic," said a soft fruity voice to the dark-skinned Indian bartender. The order was filled with quiet efficiency.

"Much obliged." Felix took a long pull from the frosted glass. "Yessir. Eighteen years I been here, ten in oil, eight in dhow trading. Don't regret a day of it. Let me tell you . . ."

His drinking companion tuned the cracked voice out of his mind. For him Bahrain was not simply an isolated pond dimensioned to the ego and croaking of a small Texas frog; it was a field of honor. At age twenty-nine, Meredith Orchard, the seventh (nonconsecutive) of that name, was earning the equivalent of a third of a million pounds a year, taking into account the rate of taxation he would face if he worked in Britain. Moreover, as a chartered accountant and self-employed accounting consultant to a score of Gulf businesses, his knowledge of how to store and nurture his money beyond the reach of any taxing authority was encyclopedic.

It had long been his ardent desire to become wealthy enough to reestablish the Orchard family in the ranks of England's moneyed class, a position from which it had fallen in his grandfather's generation. But there was more than a passion for riches beneath the exterior of his smooth, white forehead and limp brown hair.

The first Meredith Orchard had been a "free lance" in the literal sense of the term. Family lore had it that he had been a younger son of a Catholic English knight who had left England during the reign of Henry VIII and roamed through Italy taking service as a man-at-arms with one mercenary commander after another. His young descendant had always fancied the story, true or not, and one of the few treasures saved from the collapse of the Orchard fortune had been a drawing by Angelo Bronzino said to have been brought back from Italy by the Orchard knight-errant. The drawing was of two men, one with a decidedly Mongolian cast of feature and the other wearing a rakish hat pulled low over a long, aristocratic nose and a large piercing eye. Though without so much as a family legend to support him, Merrie was certain that the man with the hat was his namesake, drawn in the company of a fellow mercenary, probably a Tatar. In nose, eye, and spirit Merrie felt an unmistakable kinship.

Bahrain rather than Tuscany would be his own arena for seeking fame and fortune, however. With fortune almost guaranteed to any talented, aggressive, entrepreneurial businessman who found his way to the steamy Gulf, it was the fame that was more problematic. Meredith Orchard's tactic for seeking it out was to be a freelance spy.

The role had been thrust upon him by events, but he had grasped at it enthusiastically. Shortly after setting up his business, his own government's intelligence officer in Bahrain had asked him to run errands while following his normal travel circuit visiting clients throughout the Gulf states. Then he had begun submitting reports on topics of his own choosing, for which he found he was generously paid.

After a year of such occasional intelligence gathering, he had been approached in Kuwait by an American of undivulged affiliation seeking similar services and offering to pay well for them. Soon thereafter a Japanese businessman, this time in Qatar, had sought him out as a source of specialized information. After that, he had decided to close his roster of covert clients. With three different allied governments willing to pay for similar intelligence, Merrie felt he had reached the maximum level of financial return consistent with personal safety.

At this point his life was approaching perfection. His numbered bank accounts in Geneva were growing fat, and his inherited yen for risk and adventure was equally satisfied. His primary remaining need he filled during a month's sojourn in London by marrying the large-breasted, cream-complexioned sister of his Oxford roommate.

Installed in a newly completed villa and gifted with a Mercedes and driver and a thirty-foot yacht, Gwendolyn Orchard was content, though not thrilled, to allow her husband to practice baby making on her twice a day; but as time passed and ovum after ovum successfully avoided fertilization, the specter of being the last of the Orchards started to cloud Merrie's mind. At length, a vacation visit to a London urologist had confirmed that Merrie Orchard's semen contained a tragically subminimal number of the magic fishes of procreation.

Merrie's response had been twofold. First, he stopped screwing his wife; and second, he poured his energies instead into the avocation of spying. Previously unlearned in matters military, he now bought hand weapons of all description and taught himself, with friendly advice from Captain Aubrey of the Bahrain security police, to use and maintain them. He installed a Nautilus machine in a separate room of the villa and adopted a scientific program of body building. And he undertook study of encryption, explosives, silent killing, and other spylike activities.

When asked why he engaged in five-mile runs in torrid weather or went target shooting with weapons from his collection, he invariably answered boredom. In his heart, however, he admitted to an urgently awakened thirst for fame, for which his only explanation was the transmission of a wild gene from the original Meredith Orchard.

Fortunately, the time demands of his double life did not permit too much introspection. When not surveying the financial records of his business clients, he was usually engaged in ferreting out the sort of information that seemed to elude the professionals. One way he did this was by listening to long repetitious harangues from boozers like Felix. Until Felix had chattered his way through a half-dozen beers there was little hope of interrupting him with a serious question. When the time came, though, Merrie usually found the wait to have been worthwhile.

He knew, as any casual listener to Felix's ranting would surely have doubted, that Felix's claim to having denounced the plotters of 1981 was absolutely true. Captain Henry Aubrey, the English head of the security police, had told him as much, though without naming names, over brandy following one of his regular dinners at the Orchard villa. Aubrey, whose rumored past as a brutal interrogator of suspected subversives in Kenya and Aden set Merrie's teeth on edge, was a horse enthusiast, one of the passions he shared with the current emir and with Gwendolyn Orchard, who dealt with her marital disappointment in her own way. It was through this indirect equestrian connection that Merrie first gained such advice as he needed on how to acquire a spy's talents through home study and, as the relationship between Gwendolyn and the captain had warmed, such helpful tidbits of information as the one that led him to Felix.

So now, as he ordered the seventh Bud, Merrie took note of the telltale signs of the goose being done enough to carve. Felix's Stetson was on the back of his head instead of low over the eyes the way he liked to wear it to cover his long-departed hairline, and his patter had subsided into desultory spurts of invective.

"How's business, Felix?"

"Never been better," blurted the cowboy belligerently. "Ev'body wanna ship to Iran. Gotta come to me."

"What happened to Hajji Bayram? I thought he was taking your customers away."

"Hajji sold his boats. Fuckin' idiot. Only free country left in the world. Wanted to buy my boat. I told him to piss down his leg."

The recent removal from Bahrain's shipping roster of four of the largest wooden vessels called "dhows" was the thread of information that Merrie was trying to unravel. No one appeared willing to divulge the names of the unknown buyers.

"Who made you the offer, Felix?"

"Same as the others. Big Baluch fella named Sirri. Pile of fifty-dollar bills up to my elbow. I told him to go piss down his leg." Felix wheezed a laugh at the thought.

"Any idea why an Iranian wants to buy so many boats all at once?"

"Shit, Sirri ain't no Iranian Baluch! He's one of them Pakistani Baluchs."

11
ISLAMABAD:
THE THIRD WEEK IN APRIL

The heavy, warm, sweet-smelling night air felt deoxygenated and suffocating to the thin woman standing in a shadowy gateway across the street from the building where Carl Webster had been spotted. In the almost soundless surroundings she could hear the rushing of arterial blood reaching her head with every pound of her excited heart. Moonlight diffused through high, gauzy clouds made the scene before her seem overly bright; she feared it was light enough for a careful inspection of the gateway by a watcher in Webster's hostel to make out her profile—the sharp blade of a nose, pointed chin, slight bust, Uzi submachine gun. But no one was watching.

The plan to seize Webster had been laid almost two weeks previously. It hinged upon what surveillance deduced was a standing order to Webster's guards to remain indoors and out of sight, leaving errands to be run by the cook-servant. The hostel's front windows on the ground floor faced the inside of the building's courtyard wall and afforded no view of the street; the upper windows overlooking the street had revealed no trace of an occupant other than Webster. The front door opened onto a side porch with a line of sight covering part of the driveway, but not as far as the courtyard gate. The lock on the gate was controlled by an electrical switch inside the building.

Roxanne Samsun had gone over the plan with the CIA station chief, Anthony Zwemer, a score of times. The guards were obviously intended to keep Webster in rather than others out; their routine was simple and unchanging.

Samsun had been picked up for the job for three reasons: her normal field of operations was Afghanistan, which made it unlikely that she was known to Pakistani counterintelligence. Her small team of fanatically loyal Pathan tribesmen from Afghanistan could execute the seizure—the word Zwemer insisted upon instead of rescue—without implicating the United States if something went wrong. And she had a whispered reputation for being the meanest, toughest female agent in recent memory, a reputation based upon three years of brutal assassination ambushes of Soviet personnel perpetrated by her team throughout eastern Afghanistan.

The plan appeared foolproof. Only the temporary disappearance of its objective had delayed its accomplishment. During the surveillance period Webster had been taken away from the hostel for longer and longer periods of time until Zwemer and Samsun had begun to fear that he would be permanently transferred before they were ready to act. Then suddenly he was gone, and the edgy wait for his return commenced. During the anxious days of waiting Samsun had been increasingly upset by Zwemer's insistence that the entry of the hostel be made only by the men on her team to protect the CIA even further from discovery. Being forced into the role of providing warning or cover fire if needed was not Roxanne's usual way of working, but she had complete trust in her lieutenant Qorban Ali's ability to command the mission.

The long wait ended with word from surveillance at eleven o'clock on an April evening that Webster had been delivered back to the hostel in a car bearing army license plates, had eaten dinner, and had not left since. Immediately Roxanne gave Qorban Ali the order to drive a prepared Chevrolet van into the residential street and park it at a preselected point diagonally across from the hostel's gateway. Two impatient hours of telescopic observation assured her that the van's presence was not going to be investigated. Then she herself took up position with radio and gun in the dark gateway.

At two o'clock she radioed the Pathans into action. Their

baggy *shalwar* pants and long *kurta* shirts were Pakistani garb, but their abundant turbans were from their home territory, making it difficult to misidentify the four men who sauntered up to the black van. Their big-boned, six-foot-plus Pathan physiques would in any case have indicated their origin, but a calculated part of the plan was a fifty percent probability that someone could be found who remembered seeing them; and the CIA wanted that memory to point to Afghanistan and the Soviet Union.

One of the Pathans took tools from the van and quickly short-circuited the lock on the gate, making it possible to swing it open without tripping an alarm inside. Then he joined the three others in silently pushing the van backward across the street and into the driveway. Roxanne gritted her teeth at the almost imperceptible crunch of gravel on the driveway.

At the front corner of the hostel the van came to a silent stop. The dark outline of a man grew from its top and hoisted itself onto the flat, first-floor roof. Qorban Ali crouched by the low parapet waiting for any noise from inside the house that might signal a guard's reaction. There was none. He picked his way silently in sandaled feet across to the glassed door that had been pinpointed as Webster's bedroom. He studied the lock carefully in the moonlight.

In the opposite gateway Samsun slowly released a drawn breath when she saw his form disappear into the building. One of the danger points of the operation had been the possible need for a flashlight to assist the entry.

Moments later her feeling of relief was replaced by apprehension. Qorban Ali had reappeared on the roof, but with Webster slung motionless across his back instead of walking beside him. Two other figures appeared on the van's roof and accepted the heavy body as it was lowered over the parapet. Then all was in shadow.

Roxanne chewed anxiously on her lower lip as the van moved

with painful slowness up the slight grade that had made entry into the driveway so simple. Finally it was clear of the gate, and the gate was gently reset. With the slightest of coughs the carefully tuned engine caught. There was still no sign of alarm from the hostel. Roxanne quickly but carefully studied both ends of the street with eyes and ears to discern whether there was any indication that a blocking force was being moved into position. Then she strode to the open door of the van and stepped inside.

As they drove at a slow, unobtrusive speed toward the vehicle change-point at the foot of the forested Margala hills on the edge of the city, Samsun congratulated Qorban Ali and the other three team members in their native Pushtu. Then she turned her eyes to the fleshy, recumbent, light-haired man on the floor.

"He is drugged, Lady," said Qorban Ali. She pulled open an eyelid with long, thin fingers and nodded. It was a possibility that had been considered unlikely. She slapped the man's face sharply. The responding moan was encouraging. She opened a plastic medical kit and drew out a small bottle of ammonia. In the close air of the van the coughs produced by the acrid fumes came from the taciturn Pathans as well as the captive. She slapped the man again and twisted his ear. He winced and raised the leaden lids of his eyes ever so slightly.

"Carl Webster?" she said loudly. "Are you Carl Webster?"

"Ich heisse Dieter Lauf," mumbled the man.

Roxanne drew her head back from the ear she had shouted into. Then she leaned forward again. *"Sein Name ist Dieter Lauf?"*

"Ja," replied the man weakly with reshut eyes.

As the Pathans looked on in silence Samsun reached again into the medical kit. She carefully filled a syringe from a blue ampule and injected it into the man's arm, killing him.

"Turn around, Aslam," she said to the driver in Pushtu as she did up the medical kit. "Drop me back near the head of the street we came from. Then go with the others into Rawalpindi and put this body where it won't be found."

"I could not tell, Lady," said Qorban Ali dejectedly.

"It's not your fault, Qorban. The CIA chief is a donkey prick."

"I will go back with you."

"No. You will all go to Rawalpindi. You were probably seen by someone on the street. If an alarm has been raised, you will be too noticeable. I'm going there only to reconnoiter."

"The CIA man is waiting."

Making no attempt at modest concealment, Roxanne changed from jeans and black shirt to a flowered Pakistani woman's costume. As the truck slowed she pulled a lightweight purple shawl over her braided black hair. "Patience is a virtue, Qorban, even for the CIA. Anywhere along here, Aslam." She looked through the windshield. "Make it under those trees on the left."

The van did not stop in the shadow of the trees, but as it continued slowly on its way it left behind a shuffling Pakistani woman carrying a basket.

Three miles away in a damp-smelling clump of trees Tony Zwemer looked at his watch for the fiftieth time. The radioed word from surveillance had been that the van had gotten away cleanly from the hostel. But too much time had elapsed since then. They would have to leave and try again in the morning at the secondary pickup point. He motioned his two lookouts back to the car. As they drove down the short stretch of bumpy dirt road that gave back onto a deserted parking lot the radio spoke. The volume was set at a minimum, but the tiny voice was clear.

"The van is back. They've dropped her off alone."

Zwemer's imagination came alive with possibilities. He kept driving at a sober pace but changed the return route to pass within sight of the hostel.

Roxanne shuffled determinedly to the head of the street and

turned into it. A pause to sniff the air for danger would not have been compatible with the already none-too-credible sight of an unaccompanied woman hurrying home at an inexplicably late hour. A hundred meters from the gateway she spied a telltale sliver of a guard's face protruding far enough beyond the wall that the gate was set into to allow a single eye to search the street. Switching her left hand to the handle of the basket, she dropped the right inside where it curled around the butt of a familiar silencer-equipped pistol nestled in a pile of grenades.

The distance closed to fifty meters. An explosion of light burst upon her face from the suddenly switched-on high-beam headlights of a car directly in front of her that she knew to have been parked there for the entire day. It took scarcely a second to pop a bullet into each of the lights, but her night vision was destroyed. By muscle memory she swung the pistol toward the gateway and fired again. Her ears picked up a crunch behind her that turned into running footsteps. As she pivoted toward the sound she exchanged the gun for a grenade, but the footsteps were upon her. Invisibly from the dark a heavy body charged into her midsection and drove her backward. The basket fell free as she collapsed on the ground beneath her assailant. She recognized a skillful choke-hold constricting her throat and then nothing more.

The chilling words "They've got her" brought a single whispered curse from the carload of agents nearing the deceptively quiet-looking entrance to the street. None of them turned their heads to look as they drove steadily past. They drove two miles further on before circling back toward the embassy. Another terse report informed them that Roxanne had been carried into the hostel and then that two unidentifiable cars had arrived and discharged a substantial ("more than eight") number of passengers.

"A real fuckup," said Tony Zwemer matter-of-factly in the dark car. "I wonder where Qorban Ali is."

12
ISLAMABAD:
THE THIRD WEEK IN APRIL

Carl Webster and Roxanne Samsun faced each other without speaking. He had not expected his rescuer to be a woman. But woman she was, and her presence in the room shivered the spider web of feelings that Carl had about women. The guard who had ushered her into Webster's gilded cage had difficulty unlocking her handcuffs because her right arm was in a sling. That, too, had not been part of Carl's plan, but he was cheered by the absence of any kind of cast.

The guard withdrew and shut the double door of the spacious, lobbylike sitting room. Carl still could not find the words to begin conversation. While awaiting inspiration, he catalogued her parts: thin face and body, medium height, matte black hair, large forehead, hawk nose, dark skin touched with yellow ocher coloration, raw umber eyes. He guessed her age to be thirtyish, but her inert, unmadeup face conveyed the outward blankness of an aged blind seer. Why didn't she move?

"I'm Carl Webster," he blurted at a nervously high pitch. "I'm the man you tried to rescue."

"Seize." The flat monosyllable delivered through motionless lips had overtones of hatred and disgust.

"Please sit down. I'll ring for some tea if you like. Are you hungry?" The woman walked three steps to an ornately upholstered armchair and sat. "They didn't hurt you after, uh, capturing you, did they?" Her head neither nodded nor shook. "You know that we can't leave here, don't you? It's a splendid prison, but it's very well guarded."

"Do I have a room?"

"With separate bath, in fact. It's to the left at the top of the stairs." Samsun glanced toward the low marble steps ascending to a mezzanine level where doors opened off of a walkway running the length of the room. She got up, climbed the stairs slowly, and disappeared behind the first door on the left.

Forty-eight hours later she reappeared. Trays of food placed at her door had been taken inside and returned empty, and she had accepted an armload of clothes from a servant. Otherwise there had been no indication that she was alive inside the room.

Carl was reading Ibn Khaldun's classic introduction to the study of history. Dating from the fourteenth century, it was one of the more recent titles in the sitting room bookcase and one of only seven in English. Over the top of the page he followed Roxanne's steps down the marble staircase and over to a teakwood dining table with a dish of fruit on it. He watched her peel and eat a banana awkwardly, using mostly her left hand.

"I'd like to talk to you about why we're both here," he ventured. "It would be good for us to get to know each other since we're here for the duration. This hiding place won't be as easily found as the other one."

"Duration of what?" queried Roxanne with what sounded like idle curiosity.

"Tell me your name and I'll tell you the story thus far. If you want to know how the soap opera goes after that, you'll have to tell me some more about your side of it."

In a too large and atrociously gaudy Pakistani seamstress's version of an American house dress, Roxanne looked neither alluring nor threatening. Nor did the now-scruffy cotton sling enhance her ensemble. But her facial expression in response to Webster's proposal was that of a high school girl considering a date with an older, more experienced man. Desire to sample the water was visibly mixed with a fear of getting in too deep.

"My name is Lily Mason," she said at length.

"Good. Let's consider that. Maybe your name is Lily Mason;

maybe it isn't. Either way we can proceed. But if it isn't Lily Mason and I find out, I won't talk to you anymore. So what's the probability of my finding out your real name?"

"It depends on whom you talk to."

"And who would you guess I talk to?"

Roxanne thought. "Since we walked into a trap trying to get you out of that miserable house and there's a good indication that you left the U.S. willingly with the Paks, I would guess that you talk to Pakistani intelligence. Beyond that I can't guess. As for the Paks, they don't know me."

"Good planning. You work in Afghanistan?"

She ignored both the observation and the question. "So the question is whether the Paks can find out who I am from my employer, and that depends upon how badly my employer wants to get me out . . . and on the ability of my employer's local representative to handle things. That last, I can tell you, is a weak reed. He should have spotted this as a setup from the start. Okay, I'm not Lily Mason. I'm Roxanne Samsun."

"How interesting! My wife's name is Roseanne."

"I know." Roxanne took note of the present tense.

"Well, Roxanne, it's nice to meet you. Your actual thought process, by the way, was that the primary mission underlying the 'seizure' plan was to gather intelligence about my intentions, therefore you would employ some harmless candor and admit your real name in order to get me to talk more freely. You think I can't do anything with your name, anyway. Good. I like a logical mind that doesn't let on what it's doing. Besides, the strategy is going to work. Now that I think you're bright enough to think that out, I will tell you more than I would tell to a dummy."

Roxanne mentally surveyed the means at hand for murdering Webster. Even with a still very painful dislocated shoulder she could think of six painful ways and two boring ones. She had no intention of resorting to any of them because that was not her mission, but it was satisfying to think about crushing his skull. Not since fifth grade had she encountered as much palpable condenscension from a "great mind" addressing a lesser. But in fifth grade the great mind had been that of her grandfather and had been genuine.

"Okay, Mr. Webster . . . Carl. I've been briefed about you so thoroughly I feel like your sister. I'm all ears. Tell me what brings you to Pakistan." She seated herself demurely on the stiff, cushioned couch opposite his chair.

Carl placed a fringed leather bookmark in Ibn Khaldun. "I was just reviewing Ibn Khaldun's theory of a natural cycle of political power. A tribe rushes in from the desert full of energy and esprit de corps. It topples an effete regime and moves into the capital city. Then it fritters away its energies on wine, women, and song until it becomes dependent on mercenaries or slaves for defense and eventually falls to a new force from the desert. Have you ever read it?"

"No."

"I recommend it. You'll have plenty of time. The reason I mention it, though, is because, in a sense, that's what's going on here. Quite simply, the reason I am in Pakistan is that I have devised a plan by which Pakistan and India, working together, can capture control of most of the oil in the Persian Gulf from the effete Arab rulers who now have it and divert the revenues to the subcontinent."

Roxanne could not suppress her first thought. "But Pakistan and India hate each other! They can't work together!"

"Right and wrong. They do have a history of hatred, but that doesn't mean they can't work together given great enough safeguards and incentives. Foreign policy is determined in both countries by a very small number of people. If you can convince them of something, they can turn the country's policy around overnight."

"And you've convinced them?"

"GULFSCENE III has. Do you know what GULFSCENE III is?"

"I certainly know *what* it is, but I don't know what's in it. You didn't leave any copies lying around when you left."

"Then let me tell you about it. Leaving aside Iran and Iraq, who will probably continue to gnaw each other's vitals for another ten years, the countries of the Gulf can best be compared to a group of irascible millionaire paraplegics coasting down 116th Street in Harlem in golden wheelchairs at four in the morning. They're wearing guns they don't know how to use; they're being pushed by poverty-stricken attendants whom they despise; and their main hope of protection lies in the timely use of a police whistle. Now there's no way in the world that they're going to make it down that street without losing those chairs and ending up in the gutter. The only question is who will do the mugging: the neighborhood bad guys, the attendants, or the police? Since each of these three is uncertain about the plans and capabilities of the other two, however, the millionaires manage to keep on going. In GULFSCENE III I show how the poor attendants can make off with the gold without being clobbered by rival muggers." A surly-looking absence of interest on Roxanne's face brought the lecture to a halt. "What's the matter?"

"In the last three years I've personally killed eleven Soviet personnel, two of them with a knife, and my team altogether has made a hundred and thirty kills of Afghan collaborators and Russians combined. During that time I've lived under conditions you can't even imagine. Moreover, the reason I'm so pissed off about being here now is that this operation to get you back under American jurisdiction was the pettiest assignment I've had in a year. Do you understand what I'm saying?"

"Not entirely."

"What I'm saying is that I don't want to listen to extended metaphors! I did that in college English, and that's not where I'm at anymore!"

Carl was pushed back in his chair by the sudden and unexpected violence of her words. Then he leaned forward again. "Sorry. I'll start again. India and Pakistan at the present time have a combined population pushing eight hundred and fifty million. By comparison, the combined population of Bahrain, Kuwait, Saudi Arabia, Qatar, Oman, and the United Arab Emirates is at the very most seventeen million. That's two percent of the population of the subcontinent. Looking at it from the standpoint of wealth, the relationship is nearly the reverse. Per capita income in Pakistan and India is only a small percentage of per capita income in those Arab countries.

"Now, I am not going to make the moralistic argument that world wealth should be equalized. However, there are other consequences of demographic imbalance to consider. Most important, the citizens of the Gulf states cannot afford to protect their countries by personal service. Every citizen of Abu Dhabi or Dubai has money-making opportunities far in excess of any rational level of military pay. Through obligatory service it might be possible to levy an army, but the soldiers would all leave for greener pastures as soon as possible and would spend most of their service days working on moonlight business deals. This situation differs in degree from country to country, of course, because they don't all have as much money as, say, the Saudis. But in general, their native military manpower levels are low compared to national wealth. As a result, they resort to two ways of filling out their armor. First, they buy expensive hardware, even though they probably will never be able to sustain a native fighting force with sufficient training and practice to make it work right. And second, they hire foreign guns.

"In GULFSCENE III, it's the foreign guns that are crucial. They originate from different countries, but basically they are either Western or Muslim: Brits and Americans for technical training and Pakistanis as clerks, advisers, instructors, and troops. The Paks are cheap, and they're good. But more important, the Arabs trust them, even though they look down on them, because they're Muslim and they aren't greedy brother Arabs. So the upshot is that without really intending to, the Pakistani military finds itself in the position of having thoroughly infiltrated the Gulf armies.

"This doesn't mean, though, that they can just walk in and take over. First, they're not deployed properly. Second, the U.S. wouldn't stand for it. And third, the Russians and the Indians are in a position to cut them off at the knees. So the poor Paks just drool and hope and mutter about their right to 'Muslim oil.'

"Now look at it from the Indian point of view. There are almost as many Indians working in the Gulf states as Pakistanis, but they're not important militarily and they don't contribute as much to the Indian economy as the Pakistani workers do to their economy. Without money from workers in the Gulf, Pakistan would go broke. Still, India would like to tap more Arab money than it has. But their primary annoyance in life is Pakistan. They're convinced the Paks want to build an atom bomb and make some sort of suicidal effort to get Kashmir back. So they have to maintain a large and expensive preponderance of force to keep the Paks from biting them. Pakistan, of course, says it only wants peace with India, but after three wars the Indians don't believe them.

"What GULFSCENE III visualizes is an agreement between Pakistan and India to act jointly in the Gulf based on the following principles: India contributes its entire nuclear stockpile to the enterprise and in return Pakistan abandons its own nuclear program. After taking over the Gulf, the two countries work out a revenue-division formula taking into account the fact that Pakistan, as a Muslim power, will have to be the actual occupying force in the Gulf since the power and influence of Muslim countries worldwide would be sufficient, over time, to undermine any non-Muslim interloper in the area. I've suggested they split half and half with the understanding that Pakistan will be responsible for bailing out the economy of Bangladesh. And finally, both countries would sever their strategic connections with the superpowers and declare a nuclear-free zone in the Indian Ocean. Eventually India and Pakistan will probably work out some sort of peace and friendship treaty, but that's outside the time frame of GULFSCENE III.

"Let me finish, and then you can ask questions. Benefits: Pakistan goes from being poor to being fairly rich and gains a modest empire. It takes the place it has always desired as the world's leading Muslim country. It also gets India off its back. All it sacrifices in return is its alliance with the U.S., which it won't need anymore in any case, and a nuclear weapons program that probably hasn't gotten beyond making a single bomb yet. India, too, goes from rather poor to rather well off, and also gets rid of the Pakistani military threat. With any luck, the two countries together should be able to make themselves into a world-class military and economic power and gain complete hegemony in the Indian Ocean region.

"As for the Arabs, they get screwed; but they've got so much laid down in foreign bank accounts that nobody's going to feel sorry for them. Their plans for modernizing the desert, of course, would stop as soon as the money got diverted to Pakistan and India; but no one's going to grieve about that either. Finally, from the point of view of the superpowers, the whole thing sounds like a bad idea simply because it juggles the world balance of power too much and threatens to create a major new force by combining the resources of India, Pakistan, and the Gulf. Actually, it isn't bad for the superpowers, but they can't be expected to see it that way. They're too accustomed to acting on the principle that anything they can't control is bad, and GULFSCENE III has taken this into account. If the Indo-Paks play out the scenario properly—for which, I don't mind saying, they need my advice—they should be able to prevent either the U.S. or the Soviet Union from intervening to stop them."

Carl Webster sat back in his chair and awaited a response. "Don't rush. Think it through. It's complicated."

Roxanne sensed that he had suddenly passed from being the didactic, patronizing professor to being a twelve-year-old presenting his stamp collection to a visitor in hopes of having it admired. His high, smooth forehead sparkled with sweat generated by the effort to make a clear and concise presentation.

"I don't see why the Pakistanis wouldn't cheat, keep all the oil for themselves, and get into a war with India. The people who run this country, and India too, for that matter, are not saints. If you're right, and they've got an army and a fifth column in the Gulf already, why not take the money and run?"

"Excellent question. It brings us directly to stage two of my proposal. The Pakistanis and the Indians are now in the process of executing GULFSCENE III. But what they're doing and how it plays from here on out I don't intend to tell you until you've told me what's happening on your side."

"I'll think about it," replied Roxanne. "Changing the subject, what kind of house is this that we're being held in? I have something that looks like a Gideon Koran in the table by my bed."

Knowing when not to push people was a virtue that Carl had to work hard to approximate. But he needed Roxanne Samsun too much to risk losing her. It was the only way to remedy the one flaw in GULFSCENE III. "I'm told that this is a guest villa belonging to a Muslim religious group allied with the government. It's for entertaining pious foreigners. We're probably the first infidels ever to stay here. For all I know, we may be polluting it so much they'll have to reupholster the furniture. But I don't pretend to know much about the Islamic religion. The kitchen's through there." He pointed to a sliding door beyond the teakwood table. "They set up meals at this table. I'll be delighted if you join me. All of the other doors are locked except for your bedroom suite and mine. We can get out into the garden through that sliding glass panel down there." He pointed to the far end of the room from the kitchen door. "It's very pleasant, but it's completely enclosed by a brick wall. I've counted twenty-four different varieties of flower in bloom, but I don't know the name of a single one of them."

"What time are meals?"

"Eight for breakfast, or whenever you get up. Around twelve-thirty for lunch. Eight for supper. The same times your tray was brought."

"Do you consider yourself a prisoner?"

"Yes and no. I can't leave, but I don't want to either."

Roxanne wandered around the room looking at more specimens of carved teakwood furniture and at some beautifully scribed religious sayings framed on the walls. "Tell me, Carl, why did you arrange things so that someone impersonating you would be rescued and a follow-up scout would be captured? It seems rather pointless."

"Pointless? Not at all. That the U.S. government would launch a significant effort to get me back was one of the last proofs I offered the Pakistanis that I wasn't an American agent myself. As for the capture, I told them I just wanted one American familiar with intelligence work to keep me company. Frankly, I get tired of talking to Pakistanis and Indians all the time."

"So we played right into your hands."

"Of course. That's what GULFSCENE III is all about. The only questionable item was whether Pak intelligence could dredge up someone who looked enough like me to fool the rescue team. By the way, what will become of that German tourist they came up with?"

"I killed him."

Carl felt as if a powerful hand had reached inside his chest and squeezed his heart in an iron grip.

Consultations with the core group of Pakistani officers charged with managing the Gulf scenario normally occupied Carl's mornings. Sometimes he was escorted to an office in the guesthouse where a secure telephone line had been installed. On other days, he was picked up by car—always nondescript, never the same—and driven to a meeting. His quasi-prisoner status was not entirely to Carl's liking. He had envisaged himself in a more obvious position of control. Thinking that India and Pakistan might distrust each other so much that they would refuse to cooperate without elaborate safeguards and provisions for independent confirmation of each other's actions, he had even prepared for the possibility of acting as the sole conduit of messages between the two countries and independent guarantor of their accuracy, a kind of messenger of the gods or real-life control team. But he had not seen his computer-generated one-time cipher pads since leaving Cambridge, nor had he been asked to play such an active role.

Fortunately, however, flexibility on nonessentials came easily to him. If it was General Baber's will as president of Pakistan that he be kept confined and be deprived of ciphering materials, so be it. When he conferred with the military officers and occasional civilian officials who attended the meetings, there was no doubting their dependence upon his interpretation of ongoing developments and their utter faith in the grasp of world strategy displayed in GULFSCENE III.

To his surprise and, when he considered it, satisfaction, the sole Indian participant in the meetings was Dr. Lal Chatterjee, the short, rotund nuclear physicist he had consulted with so frequently in Cambridge and from whom he had gleaned the information on the organization of India's nuclear establishment he needed to flesh out CIA reports on weapons capability. During a break on the first day of Dr. Chatterjee's presence, the physicist explained that he had requested the job of being the conduit between Carl and the Indian government because their familiarity with one another would lessen the possibility of misunderstandings. In addition, his continuing presence in Pakistan, if discovered, would be less alarming to foreign observers than that of a senior government official. How the more senior figures were handling their participation while maintaining secrecy was a question that Dr. Chatterjee said he was not at liberty to answer. Thus one more small annoyance was added to Carl's list.

Late in the morning Carl would be delivered back to the guesthouse. Although different routes were taken in driving him to and fro, he observed enough of the guesthouse surroundings to realize that the copse of woods it was situated in totally prevented observation from a distance and made it possible to maintain a nearly invisible security guard, as well. The building itself was red brick with wide eaves and a high gable unusual in Pakistan. The wrought-iron grillwork over the glass front door contained the ingenious-looking curlicues and loops of Arabic writing, but their import was lost on Carl.

The main meal of the day was served at noon. The food, primarily rice and meat, was good but heavy. Thus, a siesta afterward was more a necessity than a luxury. The slow hours for Carl were the ones after he awoke. With the library nearly useless, solitary versions of chess and backgammon were his chief diversion—a diversion made somewhat more palatable by the availability in the sitting room of two intricately carved ivory sets with inlaid boards. Yet Carl hoped against hope that the fellow captive he had planned for would turn out to be expert at one game or the other.

Two days after his initial breaking of the ice with Roxanne, he resolved to sound her out on the subject of games, even though her insistence on portraying herself as a homicidal maniac had been very unsettling. It had, in fact, ripped to shreds Carl's spider web of feelings about women. Prior to her announcement of the German tourist's demise, he had even given a fleeting thought to the possibility of bedding her. She was skinny, but in spite of the sloppy dress he could see that she was firm and sufficiently rounded. Even her deadpan face with the sundial nose had a peculiar attractiveness all its own. But making love to a killer was out of the question. Even playing chess with one seemed fraught with risk.

In any case, Carl's resolve to raise the subject was forestalled by Roxanne's declaration over lunch that she was ready to tell Carl what she knew about the U.S. reaction to his disappearance. Groggy from three helpings of rice mixed with raisins, lamb, sliced carrots, and orange peel, Carl was dying to hit the sack, but he was still alert enough to realize that Roxanne's timing had been keyed to his predictable somnolence. He recalled that she had ladled the third helping onto his plate herself. So he goaded himself to wakefulness so as not to miss anything of importance in what she had to say.

When the servant had cleared away the dishes and left them alone with their tea and a bowl of oranges, Roxanne began to talk while peeling an orange with concentrated precision.

"What I know comes from three sources: my own experience, which amounts primarily to a realization that my bosses did not know what they were doing when they sent me to get you; a briefing paper and psychological profile that the Agency has prepared; and questions I asked of the man who flew out from Washington."

"What was his name? I might know him."

"No names," said Roxanne flatly.

"No names, no deal," replied Webster.

"Lincoln Hoskins."

"He's a friend of Morrie Gratz, the head of the Harvard-MIT Strategic Research Group. We've never met."

"So he says."

"Who did the psych profile? It should at least have been initialed."

"A.L.K. Does that mean anything?"

Carl thought then shook his head sleepily. "Probably not. Go on."

"Well, the profile portrays you as a megalomaniac genius with borderline schizophrenia, an amoralist, and a male chauvinist pig. Does that leave anything out?"

"Does it go into detail?" Carl asked as a look of morbid fascination passed fleetingly over his face.

"Like you wouldn't believe. I've never seen such detail. They have dredged up stuff on you that you've probably forgotten yourself." Carl's eyebrows lifted with surprise even while his eyelids continued to droop. "I can tell you about that later if you want. I know I'm keeping you from your nap."

"I know you know. And I resent your doing this to me."

"The briefing paper covered through mid-April. Your tracks were picked up without too much difficulty in Cambridge, but there was uncertainty as to whether you were in Pakistan or had gone on to the Soviet Union through Afghanistan. That was solved when you were identified in the hostel. Your friends back in Cambridge made sure you left nothing behind. I don't know whether you know this, but they torched your apartment at night and killed your wife and the woman she was sleeping with."

Carl's eyes opened wide with shock. "They did what!? They killed Roseanne? What an utterly asshole thing to do! Who was the woman she was sleeping with? Did you say a *woman*?"

For the first time since entering Webster's presence Roxanne smiled for a moment. "I didn't think you knew. Yes, somebody burned them both up. Death from inhaling toxic fumes. It could have been worse. The other woman was your office mate, Selma Dorfman." Her smile returned in response to the astonished look that spread over Webster's face affecting every square centimeter from unreceding hairline to second chin.

"Selma." He said the name almost in a whisper. "The little

shit floozy! Smug cheater. She must have been using Roseanne to get at the stuff I kept at home. No wonder Roseanne wouldn't tell me who she was making it with!"

"Dorfman's apartment was broken into, but there is no evidence that anything was taken away. Do you think she had a copy of GULFSCENE III?"

Carl was still shaking his head in wonderment. "I don't know. If she did, the Paks must have gotten it. But even if she didn't, she had probably read it. It's probably a good thing they killed her."

"But too bad about the wife?" prompted Roxanne.

"Yes, of course. It's ghastly," responded Carl remotely.

"Let me go on. An interagency board of inquiry was put together in Washington to make a report on your disappearance and its possible security impact. According to Lincoln Hoskins, this was a front staffed with dead wood to create a pile of paper that the higher-ups could hide behind if anything leaked. Your friends Gratz and Bonny worked with the board, but they've now been seconded to the Agency to pursue things at a more serious level."

"God help the Republic. I'm amazed that Hoskins told you things like that."

"I was their best bet for a fast, failsafe operation; and I've got the kind of reputation that makes people take me seriously when I say I won't go without an honest briefing. I scare people. I don't know how. I just do." The hell you don't know how, thought Carl. "Let me see. After the board reported, someone gave orders to spring you. That's as far as the paper went. What Hoskins said beyond that was that there's a real apprehension in high places that you're not a routine traitor, but that you're actually planning something awful." A change of expression was gradually coming over Carl's face, and he didn't appear to be paying attention. "They want to know what, and they want to stop it. But they just haven't been able to piece it together. I

might add, if I broke out of here tonight and told them everything you've told me so far, I still think they wouldn't understand it. Frankly, it doesn't make much sense to think of India
and Pakistan working together under any circumstances. On the
other hand, it's evident that someone is taking you seriously, so
now I'm waiting to hear you tell me why GULFSCENE III is
going to work."

Roxanne looked carefully into Carl's seemingly blank eyes. "I
think you'd better go lie down, Carl. You're as white as a
sheet." Without further prompting Carl stood up and dumbly
headed for the stairs. Roxanne watched him until he closed the
door to his room. She understood what had happened, and
welling up inside her she felt an identical but long-suppressed
emotion, one she had first felt on being told that her father had
been shot dead by an Armenian terrorist. It had been eight
years. The news had struck her like a razor sharp blade slicing
off a limb so surely and cleanly that it had taken several minutes
to become aware of the incredible pain and the loss. When the
realization finally hit, it had overwhelmed her. From upstairs
came the muffled sound of sobbing. Roxanne cradled her head
on her arms and wept too.

In the late afternoon Roxanne cautiously did her karate exercises in the walled garden, testing the limits of her stiff shoulder. Baggy white *shalwar* pants and chemise with a red shawl
belted around the waist made a strikingly appropriate-looking
costume. When she stepped back into the house, tired but
loose, Carl was waiting for her.

"I'm ready to tell you the rest of GULFSCENE III now." His
voice was lacking its customary patronizing overtone, but he
looked composed. He was wearing a light red robe over American-style pajamas. "Let's sit down." He led the way to the arm-
chairs where a tea service was already prepared. Roxanne
poured.

"The key to GULFSCENE III is the deployment of the entire Indian nuclear arsenal of ten explosive devices on ships in the Persian Gulf. Three times that many freighters and large dhows are being bought through dummy agents. Only the Indians will know which of them contain weapons, and the Indians will maintain exclusive control over them with one proviso, that they cannot remove any of the thirty weapons ships from the area. The Paks and Indians will then open their nuclear plants to continuous inspection by the other country to ensure that neither side makes any more weapons.

"For their part, the Paks have infiltrated complete commando units into key points in each of the six Gulf states. They're small, but they're the best. They can go into action on a moment's notice with weapons drawn from local arsenals by Paks in the supply services of the Arab armies. On D-day, India and Pakistan will issue a joint ultimatum to the six rulers giving them orders to abdicate in favor of the president of Pakistan and to surrender control to the Pakistani commando teams. The alternative given will be nuclear annihilation from ships floating in their harbors. At the same time, Pakistanis in the armies, police forces, and communications networks will blank out contact between the rulers and their armed forces and the Western embassies.

"If confirmation of surrender is not received at the field command headquarters within an hour of the ultimatum being delivered, a demonstration bomb will be detonated in a high air burst over the water east of Qatar. The ultimatum will tell the Arabs where to look, and everyone but the Kuwaitis will be able to judge the credibility of the ultimatum with their own eyes. The wind pattern should carry the fallout over areas that are almost uninhabited."

"Excuse me for interrupting, but I thought you said the bombs were all on ships. How do you get an air burst?"

"Surprising, isn't it? Let me just say that if there's no need to determine exactly where the damn thing will land, the Indians are capable of pitching a nuke into the air on a ship-borne rocket. But I doubt that a demonstration will be necessary. Most of the ruling families will be in their jets and out of their countries in less than an hour. The Omanis might want to stick it out; they're tough. But with half their army recruited in Pakistan, they should figure out the odds pretty quick.

"Obviously, the crucial element of the scenario is the U.S. reaction. That's where the Paks have to depend on me, sort of as a control team, to tell them what's happening. Since Washington is committed to the belief that any political change in the world other than the collapse of a Communist regime is probably bad, the U.S. would certainly oppose GULFSCENE III if it knew what it was about. But I can prove from a whole series of crisis-simulation games that U.S. intelligence capability, reaction time, and speed of military redeployment are so poor that clever deception and rapid execution can create a fait accompli before the Americans have a chance to interfere.

"In GULFSCENE III the deception is built in. Since no one in his right mind would ever imagine the Indians and the Paks could overcome their hatred enough to work together, simply believing that GULFSCENE III can take place strains credulity. Moreover, even if they sense something fishy going on, each superpower will have to tread very carefully because the two countries involved live under the tacit protection of opposite powers. The Soviets have to be circumspect about Pakistan if they don't want to upset the Americans, and the Americans vice versa about India. In other words, the superpowers will react first as if some scheme were being hatched by a surrogate of the opposing superpower and only secondarily consider the likelihood that Pakistan and India are acting together independently. By the time they catch on, it'll be too late. There's no way in the world they can pressure the Indians to take their bombs out of the Gulf without simultaneously jeopardizing world energy supplies. The demonstration bomb, whether exploded at the time of the ultimatum or later, will prove Indo-Pak willingness to blow the oil to kingdom come if pushed too hard.

"Then in the aftermath, I expect the Soviets will finally realize that having the Indo-Paks in a position to nuke the Gulf oilfields is potentially advantageous to them because it means the U.S. can never achieve total control of the area for itself. When the Soviets start to need oil from the Gulf themselves fifteen years from now, they will prefer buying it from the Indo-Paks than directly or indirectly from the U.S. It's already bad enough that they have to depend on American grain.

"The Americans, for their part, will probably come to realize that stabilizing the Indian subcontinent by making it rich and strong is advantageous to them because it freezes the Russians out. So everyone lives happily ever after even though neither superpower would ever countenance this degree of change in the world order if they knew about it in time to stop it."

Carl had become increasingly animated as he delivered his discourse so that by the time he finished, he was gesturing wildly and almost laughing as he spoke. Roxanne wondered whether he had ever before had an audience to whom he could lay out his whole vision from beginning to end.

"Of course, there are a lot of details that I can go into. But that's the overall thrust. Did I talk too fast?"

"No, no. It was very clear. I was just thinking." Thinking what it must feel like to believe that you are God, Roxanne mused. "It sounds fantastic. I'll have to think about it for a while before I know what to think about it. One thing, though . . . why are you telling it to me? Do you really think this guesthouse is impossible to escape from, or are you that eager to have a captive audience, so to speak, to tell your flawless plan to?"

Carl's eyes sparkled and again he seemed on the point of laughter. "Neither! I'm telling you precisely because the plan

isn't flawless. You are going to be my answer to the only flaw in
GULFSCENE III."

"How's that?"

"It's simple. Everything the CIA has done so far is exactly on
schedule. Everything is. The decision to proceed had to be
made in Pakistan and had to coincide with the beginning of the
new administration when Washington was most confused. And
that's the way it happened. It's all predicted in GULFSCENE
III. Since the Paks needed to get hold of me either to help them
or, if I proved unwilling, to keep me from revealing to Washington what they might be planning, they had to kidnap me. I
just made it easy for them. Initially the Pakistanis and Indians
knew only the broad strategic aspects of the plan because I fed
that to two Pakistani political scientists and an Indian nuclear
physicist in Cambridge. But when they got me to Islamabad and
found out I had predicted my own kidnapping practically to the
day, it blew their minds.

"I also predicted that by the tenth week the CIA would try to
rescue me. They agreed to set up the trap and were very impressed when you fell into it right on schedule."

"But we were ready to go two weeks earlier, only you weren't
available."

"Minor detail. The flaw is what I was talking about. The flaw
in the scenario is that in week fourteen the CIA will be far
enough along in guessing what's happening that they will order
me killed. I haven't written that into GULFSCENE III, of
course, because there's no point worrying the Pakistanis. They
can't protect me. What will happen is that the CIA will decide
things are serious enough to surface some Indian or Pakistani
mole who is above suspicion to assassinate me one way or another. After the first trap, they'll know better than to try another
frontal assault. So in a month's time, the third week in May to
be precise, I'm a goner and GULFSCENE III folds up only two

weeks before D-day, which is June 5, the end of Ramadan and the most chaotic day in the Muslim year."

As the implications of Webster's words sank in, Roxanne slowly nodded her head and then slowly shook it. "I would never have guessed. You want me to be your bodyguard, don't you? I'm the only person you can trust not to be a CIA assassin coming to get you precisely because I *am* a CIA assassin but under strict orders not to hurt you. Lincoln Hoskins said 'live delivery' at least ten times in briefing me. He didn't even want me to kill you a little bit."

"That's about the size of it, Roxie," chortled Webster.

"Of course, that doesn't mean I can't just stand out of the way and let someone else do the job."

"Nope. But I've still got three weeks to convince you that it's better for me not to be killed at all."

"And how do you expect to do that?"

"That's something I have yet to figure out. Maybe I should start by letting you beat me at chess. Do you play?"

"Poorly but aggressively," said Roxanne.

By the end of their sixth chess game, with time out for a sandwich supper, both Carl and Roxanne were yawning. The games had been played with Carl starting with progressively fewer pieces. He had won every one nonetheless.

"That's it. I'm going to bed," said Roxanne standing up.

Carl yawned again and stood also. "That was fun. By the way, do you mind if I ask you a personal question?"

"Normally I mind intensely, but go ahead."

"Why are you a murderer?"

Roxanne smiled. "Premenstrual tension. Why are you a traitor?"

Carl returned her smile. "Midlife crisis, I suppose."

13
ABU DHABI:
THE THIRD WEEK IN APRIL

A Boston banker boating on a breezy bay: Sargent Oakes in his element. With so few gray hairs that he could still count them in his thick brown thatch, with the still-hard rangy physique of a trophy-winning heavyweight oarsman, and with primary authority over the prudent investment of seven billion dollars of the sheikh of Abu Dhabi's money, Sarge Oakes's future was as sparkling as the crystal blue water of the Gulf gurgling past the bow of his white motorboat and as clear as his view of the shiekh's magnificent administrative palace nearing completion on an artificial spit of sand reaching out from the western promontory of Abu Dhabi island.

In the eight years he had spent as senior economic advisor to the Abu Dhabi Investment Authority, Sargent Oakes had seen Abu Dhabi city grow rich, green, and bejeweled with architectural marvels at a rate he would not have thought possible. When the boat rounded Palace Point and reached his favorite fishing grounds, he would have in sight the grand vista of a white beach backed by a palm-shaded, garden-studded boulevard as far as his eye could see. And along this corniche would be hotels, ministries, and office buildings as pristine and modern as could be seen anywhere in the world. It was simply beyond imagining that before 1960 the same line of sight would have taken in nothing but sand, a sparse scattering of mudbrick houses, and an occasional native fishing boat pulled up on the shore. No trees, no flowers, no buildings, no civilization. He had seen the photographs to prove that that was what Abu Dhabi had so recently been.

The British ambassador himself had pointed out to Sarge a

plain, concrete block building in the embassy compound that had been built in 1957. He claimed it was the second-oldest building in Abu Dhabi. To Sarge, in the reflective moments that accompanied his fishing, the survival of that small office structure seemed poignantly symbolic of the lost status of Great Britain in the land that had once been called, because of the treaties between the sheikhs and Queen Victoria, the Trucial Coast, and controlled by intrepid British political officers with gunboats on call in the event of piracy or other acts of native insubordination.

Destitute and tired of empire, the British had left the Gulf just as the oil began to come on line. One of their last important acts in Abu Dhabi had been to orchestrate the overthrow of crusty, fearful Sheikh Shakhbut, who had insisted that his oil royalties be paid in coins that he kept in sacks under his bed, and the installation of his brother, who had joyfully accepted and guided the oil boom.

As the British tide had ebbed, the incoming flood of oil wealth had washed in with it so many new foreign residents that it was now easily possible to fly into the emirate, do business, and fly out again without being sure whether one had even set eyes on a native Arab inhabitant. As elsewhere in the Gulf, an implicit social ranking of foreigners by the Arabs situated Pakistani laborers and Filipino servants near the bottom and American bankers very close to the top. It was a social order that Sargent Oakes never complained about. Indeed, the Oakes family comfortably believed itself to hold a similar rank back in Boston in comparison with the Irish, the Italians, and the blacks.

Nor was that the only similarity with home. Laser-class sailboat races at the club in Abu Dhabi were much like sailboat races on Boston's South Shore, minus the sight of Minot lighthouse and plus thirty degrees of temperature on an April Friday that substituted for Sunday in the Muslim weekend. For greater relaxation there was solitary fishing from the motorboat that Sarge kept moored in the artificial cove of a dhow construction yard east of the new palace. The fishes differed from those of Massachusetts Bay, but the solitude was, if anything, more complete.

Oakes's route in reaching the Gulf had not been unusual. His bank had sent him to serve in their Abu Dhabi office, and the Investment Authority had made him an offer he couldn't refuse, particularly after he explained to his wife Carol the tax situation and the two-month vacation allowance with free travel to Europe. It had been Carol, really, who had taken charge from there. She had created for them a living environment and life-style so similar to the one they had left behind that it deserved to be appreciated as a masterpiece of social craftsmanship, if not as a work of art.

Carol was too pragmatic in her search for perfection to set down an unworkable rule like "no Arabs in the house unless they wear normal clothes and have an Ivy education," but somehow, week after week, the Arab names on the list for the Thursday night buffet always boiled down to one; and that one was invariably a Palestinian or a Lebanese with a minimum of five years residence somewhere between Washington and Boston. In eight years, no native of Abu Dhabi had been invited to dine at the Oakes home, and no foreign language other than French had been uttered inside it, excepting, of course, whatever the Filipino houseboy may have muttered in the privacy of his own room.

The Oakes's friends were mostly American, of early middle age, and happy as clams to be raking it in in the Gulf. Their talk was of sailing, gold prices, and the sufferings of their counterparts who were stuck in stifling Qatar or Saudi Arabia instead of free-and-easy Abu Dhabi. The male social costume was brass-buttoned blazer and Madras slacks; the female anything expensive from sarongs slit to the hip to colorful floor-length dresses reminiscent of the native garb of someplace that could never quite be brought to mind. Gin, Scotch, and beer anesthetized their palates; and all-American buffets of sliced turkey, dressing, and an interesting salad did little to reawaken them.

In the Oakes's social set, serious thoughts about Abu Dhabi's future were reserved for business hours. They were not responsible for decisions like building a university in the oasis of al-Ain, constructing an administrative palace, or planting another million bottle-fed palm trees. These were made by the ruler. But they were people of importance. Every day Sargent Oakes had decisions to make concerning the movement of money around the world's capital markets in search of maximum yield with minimum downside risk. From time to time he even pondered larger issues—what investment strategy will change if the sheikh drops dead? or, will the next generation, raised with a gold ladle stuffed halfway down its throat, be responsible with its money?—but teleological questions about the relationship Abu Dhabi's tiny, diamond-studded existence might have to the final outcome of human history crossed his mind as seldom as the absurdity of shipping New England ice by clipper ship for sale in China had distracted his Yankee forebears from making money in their own day.

14
DHAHRAN:
THE FOURTH WEEK IN APRIL

The arrival of Prince Talal bin Talal at Virgil Foltz's office in ARAMCO headquarters brought to four the number of Saudi princes with whom Virgil had had direct dealings. By popular reckoning, that made up a tenth of one percent of all the princes in the family. Not all, of course, were in the ruling line descended from King Abd al-Aziz, who had shared in the creation of ARAMCO, but a prince was a prince, nevertheless. Prince Talal himself was not descended from Abd al-Aziz, but he was still a man of influence in the Ministry of the Interior, an influence deriving less from his comparatively modest official rank than from the awareness of other ministry employees that by birthright he had guaranteed access to the true wielders of Saudi power.

At Virgil's invitation Prince Talal disposed himself in one of the capacious, overcushioned, leather easy chairs that office designers working in Saudi Arabia seemed hopelessly addicted to. He was a chunky, square-headed, mustachioed man of less than average height by American standards, but he filled the chair more majestically than Virgil himself ever could do even at six foot two and with a beer drinker's paunch. The secret lay in the clothing. Prince Talal's red checked *ghutra* descended grandly from his head to cover the entire back of the chair, and the heavy, brown wool *bisht* covering his floor length white *thob* was so thick and voluminous that it spread out around him like a tent—a tent with gold braid and tassels down its front.

By the time the customary greeting formulas had been run through and the prince's preference for Seven-Up, Pepsi, coffee, or tea ascertained, Virgil had concluded that the Prince's

English accent was American made, probably in California. He put the question and was satisfied to learn that the prince's college degrees were from Claremont Men's College and the University of Southern California, both traditional watering holes for young Saudis athirst for learning.

By duplicity and threat Virgil had managed to get a Sudanese Christian named Cyril assigned to the position of servicing his office with beverages. So while other managers with Virgil's illegal avocation were served by abstaining Muslims, Virgil could count on his Seven-Up being fifty percent "white," a combination he personally labeled "Seven Heaven." Prince Talal took tea.

"I'm so happy to meet you, Mr. Foltz," said the prince for no less than the tenth time. "You are welcome. Very kind."

"Thank you. You are very welcome. I'm most pleased to have a chance to meet you, Your Excellency." Virgil took a long sip and released a breath that blistered the insides of his nostrils.

"I know that you American businessmen like to do business quickly, Mr. Foltz. So do I. It is a good way. I have come to you at the suggestion of Mr. Wilson." The mention of the vice-president in charge of government liaison seized Virgil's attention. "Mr. Wilson said he would speak to you himself, but I insisted on coming to meet you."

"I'd certainly like to be helpful if I can, Your Excellency," said Virgil warily.

"Well, that's what I thought. You see, it's about the auxiliary airstrips." The prince pronounced distinctly all five syllables in the word "auxiliary." "Mr. Wilson told me that you were put in charge three years ago of carrying out my minister's order to render them useless."

"Yes, I was." And Wilson ordered me to fake it, too, continued Virgil to himself.

"As Mr. Wilson said. Now then, let me tell you. My branch

of the Ministry of the Interior has jurisdiction over the Frontier Forces. We have a terrible problem with smuggling, as you may know. Alcohol especially. But that is not my concern. Personally, I would not care if that Seven-Up you are drinking were one hundred-proof vodka. There are others who enforce such laws."

Virgil Foltz suddenly felt like a defenseless pupa awaiting the stab of a predator wasp's sting through its soft cocoon.

"My concern in the Ministry is primarily with counterintelligence. You see, there are many countries who have citizens living and working in Saudi Arabia. Saudi Arabia is a very rich country. We would be naive if we did not assume that at least some of our visitors are here to work against us. So we try our best with the help of our friends to keep this danger to a minimum. But sometimes we cannot even be sure who our friends are."

"I assure you, Your Excellency—"

"Please, let me continue. I have had a check made of several of the airstrips that were to have been destroyed. Of course, as you know, some of them—I have a list here: A-3, E-6, B-1, and so on—are completely intact and still have aviation fuel, landing lights, and other useful things in place. Clearly, the job was not done right. The question is why?" Prince Talal forestalled intervention by raising a ring-covered pinky and holding it with the index finger of his other hand. "Number one, it is possible that you did not supervise the job properly. But I don't think that is the case." He pried his fourth finger up next to his pinky. "Number two, you may be part of a conspiracy to smuggle something into the country. This is not out of the question, but I don't believe it is the reason. That's number two." A third finger was added to the first two. "Third, you may be one of our well-meaning friends who think to protect us by flying soldiers into these desert airstrips during an emergency. But I don't even believe that to be the answer. So what is the fourth case? The fourth case is that Mr. Wilson ordered you to make a show of destroying the airstrips but to leave selected ones intact, and you followed his instructions. And I cannot blame you for that."

Virgil sat still in his desk chair, held captive by the prince's calm but incisive analysis. Only an idiot would have failed to notice that the disused runways he had been ordered to preserve from destruction were precisely the ones best connected with the company's road net, and hence the best ones for landing air force transports on if the U.S. needed to come in in a hurry.

"Since we are friends, Mr. Foltz, I will tell you something. I know why Mr. Wilson wanted the airstrips saved. There are some times when your company is asked to do favors for my government, and other times when it is asked to do favors for the American government. And I might even say that it is not entirely a bad idea. The American Rapid Deployment Force could make good use of those airstrips. You remember the mission to rescue the American hostages in Iran. But I tell you this sincerely, Mr. Foltz, it is not the best idea. We were not being foolish when we ordered them destroyed. You see, other people can use those strips, too. Not just smugglers, either. I don't care about smuggling. I mean our neighbors to the east and to the north. The Israelis, who you know are our cousins, and who we understand very well, could land planes there to sabotage, or do other unpleasant things. I am sure the Americans would not officially support such acts, but they might not prevent them either. After all, quite frankly, Mr. Foltz, in America the Jews have the WASPs by the balls. I've been there and I know what I'm talking about. And then we must also worry about the Iranians. Do you remember in 1982 a fully armed Iranian warplane flew to Saudi Arabia undetected and landed? Today we would be able to detect such an intrusion, but we still could not be sure of stopping it, particularly if the Iranians had desert airstrips to land on."

"The story that I heard was that AWACS saw the plane but communications with the ground were fouled up."

Prince Talal waved his fingers lightly. "It doesn't matter. That was old history. But it remains that it is only eight minutes flying time from Iranian airspace to our oil installations. This is a very serious problem that I don't think your Mr. Wilson and his friends understand. I come to the point, though. You followed Mr. Wilson's instructions; now you will follow mine. I want you personally—personally, Mr. Foltz—to see to it that all of the auxiliary airstrips are made totally inoperative, everything blown up. Furthermore, I do not want you to listen to what Mr. Wilson or anyone else says about this mission I am giving you. If they ask you why you are doing this, tell them to contact me personally at the Ministry. You will remember, Mr. Foltz, that my government *owns* those airstrips. You can remind Mr. Wilson of that if you wish." The prince drew in his tent about him and rose.

"Your Excellency—" began Virgil, clambering to his feet.

"No, please. You are in a bad position. There is nothing really for you to say. I know you will do what I ask. You don't have to tell me. It would make you feel disloyal." As the prince opened the door, Cyril slipped inside with an empty tray. "Good-bye, Mr. Foltz. It was a pleasure to meet you. You should have your servant bring you another Seven-Up. Make it a tall one."

15

ISLAMABAD:
THE FOURTH WEEK IN APRIL

Roxanne Samsun proved no more competitive at backgammon than she had at chess. The element of chance in rolling the dice made playing with her a bit more interesting than beating her at chess, but five victories after dinner were enough even for Carl Webster. Sitting back from the mother-of-pearl and mahogany board, he felt acutely in need of something alcoholic to drink. One of the drawbacks of being detained in a Muslim religious surrounding was enforced abstinence. The guesthouse boasted neither bar nor wine cellar. Ordinarily, it would have made little difference, for Carl was not habitually a drinker; but alone of an evening in the company of a woman he found it helped.

"Well, one week gone," said Roxanne cheerfully. "Three more before your executioner comes, isn't that right?" Carl nodded. "I thought you were going to convince me that I should protect you? Here I've been working to get the old shoulder back in operation so I can break a few bones and you haven't told me anything new about why I should help make your wonderful plan succeed."

Carl looked at the backgammon board and began to make a tower out of the round pieces. "What did that psychological profile you read say about my being a megalomaniac, schizophrenic genius?"

"Don't forget male chauvinist pig." Carl did not look amused. "You're not amused. You seriously want to know all the dirt?"

"It would help if I knew what you already believe about me."

"Are you sure that's the only reason you want to know?" It was Roxanne who seemed greatly amused by the conversation.

"No, I have another reason."

"What's that?"

"I'll tell you after you tell me about the profile."

"Really eager, aren't you? Are you sure you can take it?"

"Stop teasing," said Carl testily.

"Okay, okay. Here goes. Remember, you asked for it. If you don't like it, don't blame—"

"For Christ's sake!"

"You *are* anxious. Well then, the psychological profile said that you are highly introverted and romantic with a strong self-image as a megalomaniac genius bordering on schizophrenia. I threw in the male chauvinist pig part on my own because you were such a condescending snot last week when you were trying to see if my tiny brain was capable of grasping your magnificent scenario. Actually, according to the profile, you are at best ambivalent about women because of a strong attachment to your stepmother who then betrayed your love for her by leaving you and running away with your uncle. The analyst was of the opinion that your sexual experience is probably very slight and that you are possibly homosexual even though your original security check found no evidence to that effect. Your wife was described as a social ornament whom you essentially bought in order to convince the world that you could attract a beautiful woman."

Carl's attention appeared to be focused entirely on trying to pile all thirty backgammon pieces in a single stack of alternating red and white.

"You see, when I told you that the profile said you were a megalomaniac genius, I only did it because I knew that was what you wanted to hear. I thought, since you probably weren't going to like me as a woman, I might at least try to flatter you into trusting me. Telling you that you were crazy seemed like a good way to make friends."

Carl cleared his throat noisily. "Why did the profile say I had this so-called self-image? What did it say about being introverted and romantic?"

"You don't really want to know all this, Carl. But if you ask me, I'll tell you. According to the profile, you were socially unsuccessful as a child and became fixated on academic accomplishment as a result. You were very bright and imaginative and very good at board games. You loved to win so much that winning a game took the place of all other forms of relationship. You made up complicated new games just so you could win them.

"When your uncle from Hungary moved into your house, you became even more introverted because your uncle and your father fought. The only love you got was from your stepmother, and finally she deserted you. Then as you grew older, you became worried about the fact that the only thing that meant anything to you was winning games. You wondered if you were becoming schizophrenic and out of touch with the real world. At the same time, you got into crisis-simulation gaming, which put a high premium on inventing and winning highly complex games. The upshot was that you were so good at your work and so screwed up otherwise that you convinced yourself you were a schizoid, megalomaniac genius while secretly you were afraid that you were just an isolated wimp living in a romantic dream world. Your gorgeous wife and that limp you nursed to keep your Achilles tendon from healing properly were both part of your self-image. You thought having Roseanne would make you look like a stud—the genius and the goddess—and you had the idea that some sort of physical imperfection, a limp, went with the image of being a genius." Roxanne stopped but Carl made no sign of responding. "I'm sorry, Carl. You wanted to know what the profile said, so I told you. If it's wrong and you really hope to get me over to your side, you'd better tell me what's right."

Carl sighed and looked up. Roxanne thought his blue eyes looked misty. "I don't know if it's right or not, but one thing I am sure of is that my Uncle Andras wrote it." Roxanne's mouth fell open in astonishment. "I don't know how or why or when Uncle Andras went to work for the CIA. The last I heard anything about him, around my senior year in college, he had just taken a job with the government and moved from California. That might have been it, but his profession before that was mechanical engineer, which doesn't seem like a normal route into the intelligence business. It doesn't make much difference in any case; he's the only one who could possibly have written a profile like that talking about my stepmother."

"Incredible. Do you suppose he was somehow found and persuaded to write the profile just in the last few weeks?"

"No, he couldn't have been cleared in time to be told what they wanted him to do. Besides, he wasn't all that close to me when he lived with us. A profile like this must have taken a good deal of time to prepare even for him. In fact, I can hardly believe he would have had enough time to do it at all if it was in your hands only seven weeks after I left the country. It's almost as if it was already prepared and just pulled off the shelf."

"You know, listening to what you are saying and looking at you saying it is very odd. You don't look at all shocked. You didn't write all this in GULFSCENE III, did you?"

Carl laughed and pushed over the high stack of backgammon pieces so that they clattered noisily on the board. "I wish I had. It would be easier to explain. But you're right; I'm not particularly shocked. Late in the afternoon after our last long talk it came back to me that you had said the initials of the profile's author were A.L.K. My uncle's name is Andras Lajos Kovacs, and I've been wondering ever since you mentioned those initials whether he could be the author. Now I know."

"But something like this can hardly be a coincidence, can it?"

Carl shrugged. "I don't know. Even the most improbable event can happen once. I don't know how else to explain it."

"How about a good psychologist with the same initials having a detailed interview with your uncle? That could have produced the same result."

Carl shrugged again. "It sounds like a damn good profile. That's all I can say. One way or another, Uncle Andras must have been the source. He probably knows things about me that I don't know myself."

Roxanne was suddenly looking puzzled. "You know, for the first time, talking about your precious psyche makes me realize that there is something very important that I don't understand about you."

"What's the problem?"

"I don't know why you're doing all this, why you're holed up here in Islamabad. And it's something I need very much to understand if I'm going to go to the trouble of saving your life from the famous unknown assassin." Carl brightened inwardly at the implication of the remark. "The reasons you gave me before for being here went along fine with the megalomaniac genius image. 'GULFSCENE III is a brilliant new strategic concept by means of which I shall utterly transform the shape of the world' and all that crap. Carl Webster, the puller of the lever that moves the planet from its orbit. Fine. I don't doubt that some part of you believes that that is what you're doing. But on the other hand, it's one thing to dream about such a thing and it's another to do it, and I have a hard time seeing how an introverted romantic, who would rather limp than walk right, ever got up the courage to act his fantasy out. I just don't see why you went ahead with this. Aren't you scared to death of how this might come out? Things don't have to go very far wrong for you to end up dead. In fact, you're even predicting as much and telling me that I'm the only one who can save you. According to that profile, you don't have the balls for this sort of game."

"I'm absolutely petrified," said Carl seriously. "I think that's why kidnapping was the only way I could think of to start. It took the decision out of my hands. The window of opportunity on the calendar ran from the presidential inauguration to the end of Ramadan. All I had to do was sit on my park bench and make myself available. Whatever happened after that was beyond my control. You can't imagine how cold I got sitting out there night after night waiting to see if they would come for me. It's the sort of thing that really does make you feel schizophrenic because it's so remote from normal life."

"But you're still not explaining why you decided to let yourself be kidnapped. It would have been more comfortable to sit home and just dream about GULFSCENE III. Nothing in the profile and nothing you've said now tells me why you did it for real."

A fleeting smile played over Carl's face. "That's because the profile was written by Uncle Andras, and there was one thing Uncle Andras couldn't have understood about me because we were never close enough for him to realize how much he himself affected me. When I was in junior high school, he used to go on and on about socialism and the unjustness of societies in which a few rich people own everything while the masses starve. Then my stepmother would echo the same thing to me. And you know what? Deep down all that preaching got to me, particularly after I realized that my father was one of the rich ones who owned everything and thumbed his nose at the poor. You're right in thinking that I sometimes believe this 'genius controller of the world' business. That's because there's a hell of a lot to it. I'm proving it right this minute. But I don't think I would have ever gotten this far if I didn't also believe somewhere deep down that it's simply wrong for so incredibly much money to be hogged by those few Arabs while tens of millions of Indians and Pakistanis live in poverty. I know that sounds mushy, and maybe it is romantic, but that's the way I feel. Since in general I don't hold much by noble thoughts, I feel almost ashamed of having such an idealistic feeling. In fact, I wouldn't even admit it to you if I didn't need your help. But I have it nevertheless. The Arabs in the Gulf don't allow foreign workers to become citizens and share the wealth; they're stingy with gifts; and they flaunt their money everywhere in the world. That's just wrong. They deserve what they get." Roxanne crossed her arms and sat back in her chair with the semideflated look of a person who has just had a puzzle explained that she should have been able to figure out for herself. "And while I'm at it, I'll tell you another secret that I'm not very proud of. The basic idea of GULFSCENE III isn't original."

Roxanne's look changed to one of sudden surprise. "It's not?"

"No. It was actually handed to me unwittingly at a cocktail party in Cambridge. Morrie Gratz had dragged a big shot up from Washington to prove to the Harvard and MIT deans that he had important contacts, and we all had to show up at the party to help Morrie con everybody. It was the guy from Washington who brought up the idea of an Indo-Pak coup in conversation as a kind of joke. We spun it out a bit for fun; then the next day I realized that it was probably too good an idea to let pass."

"Some persons are born megalomaniac geniuses and others have the role thrust upon them. Is that it?"

"I wouldn't go that far. All my original ideas aren't stolen. In fact, I don't really consider this one stolen because sometimes genius is simply the recognition of value in something that no one else has thought important."

Now Roxanne was trying her own hand at stacking the thirty backgammon pieces. "I'm beginning to be disappointed in you, Carl. Next you'll be telling me you do volunteer work in a children's hospital and have never had a truly arrogant thought in your life. But tell me, on a different subject, has General Baber ever actually met his kidnapped genius? Or are these meetings you go to every morning just attended by subordinates?"

"Yes, I've met him. About five weeks after coming here, right after being passed by their interrogation team, I was taken to his home late at night for a meeting. He asked me a few questions about the scenario. Not many. Mostly about my estimate of Indian reliability. I think he really just wanted to see what kind of person I was. Eventually, he gave me a little speech about greatness and about rising above petty squabbles with India and achieving leadership in the Muslim world. The same kind of thing he says publicly, only in English, very good English. He's an impressive man, you know: distinguished looking, very trim, taller than I had expected. But his head is in the clouds, I think."

"Did he say—"

"Oh, one more thing! We played backgammon. He said he had read in a report that I was an expert."

"I suppose you beat him."

"Of course. At least I did at first. Then he taught me a version I wasn't familiar with called *mahbooseh*. He said it meant 'in prison' in Arabic. I'll show you." Carl arranged a configuration of pieces on the board between them. "You know normally when you land on your opponent's isolated piece—like this— you kill it and send it back to the beginning. In *mahbooseh*, when you land on it, you freeze it, put it in prison; and your opponent can't move it until you let him go by moving your own piece. The winning strategy is to imprison one of your opponent's pieces so far back toward the beginning that even if all of his other pieces have reached home and been taken off the board, he still can't win because his last man is too far away from home, after you let him out of prison, to get there before you get your own last man off. At first General Baber beat me, but after a few games I caught on to the proper strategy and played him even. I remember it in detail because I tried to draw an analogy for him between *mahbooseh* and GULFSCENE III. I told him we were trying to keep the Russians and the Americans imprisoned by their own lack of knowledge of what's going on so that despite their power, by the time they put the pieces together, so to speak, it will be too late to stop the scenario from playing itself out."

"It doesn't sound like a very precise analogy."

"It's not, but the general liked it. Then he turned it around on me. He said that surely I was the one who was '*mahbooseh*' since he intended to keep me in confinement right up until June fifth. That was the first time I realized that I wasn't going to have quite the starring role in GULFSCENE III that I had planned on."

"Not going to get to rule the world? Poor you. It must have been hard to take."

Carl was laying out the pieces for the start of a game. "Let's play one more. I suddenly feel a neurotic need to win big in order to compensate for my disappointment."

16
WASHINGTON:
THE FOURTH WEEK IN APRIL

Open and direct but suspiciously impassive like a northern Baptist preacher trying to conceal knowledge of a dirty joke, Roger Mudd opened the tap on a leak whose haunting drip had been filling the ears of Washington's intelligence community for the previous three days.

"NBC News has learned that an American strategic research specialist has defected and taken with him some of this nation's most important secrets. Dr. Carl Webster of the Harvard-MIT Strategic Research Group, a high-powered think tank frequently consulted by the Pentagon and U.S. intelligence agencies, was last seen in Cambridge, Massachusetts, on February third. His current whereabouts are unknown, but it is believed that he is either in Pakistan or the Soviet Union. Initially, we are told, a government board of inquiry issued a report saying that no significant breach of security had occurred. But NBC News has learned that there is now serious concern in Washington not just about the missing documents but about the possibility that a large-scale international conspiracy against United States interests may be in the works. We have two reports: one from Washington and one from Cambridge."

Arch Thornton turned off the television set. He had seen the tapes from Cambridge and Washington earlier at the Agency when the NBC news bureau had made one last attempt to find someone to comment on the story. He had only switched the set on to see how Mudd would play the lead-in.

In and of itself, the story was still thin. No one was talking except the leaker, and as yet he did not appear to be saying very much. Still, it was vexing in the extreme that information as closely held as that surrounding the Webster probe could leak. Thornton had long argued that a mole was nesting somewhere in the higher echelons of the Agency, but all he had ever gotten back was the repeated instruction to factor that possibility into all of his plans.

The parts of the story emanating from Cambridge were the most suggestive as well as the most lurid. The murders of Rose-anne Webster and Selma Dorfman were listed as unsolved crimes but were sensational nevertheless. To that the news report had added the bizarre unsolved shooting of the Cambridge police detective in charge of local aspects of the investigation and the bludgeoning death, on the same day, of Morris Gratz's secretary, Peggy Inman, in the apparent course of a robbery of her home. Yet there seemed little likelihood that the story had far to run at the Cambridge end. There had been a semi-coherent quote about disappearing Pakistanis from an interview with a beefy Irishman on the Harvard police force, but the FBI agent in charge in Boston, Michael Littlefield, had sounded decisive in saying that there were no remaining clues to follow up.

If a pothole lay in the road ahead, and Thornton was certain that one did, it would be at the Washington end. The pattern was altogether familiar. A leak to the press followed up by shreds of new intelligence to keep the story on the front page long enough to prod some publicity-hungry congressman into calling a hearing. Meanwhile the Soviets would get enough from the public record and from congressional leaks to the press to make it impossible to prove that their real source was a spy on the inside. The usual outcome: a blown operation and no way of proving that a mole existed.

Might as well start preparing for the goddamn congressional committee hearing now, thought Thornton. This was his baby, and the Agency would expect him to do any necessary diapering. Thornton rose from his couch and went into the tiny lavatory built into what had originally been a coat closet outside his study door. He turned on the light and looked in the mirror. He visualized the senior senator from Washington and beetled his brows ferociously. Long silvery strands jutted upward from their peaks toward his graying brush-cut hair. He clenched his teeth and approved the way the knotted muscles shaped his jawline. "The bastard likes to deal with professionals," he said aloud. "I'll show him the most professional goddamn spy he's ever seen."

Lincoln Hoskins's suggestion that Morris Gratz make himself useful and loved by lending his team to the effort to reconstruct GULFSCENE III had undergone a metamorphosis. Colonel Seymour's inquiry board had dissolved itself after making an obfuscating report and then, a week later, reconstituted itself as an interagency task force working under significantly higher security procedures. Hoskins had been officially added to the task force as an operations specialist, but the more crucial additions had been two more strategy theorists from Gratz's Group and one from a rival team within the District.

The line of analysis proposed by Gratz on Ted Bonny's suggestion had been accepted. What would it take for Pakistan to grab a piece of the Gulf oil pie? What would be the military requirements? What would be the possibility of making such a coup work? How would the U.S. and the USSR react? What would be the time frame? And what role might Carl Webster play in such a scheme?

As the data had been acquired and fitted together, a clear scenario of what GULFSCENE III might have been failed to emerge. Carl Webster's work had always been characterized by the unexpected, and try as they might, neither Ted Bonny nor anyone else could see anything particularly ingenious in what the task force was coming up with. Nor could they convince themselves that there was any possibility at all of Pakistan pulling off such a coup if the U.S. disapproved. Even with prepositioned forces, a conceivable factor, the supply and communication link with the nearest Pakistani support bases in Baluchistan would be beyond the capacity of either the Pakistani navy or air force. Troops in the Gulf could easily be cut off. The American fleet in the Indian Ocean was simply too strong. To hold their position the Pakistanis would need the equivalent of a credible nuclear threat to the oil fields themselves, and that was out of their league.

From there the task force had branched out into appraisals of Pakistan's chances of taking over the Gulf in collusion with another country. The four possibilities were Pakistan-Iran, Pakistan-Iraq, Pakistan-Egypt, and Pakistan-Israel. Of the four, the last seemed the most promising from a military standpoint. Iraq and Iran could chip in troops and provide supply bases and other logistic support, but to the degree that these would materially improve Pakistani capabilities they would suggest that the Iraqis or Iranians might prefer to go it alone. At the very least, Iraq or Iran would demand senior partner status since they were already Gulf states. But Webster had chosen to be kidnapped by Pakistanis, which was a sure indicator that whatever GULF-SCENE III was, it was centered on Pakistan and not elsewhere.

Egypt offered an advantage of a different sort, the possibility of dissuading the United States from interfering. If the Egyptians made the case to their American friends that their brother Arabs in the Gulf had brought deserved calamity upon themselves by their greediness, and the Pakistanis promised to share the loot with other "moderate" Muslim countries, the Americans might decide that the oil was better off in Pakistani and Egyptian hands. It was a big "if" to rest such a colossal gamble upon, however, particularly since the Israelis might take the view that a rich Egypt less dependent on the United States might become a less friendly neighbor and move militarily to forestall the possibility.

When it came to a tandem Pakistani-Israeli operation, the

odds in favor of success rose markedly, but so did the political improbability. The Israelis might leap at a chance to get a share of the Gulf by lending military backup, nuclear capability, and pressure on the U.S. to a non-Arab Muslim collaborator like Pakistan; but the success over the long term of a Pakistani coup in collaboration with any other country would have to rely in part on selling the idea of Gulf oil as "Muslim oil" to the Arabs, Iranians, Indonesians, Nigerians, and other Muslims capable of undermining Pakistan diplomatically and economically. Alliance with the Zionist state would effectively nullify any such sales pitch.

As a consequence of having assigned prohibitively high risk values to the scenarios under examination, the interagency task force was in a state of casting about for fresh ideas when NBC News exposed their problem to public view.

"I wish Roger Mudd had told us what the large-scale international conspiracy was last night," drawled Walker Rankin as he munched on a sweet roll at the morning meeting of the task force. Normally, only the strategy specialists convened every day, but advance notice of the news announcement had given Colonel Seymour time to corral the full group for a "planning and assessment" session.

"Walker, come over here and sit down," ordered the colonel. "We're not here to chat about the news. We're here to make it."

Rankin raised his eyebrows at the unexpected bit of rhetoric from the military. "If any of us has been making the news so far, we're all in for a mite of trouble."

Colonel Seymour looked as if he had had a door slammed rudely in his face. "What I meant—"

"Oh, I know what you meant. Let's get on with it."

"Gentlemen!" announced Ted Bonny, his Adam's apple bobbing. As Bonny had never previously spoken at a meeting without specific authorization, all eyes but the colonel's looked in his direction.

"Let's be orderly," said Colonel Seymour perusing a small notepad with neatly numbered items on it. Bonny subsided. "We'll start with a review of where we've been and where we are, and then we'll go on to discuss our best course of action. Then I will finish with a reminder to you all to guard yourselves against inadvertent leaks of information in the coming days." The last item did not sound like something the colonel had intended to read aloud as an agenda item, but the group had learned to accept the compulsive side of its leader's orderliness.

"A point of order, Colonel Seymour," put in Rufus Snipe diplomatically. "I wonder if we might suspend the agenda in order to ask Mr. Bonny if what he has to say affects the order of the agenda."

"Yes, I think that is in order," replied the colonel. "Dr. Bonny?" All eyes shifted to the emaciated, reddening face of the strategist.

"I know what GULFSCENE III is," he said with forced firmness. "I don't know if that affects the agenda, Colonel."

"That will come under 'best course of action'—"

"For Christ's sake, Seymour!" ejaculated Link Hoskins, his face lit with a mixture of annoyance and excitement.

"Would you please ask for those in favor of suspending the agenda, Colonel," said Snipe quietly.

"Those in favor?" muttered the colonel. Everyone around the table raised a hand. Seymour jotted the total on his slip of paper. "Dr. Bonny."

"Thank you." The Adam's apple bounced several times as if priming the pump. "GULFSCENE III envisions a collaboration between Pakistan and India to capture some portion of the Gulf using Pakistani armed force and Indian nuclear deterrent." The attending faces registered looks ranging from astonishment to dismissal. "I know this is hard to believe. In fact, that's the main reason I'm sure it's what Carl Webster planned. His work always seems off-center until you look into it more. But I'm only half-guessing on this. Three weeks ago you will remember I asked Colonel Seymour if DIA had monitoring information on radiation sources passing through the Strait of Hormuz into the Gulf. As it turned out, there is a monitoring station in Omani territory on the Musandam peninsula. Obviously, I had no reason to ask for a log of radiation sources since the movements of our own or Soviet submarines are not the concern of this task force. But I did ask to be notified if there had been any doubtful or unattributable passage of the strait by a radiation source in the last three months. The report came back last week that there hadn't been any. Then on Monday I got an addendum saying that two weeks ago there had been an unattributable passage.

"After that I asked for a list of ships that had passed during the period in question, and I got two: one from the Omani navy taken from sightings and the other a radar count from our navy. As it turned out, the counting time for radiation collection has to be quite long because of low emission levels and the high degree of shielding, so there were over thirty ocean-going ships on the two lists. But if you exclude tankers and American ships, only five came from nuclear fuel-exporting states and three more from a state with nuclear weapons capacity. Then I asked the NRC to find out whether any international transfer of nuclear fuel to the Gulf had been registered anywhere and, if not, what the probability was that some Gulf state would be importing nuclear fuel at this time. They answered that they thought it could not be nuclear fuel. So that left a weapon. And if it wasn't ours or the Soviets', it must have been Indian. All three unaccounted-for ships were Indian freighters."

"Typical Webster," murmured Morris Gratz.

"Now, I know that's not a whole lot to go on," continued Bonny, "but a Pakistani-Indian collaboration would fit a lot of our projections. Moreover and most importantly, I believe it fits the way Carl Webster thinks."

"If he thinks those sillies could ever work together on any-thing—" started Rankin.

"If we want to pursue this interesting new thought, Dr. Bonny," interjected Colonel Seymour decisively, recovering the floor and surveying the room for dissenting looks, "we will want to put together a list of further information needed and divide up our duties in an orderly fashion. Just where, Dr. Bonny, do you think this Indian bomb might have been headed?"

"Heavens, I haven't the slightest idea," said Bonny.

Michelangelo Castrodigiovanni, Republican representative from the state of California and junior member of the reformu-lated Joint Committee on Intelligence, read carefully between the lines of a *Wall Street Journal* editorial deploring with equal vigor the existence of leaks in the intelligence community and of spies and defectors in overpaid and overpraised university think tanks. A decade before, many a politician had been pun-ished by campaign contributors for taking part in what was con-sidered the dismemberment of the nation's intelligence arm. Now the problem was whether to get out front in a move to smoke the incompetents out of the CIA and risk being tagged as too far left or too far right, depending on who the incompetents turned out to be, or to lay low. A video clip of Mickie Cazz socking it to the big guys would make good reelection mate-rial—just like the old state's attorney stuff. But what if the big guys also came across as good guys?

"Skip, would you come in here!" he shouted over his shoul-der into the outer office.

Skip Mittelman appeared in the doorway oozing political savvy and legislative know-how in the obnoxious fashion re-served for legislative aides under thirty years of age. "Boss?"

"The Webster spy case, where's it going politically? Is it something to run on?"

"Scuttlebutt has it someone in the CIA has given the chairman a green light. I'd say go for it."

In a temporarily borrowed office in the Senate office building a White House official known to Soviet intelligence by the code name "Ghostwriter" carefully scrutinized a single sheet of paper in a final check for errors in the five numeral groups into which he had enciphered a message to General Maxim Tejirian of the KGB.

CONGRESSIONAL HEARINGS ON GULFSCENE III CERTAIN. DEEP CONCERN IN WHITE HOUSE OVER UNKNOWN FACTORS. CONTENTS OF GULFSCENE III STILL UNCERTAIN.

Satisfied that the numerals were correct, he burned the piece of paper in an empty metal wastebasket. A single tiny photographic negative resting on the red blotter of the otherwise unburdened desk was the sole remaining repository of the message. He withdrew from his coat pocket a paper bag and from the bag a thin square box covered with a lurid color photograph showing a blond woman wearing nothing but a black ribbon around her neck sexually accommodating a black man and a white man simultaneously. He extracted a four-inch reel of movie film from the box and pulled three feet of film onto the desk. Then he carefully taped his own bit of film over several of the orgiastic frames and repacked the box.

Fifteen minutes later he walked into an adult book store a few blocks north of the Capitol and negotiated an exchange of the film he was jaded on for something more in the S-and-M line.

17
BAHRAIN:
THE FIRST WEEK IN MAY

Being men of financial worth, the cordiality with which the Bahraini merchants received a visit from a successful British businessman, particularly one like Meredith Orchard, who could converse in the Persian they used among themselves in preference to Arabic, went without saying. On the other hand, being for the most part Shi'ite Muslims and pillars of their religious community, and as such regarding the Sunni ruler of Bahrain and his entourage of Sunni supporters as usurpers at best and oppressors at worst, the merchants of Bahrain were quite accustomed to keeping their own counsel and divulging nothing to strangers that could possibly disadvantage one of their own. Consequently, Merrie's quest for more information about Sirri the Baluch, the mysterious buyer of large dhows, produced nothing that he had not already learned from Felix the cowboy. Huge sums of cash had been offered for large boats by a Baluch named Sirri of Pakistani nationality. Full stop.

Yet it was precisely in the confirmation of Pakistani nationality that an unexpected window of information opened for him. His interlocutor was a prosperous, well-fed, trader named Ali Akbar Shirazi. In snow white gown and headdress, with a neatly trimmed short black beard, large round eyes, and a small, pursed mouth in an altogether owlish face, Ali Akbar was almost a parody of bourgeois rectitude. His commercial interests were in the importation of foil-wrapped butter patties and other commodities from Denmark, but his conversation habitually ran to the neglected state of his fellow Shi'ites, particularly in his home village in the middle part of Bahrain island, and to his own good works on their behalf. It was in expatiating on the

latter subject that the issue of Sirri the Baluch's Pakistani nationality arose.

"My friend, I will tell you something about this Pakistani
Sirri you are interested in. It is something you will not believe.
He claims to be a Shi'ite! Have you heard of such a thing?
When have you ever met a Baluch who was Shi'ite?"

"Perhaps he felt you and your friends would be more interested in doing business with him if . . ."

"No, I am sorry; that is not it. For two reasons: first, everyone
knows we do not refuse to deal with Sunnis. How could we?
They rule us. And second, he never told us that he was Shi'ite.
So you will ask 'How does Ali Akbar know this?' I will tell you.
It is because since ten years I am trying to get the emir to allow
me to build a mosque for my people, and he will not allow it.
But now I see a mosque being built just where I had wanted.
And who, you ask, is building it? A Pakistani construction com-
pany owned by this Sirri."

Merrie politely put on an expression of interest and sympa-
thy. "That must be rather an affront, having a foreigner building in your own village."

Ali Akbar held up his hand. "No, no. It's not in my village.
The emir would not have stopped me from building in my village. But I've already built a mosque there. It is in Hoorah
quarter. All Shi'ite and without a good mosque. But very close
to the palace. Very close. That is why I never received the permission. But now this Sirri, who probably is not even Shi'ite, is
building my mosque. And," Ali Akbar leaned forward and
tapped Merrie's knee, "and many of the workmen from Pakistan
are not Shi'ite either. I have watched them. When they say
their prayers, even when they wash for their prayers, they do it
as the Sunnis do. Can you believe such things? Never, never
will my people use that mosque. If the Pakistanis wish to use it,
that is their business. But we shall build another one for ourselves right next to it."

"Ali, why are you telling me all of this? I asked you about Sirri buying boats, and you knew nothing. But you tell me everything about his mosque building."

Ali Akbar ballooned his substantial belly a bit further and settled himself deeper in his chair. "Mr. Merrie, you are right to ask it. The truth is that I want you to do something for me. I cannot myself ask our emir why he has let Sirri do this insulting thing. But it is something I wish to know. Perhaps you could find this out for me. And in the meanwhile I will ask my friends whether possibly they know anything more about Sirri's plans for the dhows he has bought. They may know something. It is possible."

Judging from the concrete footings in the capacious excavation, the Hoorah mosque was destined to be a very large structure indeed. So much had been obvious at first sight. But this was not Merrie's first sight. In fact, it was his fourth day of observation.

At the emir's weekly reception, an institution designed to promote his popularity but attended mostly by foreigners, the ruler had been only too happy to tell Merrie about the favor he had done, in the name of Muslim brotherhood, for Pakistan's president. General Baber had requested the permission for the mosque to be built for the benefit of the Shi'ite Pakistanis living and working in Bahrain at the same time he had offered to expand the provision of military advisers and trainers for the island country's fledgling armed forces. Since the president and the emir were both Sunnis, granting the request would be universally seen as evidence that Sunni-Shi'ite differences in both countries were of no consequence. And, the emir added conspiratorially, it solved the problem of a long-standing request for use of the same site by a certain self-important Bahraini Shi'ite who was surely interested in it for political reasons.

The last part of the brief conversation Merrie did not report to

Ali Akbar Shirazi. The first was sufficient to pry from the butter importer's pursed lips a rather full account of dhow and also freighter purchases in Bahrain, Dubai, and Abu Dhabi involving Sirri the Baluch.

Yet while he was satisfied with obtaining the desired intelligence on shipping, Merrie could not get out of his mind the peculiar vehemence of Ali Akbar's assertion that the workers building the mosque were not Shi'ite. Why negate the impact of a generous and pious act by giving affront to the Shi'ite community? The question had drawn him to the worksite, and what he saw there had drawn him back again and again. The differences in ritual at prayer time were too subtle for him to make out, but other differences between workers were unmistakable. A crew that Merrie estimated to number about twenty men stood out clearly from the rest of the work force. They were young, they were tall, they were robust, *and they saluted their foreman.* Three times in four days he had noticed it, and three times was sufficient.

When Captain Henry Aubrey, a red-faced, ginger-haired man of fifty, dined with Merrie and his wife at their villa, the talk before dinner was usually of guns, with Gwendolyn listening in polite boredom. Over the food, matters English were discussed, but Aubrey had been an expatriate so long that his stories were rather more quaint than amusing. With brandy in Merrie's den, serious questions relating to intelligence gathering were dealt with by the men while Gwendolyn retired to her boudoir to change for bed. Then the men would say good night to each other and Merrie would turn to his evening's work while the captain tipsily climbed the stairs to share an equestrian passion with the hostess. It was an arrangement that was satisfactory to all concerned. It gained Merrie access to the stimulating world of spying and secrecy. It gained Henry and Gwendolyn access to one another. And on occasion, it provided a useful mechanism for the serious exchange of information.

It was on one such evening that Merrie informed Captain Aubrey of his opinion that a Pakistani military unit had taken up station, under the guise of common laborers, on the mosque construction site two hundred meters from the emir's palace. The captain did not permit the revelation to detour him from his scheduled evening activities, but he had not acquired his reputation or his job by ignoring tips or being timid in exploiting them. The following day Bahraini security police descended on the site and unceremoniously bustled a worker whom Merrie had identified as a probable officer into a car.

It took forty-eight hours to break him. On the first day, at Aubrey's invitation, Merrie had watched from an observation room with one-way glass. On the second day, to avoid becoming sick, he pled illness. Aubrey telephoned at five.

"You were right, old boy. Special Services Group. Commando types. Tough as nails. Our man turned out to be a captain."

"Did you find out what they're doing here?"

"I believe so. It's rather ironic, really. They're here to be a bodyguard for the emir, of all things. The Paks don't feel we can handle the job apparently. If there's a coup, these boys are supposed to act independently to stop it. Seems old General Baber feels that Pakistan needs money from the Gulf too much to tolerate any radicals getting in. Not a bad thought. A shame we had to go to such an extreme to find out we had an ally, though, isn't it."

"That's all there is to it, then?"

"Seems so. Can't really pry much further, can we? I mean, if the general is doing us a favor, it really doesn't do for us to go about roughing up his officers."

"Quite."

"Righto. My best to Gwen."

Merrie was on the point of asking the condition of the captain who had been interrogated and then decided he didn't want to know. The telephone clicked dead in his hand.

It had not seemed necessary in divulging the information about the soldiers masquerading as workers to give Aubrey any particulars about the far-flung enterprises of Sirri the Baluch. After all, such information was better sold than given away. But in light of the captain's discovery of the soldiers' purpose, the mysterious Sirri's activities became a matter of considerable puzzlement. What conceivable contribution could ten large dhows and freighters make to the covert protection of the emir of Bahrain?

In Abu Dhabi, Sargent Oakes was not sure what to make of a letter from Meredith Orchard. It was so obliquely worded that it was not at all clear what he was driving at. The part about the possibility of certain matters being of vital interest to the government of Abu Dhabi was straightforward enough, although completely unexplained. But how that could possibly tie in with a friendly request for a list of construction contracts recently let to Pakistani firms was beyond conjuring. And hush, hush, too. Sarge grabbed hold of his apple-sized chin to help himself think. The list would be no problem. He could have it for Merrie by the time of his visit. Only what in the hell did he want it for? Merrie Orchard was no one's fool even if he did have an overripe Oxford accent. Sarge tapped out some code words and numbers on his computer keyboard. In a moment the monitor glowed green with data on the investment status of Pakistani construction firms. Downside with a capital D. Sarge shook his head in bafflement.

18
ISLAMABAD:
THE SECOND WEEK IN MAY

*Kabul again. Wet glints from mud-covered cobbles. Water drip-
ping off thatched roofs. Lime, orange, apple, and quince splashes
of color among the market-goers. Around the sharp corner the
heavy engine whine of an armored personnel carrier, then the full
noise as it maneuvers into the narrow street, its outboard front
tire crushing a trayful of pistachios. Fists and voices raised from
the nutsellers' row. The roof turret pivots threateningly in their
direction. Suddenly five men rush from the near side slinging
gasoline bombs under and on top of the vehicle. The whoosh of
ignition. I am trying to run with the rest. My chador is too
clumsy. I can't see through its eyescreen. Gunfire behind me.
One of the men falls, knocking hard against my hip. Blood is
pouring from his head.*

. . . *ahimsa* . . .

*Five Russian soldiers walking back with the other four Afghans.
There, out the shoe seller's door. "Don't take my husband!" Why
am I screaming? I can't run in my chador. "Don't! Don't take
my husband! He hasn't done anything!" The blond Russian boy
is recoiling from my grasp in revulsion. My knife rips through the
chador and his shirt into his liver. The look on his face goes from
fright to horror. He seems to be handing me his gun as he lurches
backward.*

. . . *ahimsa* . . .

*"It's the system that killed your father and grandfather, Roxie.
Don't you see that?" So slow, logical, rational. "The system
forces people to become terrorists and killers. You can't avenge
your father by killing some poor deluded Armenian teenager.*

Don't throw you life away. Join us. We're going to attack the system directly."

. . . ahimsa . . .

Such an old, old man. There was no need to kill him. Forty years since he had set foot in the USSR. His hair was snow white. Father should not have forbidden me to look at his body.

. . .ahimsa . . .

The blond Russian is still alive. Why won't the gun fire? He's still moving, but the gun won't fire. The four are waiting for me to come. The gunsight is hooked on the chador.

. . . AHIMSA . . .

Slowly. "Just walk in as if you are going to make a deposit. Put the case down next to the counter. Pretend to make out a deposit slip. Then walk out. Is it okay? Can you do it? It's for your father."

. . . AHIMSA . . .

"I'm sorry to have to tell you this, Miss Samsun, but your father is dead. He was shot to death leaving his hotel to go to the meeting. I'm terribly sorry."

. . . AHIMSA . . .

"I'm giving you and your boyfriend a choice, Roxanne. You can stand trial and spend the next twenty years in jail, or you can join us and find out how to make more acceptable use of all your anger." All your anger.

. . . AHIMSA . . .

. . . AHIMSA . . .

. . . ahimsa . . .

. . . ahimsa . . .

. . . ahimsa . . .

"What were you doing?"
"Meditating."
"Meditating. Just what I need. You sitting like that on the

couch with a blissful smile on your face when my assassin shows up. Are you going to be too placid to protect me?"

"I wasn't doing it to make myself placid. It's part of a rage-control plan worked out for me by a psychiatrist. I have these recurring moments when I get grooved into a set of memories and can't get out of them, like being fixated on a melody that goes over and over again in your head. It builds up a rage in me that I can't really control. So the meditation is a way of short-circuiting the pattern."

"You *are* complex, aren't you. Do you want me to give you a shoulder massage? Your arm might as well be in shape even if your mind isn't."

"Is it protection against your fantasy killer you care about, or do you just want to get your hands on my body?"

"Move over and lean forward." Carl slid behind her on the couch and began kneading her right shoulder. There was no flesh on the bony protrusions, but the muscles of her neck and upper arm were as hard and sinewy as cables. "It's not really fair, you know. You read all about me in that psychological profile, but I don't know anything about you except that you seem to be at least as psychologically screwed up as they say I am."

"Mmmmm . . . more up toward the neck. What do you want to know about me?"

"Do you mean that? You'll tell me?"

"Sure, why not? First, I want to do to you what you do to me, though. Try to figure out why I've changed my mind and decided to be nice."

Carl thought.

"Can't you think and rub at the same time?"

He resumed the massage. "How about this? For the last two weeks I've been giving you a day-by-day rundown on how GULFSCENE III is going, and you finally believe that it is really going to happen. But you still don't believe I'm right about a CIA assassin because you feel you know more about that subject than I do and you don't trust the station chief in Islamabad, whatever his name is—"

"Tony Zwemer."

"—to handle things right even if an assassination is ordered. Consequently, you have concluded that you yourself are the best hope of derailing GULFSCENE III, and you wish to win my trust in order to gain leverage for persuading me to call the whole thing off. How's that?"

"Close enough. So what do you want to know?"

"Just start, and I'll ask questions."

"Okay. Here, then, is what I think is important about me. My grandfather was a minister in the national Bashkir government between 1917 and 1919. Have you ever heard of the Bashkirs?"

"Not recently."

"They are a people in the Soviet Union related to the Mongols and Tatars. In 1917 the nationalist intelligentsia declared an independent republic, but they were defeated by the Soviets and Bashkiria was absorbed into the Soviet Union. My grandfather was their greatest poet as well as a statesman. He went into exile in Turkey, where my father was born. Grandfather was a great admirer of Mustafa Kemal Ataturk, the founder of the Turkish republic after World War I, and he even took as our family name the name of the city of Samsun where Ataturk began his campaign to save Turkey from foreign domination.

"Then after World War II the Americans asked him to come to the United States and work on a program to broadcast what I suppose was propaganda to the Bashkirs and other Turkic minorities in the Soviet Union. He had edited an anti-Soviet newspaper in Turkey and was very patriotic so he accepted, and my whole family emigrated. My father married my mother, who is American, but kept Turkish nationality. They had me in

1953. Then in 1959 my grandfather was assassinated by Soviet agents. They placed a bomb in his car.

"Since my father was a forgiving sort of man, our family life continued normally, at least as far as I knew at that age. He worked as a Turkish official for a series of United Nations agencies, and we lived sometimes in New York and sometimes in Geneva. Then eight years ago, when I was in medical school, he was shot to death by an Armenian terrorist on his way to attend a meeting on international air safety. I remember being called out of a biochemistry class in San Francisco and told about it.

"After that I cracked up. I was already under a lot of study pressure, and this was just too much. I went wild and tore up my apartment. That landed me in the hospital for six weeks with orders to take tranquilizers and rest. So all I did was lie in bed and think about Daddy and Grandfather. When I came out, I had the idea of doing something really violent to get revenge. I didn't know what.

"Then I met a wonderful man named David Storm. He had had problems too, and shock treatment had left him with an abnormally slow way of talking, but he had almost a magnetic attractive power. We talked together endlessly, and instead of discouraging me from wanting to take revenge, he persuaded me that the way to do it was to strike at the entire ruling system. So together we found and joined what we thought was a revolutionary cell and helped plan an attack on three Bank of America offices in the Bay area.

"But the irony was that our dedicated cell leader was actually a recruiter of CIA operatives. Have you ever heard of such a thing?"

"It sounds very strange."

"Apparently the whole project was the brainchild of one of the Agency bigshots who felt that the regular Agency recruits at that time were of poor quality and that there was a lot of good talent going to waste trying to foment revolution in the U.S. His theory was that anyone violent enough and simple-minded enough to become a Weatherman, for instance, probably had the makings of a useful agent. So our bank-bombing project turned into a trap, and we were virtually blackmailed into going into Agency training."

"What was the name of the man whose idea this was?"

"David told me it was Arch Thornton." Carl started at the name. "I know, Chief of Field Operations. I've never met him or heard anything official to the effect that he was the one, though. In any case, the project was a dud. David was told that he and I were the only ones to make it through both the technical and political training—you might want to call it brainwashing—and the security clearance. And I only made it because they had some damn good psychiatric personnel. They couldn't get rid of my feelings of revenge, or else they didn't want to, but they taught me how to use my anger instead of letting it use me."

"You mean when you do your cold-blooded murderer routine it's not genuine?"

"I wouldn't say that. It's genuine, but it's controlled. I use it primarily to scare people."

"But what about that German tourist? You did actually kill him, didn't you?"

"Yes, but that was because of something else altogether. You see, after training I was sent to Afghanistan to serve as liaison with a resistance group. The theory was that a woman would not be suspect and that in an Afghan *chador* she would be practically unidentifiable because she would be covered up all the time. The theory had been thought up by some dodo who had never tried to walk in a *chador*, but that's why I went. Shortly after I arrived in Kabul I was told that I could make contact with the leader of the group at a certain spot in the market. I went there and stood around waiting to be contacted, trying to look like an Afghan woman, when a Russian APC pulled around the corner and five Afghans attacked it with gasoline bombs. There was panic all around and shooting. One of the Afghans ran into me when I couldn't get out of the way and then collapsed with the back of his head blown off. As the Russian troops ran by I made it into a shoemaker's stall. From there I watched the other four Afghans being marched back by the Russians. Then I just went berserk. I ran out yelling in my bad Pushtu that they couldn't take my husband away, and the first Russian I got to I stabbed in the side. When he dropped his machine gun, I picked it up and shot down the other four Russians before they could grasp what was happening.

"After that, I escaped with the Afghans into the mountains. As it turned out, one of them, named Qorban Ali, was the resistance leader I had been assigned to contact. But more importantly, Qorban Ali was the principal chief of the Khaledzai tribe, which is one of the biggest Pathan tribes in the border area between Pakistan and Afghanistan.

"He and the others had a problem dealing with me because I had saved their lives and killed five Russians in the process, but I was a woman and a foreigner. When they found out I was also supposed to be their conduit to the CIA, Qorban Ali told me there was only one possibility. So in a tribal ceremony I was taken into the tribe and made the foster sister of each of the four whose lives I'd saved, including Qorban Ali.

"From there to constituting ourselves a special resistance team was an easy step. The assignments and equipment came through my controller in Quetta—that's in Pakistani Baluchistan—so I functioned as team commander. But I also had to accept the rules of war of the tribe, one of which was to take no prisoners and leave no one alive who might identify a tribesman. It's a rule I can't break, so that poor German tourist had to die. I made it as painless as possible."

Carl had long ceased his massage to better concentrate on her story. When Roxanne stopped talking, he continued to sit silently as if waiting for the information to be properly recorded and analyzed and an appropriate response forwarded to his lips.

"Odd story, isn't it? I sometimes imagine telling it to my sorority sisters at a college reunion."

"Which sorority? Never mind. I don't know one from another. Let me ask you this, though. What is your actual—what would you call it?—disposition toward violence and killing at the present time?"

"Not too far from normal, I think, considering I'm in the business, and I actually believe that what we're doing in the world is right and that we're justified in doing it the way we're doing it. But I don't get any special thrill out of killing people, if that's what you're driving at. If it weren't for Qorban Ali and the brothers, I probably would have asked for a different assignment two years ago. As it happens, the Khaledzai have truly become my family, and I feel the occupation of Afghanistan by the Russians as intensely as any of them. So I stay to help them fight. And I do a damn good job of it—by the rules."

Carl scrutinized her angular features as if looking at someone he had never seen before. "Since the first time you mentioned what happened to that German, I have been scared to death that I might do something to irritate you and unintentionally goad you into murdering me. I can't begin to tell you how frightened I've been."

Roxanne smiled archly. "Little me? Don't feel bad about it. Men grow wary of being taken in by women who are deceptively sweet and sexy, but the only one I've ever run into who knew how to deal with real rage in a woman was David Storm. Besides, with your record on women, I imagine it was shattering just to discover that the rescuer you wanted to serve as a bodyguard was female."

"My record on women, as you call it, isn't all that bad. I don't trust them, but aside from that I get along just fine."

"You don't trust anyone, Carl."

"Look at Selma Dorfman. What better specimen of a treacherous woman could you possibly want?"

"Oh, come off it. You're just bringing that up because you've been brooding for two weeks about your wife becoming attracted to another woman. Face it. You don't do 'just fine' with women. You couldn't keep your wife's interest in men alive enough to prevent her from looking around for something more interesting."

"Is that what you've been imagining? I suppose that's more of what Uncle Andras wrote. How utterly ridiculous. I grant that Roseanne got left alone a lot while I was working on GULF-SCENE III, but if she preferred to share her frustration with a woman rather than a man it wasn't because of dissatisfaction with me. If anything, it was probably because she realized that no other man could hope to offer her quite as good a buggy ride as I could."

"What a piggish thing to say! Is that what people who dream of ruling the world believe about themselves?"

Carl grinned. "Well, at least it's a testable hypothesis. Either I'm the greatest or I'm not." He replaced his hands on Roxanne's shoulder and then somewhat lower. "Of course, I don't want to aggravate your injury."

Roxanne's eyes were shut as she savored the ministrations of his fingers. "You know, if Qorban Ali finds out, he'll kill us both and display our heads in the village."

"What a touching thought. Shall we go upstairs?"

"I'm cold."

Carl reached over and enfolded Roxanne's thin, naked body in his own warm flesh. "I can't imagine anyone being cold in this climate."

"It was just an excuse to get you to hold me. This is the first time I've been in bed with a man in three years. I thought I'd forgotten how."

"I take it your four Afghan brothers haven't tried to take advantage of you."

"If one of them tried it, the others would kill him. And if they didn't, I would, just to protect my honor."

"There you go talking about killing people again. Do you have any idea how often you say something like that?"

"Turns you off, doesn't it?"

"At the very moment when I have just sullied your honor it certainly does. Incidentally, if you really never make it with your Afghans, why do you shave your pubic hair? It's scratchy."

"Tribal custom. The women insist on it. They say it's for cleanliness. Why do you shave your face? It's scratchy too."

"It goes with my image as a great lover, which, by the way, I am still waiting for you to confirm."

"*Great* lover? I'd say distinctly above average. Maybe a six on a ten-point scale. But on the other hand, I don't feel disgusted with the entire male sex after making love to you. Possibly both of our hypotheses were overstated."

"Certainly yours was. Mine has yet to be adequately tested because you have been out of action so long you've lost the sensitivity to appreciate really fine lovemaking when you find it."

"Judging from that macho comment and what you are doing with your right hand, I gather you think I should get in some more practice right away."

"I'd say that's a logical deduction."

"If we don't go down for dinner, the guards are going to come up to find out if we've escaped," said Roxanne, slipping out of bed. "We can take up the question of whether you really merit an eight later. You don't have any appointments scheduled do you?"

Carl resignedly heaved himself to his feet and looked about for where he had left his clothes. "No appointments. No appointments. In fact, I'm not certain that I'm going to be in the picture from here on out as much as I had planned."

Roxanne looked at him quizzically as she tied the cord of her *shalwar*. "Don't tell me your puppets are taking their strings out of your hands. I thought your great GULFSCENE III was foolproof."

"It's proof against being fooled, but it's not proof against fools. And it's beginning to look as though General Baber may be a fool. Either that, or they're deliberately keeping me in the dark about Indian participation."

"You mean the Paks are planning to go it alone?"

Carl had sat down again on the bed to put on his shoes and socks. "I think so. The only Indians I have actually talked to are a woman psychologist, who could well have been a Pakistani pretending to be an Indian, and Dr. Chatterjee. By this time the Indian nukes should be in the process of deployment to the Gulf. So I have been expecting a request from them for information on U.S. capabilities: detection of nuclear materials, naval procedures for monitoring Gulf shipping, things like that. In a crisis-simulation game, that's the kind of question the A and B teams are supposed to ask Control. If the Indians haven't asked, it makes me wonder whether they are in the game at all."

"But didn't you tell me that Pakistan alone didn't have the ability to take over the Gulf?"

"Of course they don't. Over the long term, the energy reservoir in the Gulf is so important to the world economy, including the Soviet bloc, that no one can hope to control it if they lack either one of two things: claim to legitimacy and a nuclear threat. Obviously, the Arabs and Iranians can claim to be the legitimate owners of the oil because they were living there before the oil was found. But the Pakistanis can also put forward a claim on behalf of the Muslim world as a whole by saying that the Arabs and Iranians were living there as Muslims in a religious society rather than as nationalistic groups and that therefore the Pakistanis have a right to protect the Gulf oil as the common property of all Muslims. But the Pakistanis lack a credible nuclear capacity."

"As do the Arabs."

"True. But the U.S. has practically announced oil from the Gulf to be something the U.S. would go to war to protect. So from a Russian point of view, the U.S. nuclear umbrella implicitly shelters the Gulf as well as Western Europe and other allies."

"Why wouldn't Pakistan enjoy the same protection? They're our allies, too."

"Ah, now there we run into a very fine point. If Pakistan tries to take over the Gulf alone and present the U.S. with a fait accompli, the U.S. would probably be so angry at being manipulated by a third-class power that it would stand by and let the Indians and Russians dismember Pakistan, effectively returning the Gulf to Arab hands. If, on the other hand, the Pakistanis should try to take over the Gulf in collaboration with the U.S., the Soviets would quite understandably view this as an American scheme to alter fundamentally the world balance of power. For the U.S. would then effectively control Gulf energy supplies, instead of simply protecting them, and when the USSR begins to run out of her own oil in ten or twenty years, the U.S. would be in a position to strangle it. Therefore, the Russians would view a joint Pak-American move as a direct threat and take appropriate countermeasures."

"Such as?"

"Well, war is probably the most obvious."

"So one way the Pakistanis get wiped by the Russians, and the other way everyone else does. This leaves only your way."

"That's the way it is."

"Then what do you suppose the Pakistanis are actually planning to do if they aren't following your scenario?"

"Aren't you hungry? I'm starving."

"How can I eat with world peace hanging in the balance?"

"Maybe we could just go down and have a piece of fruit while the ICBMs are in the air."

"Oh, come on, Carl. Don't turn into a prick again just when I'm beginning to like you a little bit."

"All right. Very quickly, what I suspect they are planning is a fake. There's no consensus on the question of whether the Pakistanis have actually built a single atomic weapon. But if they have, they could use it for demonstration purposes, just as I envision the Indians doing in GULFSCENE III. This would then have two possible effects. One, it would make the Russians and the Indians think twice about dismembering Pakistan because they couldn't be sure whether there was a second Pak bomb somewhere. And two, it would make the U.S. think twice about letting the Pakistanis take their punishment alone because a Pakistani nuclear strike against India or Russia followed by the predictable massive counterstrike would lead other U.S. allies to wonder if the U.S. was really willing to go to the wall with its nuclear arsenal in other sorts of crises. In other words, the U.S. might have to overlook the effrontery of the Pakistani coup and come to its support anyway. Except for one thing."

"Which is?"

"That if the Paks *do* have a bomb, it's bound to be small, cumbersome, and limited to being detonated on the ground or on a ship. Hence, if they want to make a visible, convincing demonstration of their ability to carry out the threat in their ultimatum to the Arab rulers, they will almost have to detonate it right in somebody's backyard. In Mina Sulaiman harbor on Bahrain, for example."

"Killing tens of thousands?"

"And so disgusting American public opinion that the U.S. could never gain support for a pro-Pakistani policy."

"That's what you think they have in mind, though?"

"Sounds like they're being stupid, I know; but I think that's it. And I'm more than a little pissed off that they're not following the plan I wrote for them."

"Pissed off? That's all you are? Your friends are planning to sink Bahrain island three weeks from now, and all you really care about is your plan? And you call me bloodthirsty! If you think that's what they're doing, why the hell don't you stop them?"

Carl said nothing.

"Well, why don't you stop them?"

"I'm not sure I can," replied Carl in a small voice.

Roxanne gave him a look of disgust, turned and walked to the door. "Maybe this is what General Baber meant when he said you were—what was it? 'mahbooseh'?—kept in prison too long to make it to the end of the board and win the game?" She walked out of the room.

19
IN TRANSIT:
THE SECOND WEEK IN MAY

TO: ANTHONY ZWEMER, UNITED STATES EMBASSY, IS-
LAMABAD
FROM: ARCH THORNTON, CIA, LANGLEY, VIRGINIA
APPARENT THAT CARL WEBSTER'S ACTIVITIES IN PA-
KISTAN CONSTITUTE SERIOUS THREAT TO UNITED
STATES INTERESTS. CONTACT FROG AND INSTRUCT TO
ELIMINATE HIM. POST EXECUTION ARRANGE FROG'S
RETURN TO U. S. ASAP.

* * *

TO: AMBASSADOR VLADIMIR KARPOV, EMBASSY OF THE
USSR, NEW DELHI
FROM: GENERAL MAXIM TEJIRIAN, KGB, MOSCOW
GHOSTWRITER CONFIRMS GULFSCENE III EXISTS AND
IS IN OPERATION. QUERY FOREIGN MINISTER IMME-
DIATELY RE MOVEMENT OF INDIAN NUCLEAR MUNI-
TIONS, SECRET COLLABORATION WITH PAKISTAN,
GENERAL INTENTIONS IN GULF AREA. IF SATISFAC-
TORY ANSWERS NOT FORTHCOMING, GIVE WARNING OF
POSSIBLE CONSEQUENCES.

* * *

TO: AMBASSADOR MAHENDRA RAO, INDIAN EMBASSY,
WASHINGTON
FROM: GOPALA NARAYAN, FOREIGN MINISTRY, NEW
DELHI

URGENTLY NEED INFORMATION RE DOCUMENT ENTITLED
GULFSCENE III. SOVIET INTERROGATIVE INDICATES
POSSIBILITY PLAN FOR INDIAN-PAKISTANI COLLAB-
ORATION TO CHANGE POLITICAL REGIME IN PERSIAN
GULF BEING FALSELY DISSEMINATED. RUPTURE RELA-
TIONS WITH MOSCOW THREATENED IF MATTER NOT
PROMPTLY CLARIFIED.

*   *   *

TO: GENERAL MAXIM TEJIRIAN, KGB, MOSCOW
FROM: AMBASSADOR VLADIMIR KARPOV, EMBASSY OF
USSR, NEW DELHI
INDIAN FOREIGN MINISTRY DENIES ALL KNOWLEDGE
OF GULFSCENE III. NUCLEAR STOCKPILE ASSERTED
TO BE ENTIRELY IN PLACE. AUTHORIZATION FOR ON-
SITE INSPECTION DENIED. IMPRESSION IS THAT
MINISTER'S IGNORANCE TOO OVERSTATED TO BE
REAL. HAVE THREATENED BREAK IN RELATIONS.

*   *   *

TO: GOPALA NARAYAN, FOREIGN MINISTRY, NEW
DELHI
FROM: AMBASSADOR MAHENDRA RAO, INDIAN EM-
BASSY, WASHINGTON
GULFSCENE III CONNECTED WITH CURRENT U. S. IN-
TELLIGENCE SCANDAL. CONGRESSIONAL HEARING TO
BEGIN MONDAY IN CAMERA. SUBJECT IS CARL WEB-
STER, DEFECTOR IN STRATEGIC RESEARCH ESTAB-
LISHMENT, AUTHOR GULFSCENE III. SOURCES HAVE
NOT DIVULGED DOCUMENT'S CONTENTS. SUGGEST
PLAN COULD BE SOVIET OR AMERICAN INVENTION.

*   *   *

TO: CONGRESSMAN MICHELANGELO CASTRODIGIO-
VANNI, SAM RAYBURN OFFICE BUILDING, WASHING-
TON
FROM: SKIP MITTELMAN, CAMBRIDGE
HAVE SPOKEN WITH HARVARD UNIVERSITY POLICEMAN
NAMED TOM O'MALLEY. COLORFUL CHARACTER. WOULD
MAKE GOOD MEDIA WITNESS. WILL TESTIFY THAT
INVESTIGATION WAS CONDUCTED BY SPECIAL AGENT
DAVID STORM OF THE FBI, WHO WAS APPROPRIATELY
CREDENTIALED BUT INSISTED ON OPERATING OUTSIDE
OF THE BOSTON AREA OFFICE BECAUSE OF ''SPECIAL
NATIONAL SECURITY CONSIDERATIONS.'' MICHAEL
LITTLEFIELD, BOSTON AREA AGENT IN CHARGE,
MAINTAINS FBI HAS NO AGENT BY THE NAME OF DAVID
STORM!!! COVER-UP BY BOARD OF INQUIRY BECOMING
MORE OBVIOUS. THEIR REPORT LISTS DAVID STORM AS
WITNESS. ROAST 'EM MICKEY!

* * *

TO: ARCH THORNTON, CIA, LANGLEY, VIRGINIA
FROM: ANTHONY ZWEMER, U.S. EMBASSY, ISLAMABAD
FROG HAS BEEN CONTACTED. PLAN FOR ELIMINATION
BEING FORMULATED. ESTIMATED TIME FOR ACCOM-
PLISHMENT ONE WEEK.

* * *

TO: GENERAL MAXIM TEJIRIAN, KGB, MOSCOW
FROM: GHOSTWRITER, WASHINGTON
CONFIRM WITHOUT POSSIBILITY OF DOUBT EXIS-
TENCE OF GULFSCENE III. THE PRESIDENT PERSON-
ALLY BELIEVES IT IS HAPPENING AND IS THREAT TO
UNITED STATES. HAVE SEEN LOG PROVING MOVEMENT
OF INDIAN NUCLEAR WEAPON TO GULF.

* * *

TO: VLADIMIR KARPOV, EMBASSY OF USSR, NEW
DELHI
FROM: GENERAL MAXIM TEJIRIAN, KGB, MOSCOW
GULFSCENE III RECONFIRMED BY GHOSTWRITER.
FOREIGN MINISTER IS LYING. EXERT UTMOST PRES-
SURE FOR FULL EXPLANATION.

* * *

TO: BRIGADIER FAIZ, ABU DHABI
FROM: GENERAL BABER, ISLAMABAD
PREPARE FOR FINAL PHASE OF OPERATION TANZIM.
DECEPTION COMPLETE.

20
ABU DHABI:
THE SECOND WEEK IN MAY

The older generation of luxury hotels in Abu Dhabi, already pushing fifteen years of age, had been sited near the island's northwest corner where the breezes that occasionally arose to stir the humid, hundred-degree air were apt to be found. Though every interior was air-conditioned and breezes, therefore, a matter of only secondary importance, it was still nice for the visitor who wanted to stroll on the beach opposite the Hilton and gaze out to sea to be able to do so with at least a chance of enjoying himself.

With its helicopter pad and drive-through entrance the Hilton was a trifle newer than the Khalidiya Palace Hotel. The latter had been built right at the island's tip, however, with its back to the crystal-clear water. Or at least that had been the original plan. In actuality, every day brought closer the moment when the hotel would find itself on the edge of a forest of palm trees instead of a beach.

The view from Merrie Orchard's window was of the long promontory of white sand dredged from the floor of the Gulf, barged to the island's tip, and there molded into an ideal location for the emir's new administrative palace. The gleam of the sand under the morning sun was still brilliant, but it was a gleam destined in time to be transformed into deep shade. Behind the ten-foot fence that restricted access to the sandspit to a single gate, over a hundred thousand palm trees were in the process of being planted to form an immense grove sealing the palace off from the rest of Abu Dhabi city.

The magnitude of the effort to force the color green upon the lifeless desert bespoke the unlimited funds available to carry out whatever the emir of Abu Dhabi desired. Every three-foot-high shoot was nested in its own shallow, fertilizer-filled crater into which a buried pipe dribbled a constant supply of water. Natural forests had been gone from eastern Arabia for ten thousand years, and without the artificial irrigation this nascent grove of trees, too, would quickly wither and blow away.

As always when first observing such a project, Merrie was struck by the combination of hope and fragility that it represented. It was common knowledge that if saboteurs should take out Kuwait's giant desalination plant, the entire country would have to be evacuated within two weeks, and that an explosive charge properly placed in the ganglion of pipes and valves known as the Qatif Junction in Eastern Province could put Saudi Arabia out of the oil business for years; but the everyday routine of such disasters not occurring dulled the senses to the fundamental fragility of the Gulf's economy. Only when one encountered a new example of the miracles wrought by money, and one as delicate looking as a plantation of baby palm trees nursing at their pipes, did the unlikelihood of the entire boom world of the Gulf come forcibly to mind.

The massive, sprawling administrative palace rising in the distance beyond the forest-to-be was more reassuring. When the oil was gone and the boom was at an end, such buildings would long remain for the descendants of today's millionaires to wander through, and beyond that for their buried ruins to amaze future archaeologists. The east wing of the symmetrical, marble-sheathed structure was obviously still under construction, but its west wing and the small, modern mosque slightly beyond at the farthest tip of the promontory looked entirely finished.

Merrie took a long time to examine the palace closely through powerful binoculars he had brought with him from Bahrain. It was for exactly this purpose that he had taken a suite with a western exposure in the Khalidiya Palace instead of pa-

tronizing his customary hotel. According to the long list, com-
piled by Sargent Oakes, of construction contracts in Abu Dhabi
let to Pakistani firms, the outfit that had been granted a sub-
contract two months previously to install a carved marble railing
around the porch that ran the full length of the building's front
was the same as the one Merrie had seen working on the
Hoorah mosque in Bahrain. The Bahrain discovery had in-
spired a hunch that Pakistani military units might be concealed
in dangerously close proximity to the rulers of other Gulf countries in which Sirri the Baluch had shipping interests, and this
was Merrie's first attempt to test the idea out. If Pakistani com-
mandos were in Abu Dhabi, Merrie was confident that he
would find them toting marble for the palace railing.

Unfortunately, to Merrie's great disappointment, two consecutive days of intermittent but careful observation failed to
reveal the slightest trace of such a group. The stone chippers
squatting on the porch with their mallets and chisels were obviously Pakistani, but they all looked to be highly skilled crafts-
men. No more than one or two were of military age.

Merrie looked at his watch and replaced the binoculars in
their case. To compound the problem of broiling heat, the
Muslim fasting month of Ramadan had begun, and there would
be nothing more to see until dusk as the hungry and thirsty
workers waited out the hottest hours of the day in whatever shel-
ter from the sun they could find. Watching intently through
binoculars had, in itself, been an arduous job, and Merrie
thought briefly about stretching out on his bed with a beer from
the minibar in the closet of his sitting room; but even in his
disappointment at the apparent collapse of his theory that Pakistani commando teams were lurking about the Gulf waiting to
pounce, he realized that a full test of the theory required one
more thing: a boat ride with Sargent Oakes.

Beneath an improvised canvas awning at the point where the

most northerly row of young palms met the sand of the beach, Major Hamza Rahim lay still on his back, breathing shallowly. Ramadan in the heat of the Gulf was more trying than anything he had known in Pakistan, but he regarded fasting as a religious discipline and an act of devotion in its own right. Every year he felt spiritually uplifted on completing the month's fast, and this year he had even looked forward to its coming for the opportunity it would afford to renew his sagging morale.

Until two weeks previously he had fully expected to be spending the holy month in the air-conditioned barracks at Jebel Ali, but suddenly orders had arrived. They had been delivered by word of mouth through a new worker who had just arrived in Dubai from Pakistan. The man had positively identified himself to Major Hamza as Colonel Rahmat Ullah, an emissary from Brigadier Faiz. His message was that Major Hamza and his troop were to be immediately transferred for special duty in Abu Dhabi.

The transfer had been carefully worked out and easily executed. Letters from the original labor exchanges in Pakistan through which Major Hamza and his men had been infiltrated into Dubai were sent over a period of several days to the Japanese contractor, giving a variety of reasons why each worker belonging to Major Hamza's troop had to return home immediately and announcing the sending of a replacement. Even as he boarded the PIA flight for Karachi in full awareness that at the Karachi end he would simply transfer to another plane and be flown back to Abu Dhabi airport, barely over the horizon from Jebel Ali, Major Hamza wondered at the elaborateness of the plan. He dared to imagine that some special sort of action was finally at hand. Why else transfer his troop so quickly from one country to another? Or had their presence in Dubai been discovered and the transfer been dictated by security considerations?

On arrival in Abu Dhabi, which looked indistinguishable to

him from Dubai, the major's heart had sunk, for it appeared that there had been no profound reason for the transfer. Each of his men following the same route from Dubai to Karachi to Abu Dhabi over the next ten days felt the same sense of letdown.

At Jebel Ali they had worked on building roads and digging foundations. In Abu Dhabi they discovered that their job would be to plant palm trees and lay irrigation pipe on several acres of sand in front of a huge palace under construction. The work was lighter than at Jebel Ali, but disappointment was keen, nevertheless. Even the uplifting speech about service to the faith and the nation that Major Hamza gave at the first opportunity lacked enthusiasm.

Staring up at the pendulous yellow swell of the awning, the major wondered whether the months of civilian life were beginning to affect him. His twenty years to retirement would soon be over. He had never before considered retiring, but pride in being an officer could not carry one indefinitely if that was the only attribute of being an officer that one was permitted to possess.

"Major Hamza." The major instantly recognized the commanding strength of Brigadier Faiz's voice and sprang to his feet. Stern of visage but resplendent in mustache, braid, and epaulets, the brigadier was standing at the edge of the awning with his head bent down to look under it.

"Yes, sir!" Not saluting or stamping to attention was by now a reflex.

The brigadier stooped under the awning. "Let us sit. This is a pleasant, isolated place where we can talk without fear." Major Hamza waited for his superior to seat himself on the sand and then squatted in front of him. "I have come to say that the hour is almost at hand. What I am going to tell you you must not repeat to anyone. In twenty-five days the most glorious moment in the history of Pakistan will arrive. In the name of Islam, we shall do something here that will change the world. On the last day of Ramadan, June the fifth, Pakistan shall become the ruler of the Gulf." Brigadier Faiz paused to let the words sink in. "Kuwait, Saudi Arabia, Bahrain, the Emirates, Qatar, Oman, all will come under our control on that glorious day. In the name of Islam we shall broadcast from this palace to all the peoples of the Gulf a demand that the Arab rulers immediately renounce their thrones in favor of General Baber. The alternative will be destruction by our nuclear weapons. In every country carefully chosen and concealed forces like yours will take action at the first announcement to seize the rulers' palaces and the airports. If there is failure to comply with the ultimatum, we shall demonstrate the power of our nuclear weapons with a single explosion. In the name of Islam and for the good of all Muslims, General Baber shall accept responsibility for the oil supplies of the Gulf and guarantee their safety. Now what, you are wondering, is the mission of Major Hamza Rahim's troop in this great venture? I will tell you."

Stunned by the brigadier's announcement that the greatest of days was nigh and the simultaneous revelation that his country's rumored nuclear capability was real, the major was wondering at everything the general said.

"We have monitored the performance of each of the groups assigned, as you were, to work in concealment. All have done very well, but we have been especially impressed by the thoroughness and effectiveness of your troop's endeavour. There has been no betrayal of identity and no loss of morale under the most trying condition for a true fighting man, the condition of waiting. This has not been true of all units, but our planning has been so complete that no breach of security has had a serious impact. Still, the element of surprise is paramount. That is why we have chosen the last day of Ramadan when everyone will be preparing to celebrate the Holy Day of Fast Breaking.

And that is why we have chosen you for the mission of guarding our command center."

"Where is our command center?"

Brigadier Faiz smiled. "It is here, on this point of land. Tomorrow we begin installation of the communications equipment we shall need. We have already deleted it from the supplies of the U.A.E. army. In preparation, we have stored in the palace an arsenal of weapons and everything else your men will need to carry out their mission. This afternoon you will inspect the munitions and then prepare a plan for my inspection. The fence and gate must be controlled completely, and the sea, too, must be watched. It will be difficult for twenty men. Above all, you must accomplish everything without visibly departing from your job of planting palm trees. Most of the few who will be working at the palace during Ramadan are our men; there are no Arabs. Still, no one must suspect that you yourselves are not ordinary workers. You will be too visible. Your mission is not an easy one, but I have complete confidence in you."

Tentatively the major voiced his first thoughts. "Mines. We can plant them while we plant trees. Booby traps. Night patrol. The pipes—possibly we could pump petrol through the ones by the road and set it on fire if we need a roadblock."

"Gradually. Plan it step by step. Look first at what is available. You have until five o'clock. Present the plan to me then for my approval. After that, I shall not be seen here until the first of June. It will be on your shoulders to protect the plan. We have called it Operation Tanzim because it will change the order of the world."

Great wooden skeletons of dhows under construction held upright by rows of wooden supports, like giant petrified oars reaching downward from ghostly galleys, provided a sepulchral backdrop against which Sarge Oakes's small motorboat rocked listlessly at its mooring, a living mouse in the elephants' cemetery. Not a soul stirred in the shipyard. Barred by religion from drinking during daylight hours, a Muslim carpenter would risk death working outdoors under the blazing sun. As Sarge and Merrie waded out into the shallow, tepid water and climbed into the boat, Merrie was reminded of the phrase "mad dogs and Englishmen go out in the midday sun." Identifying himself as the Englishman, Merrie invited his American friend to draw the logical conclusion. Sarge either missed the joke or was too engrossed in his outboard motor to pay attention to it. With a cough and a wheeze the motor caught on the second pull and Sarge carefully steered his way out of the artificial cove where foreigners kept their vessels.

Merrie did not unlimber his binoculars until they were well away from land. To the naked eye the white marble administrative palace rising in the distance above the sandy beach looked like a molded sugar decoration resting on white cake frosting. Only through the powerful glasses could Merrie make out the numerous traces of construction work in progress—but not a single human movement. The absence of a posted guard was a further disappointing indicator that his elaborate conception of a grand Pakistani conspiracy was a figment of his imagination, and his dream of achieving fame for the Orchard name by thwarting it even more so.

"Sarge, can we drop anchor about a hundred meters off the point, or is there too much current?"

"No problem." The athletic-looking banker was wearing red swimming trunks, a white cotton Lacoste shirt, and a Boston Red Sox cap. "The water's very still through here. A hundred meters out we should still be able to see the bottom. Do you really think someone is keeping a lookout?"

"Doesn't look that way, but I can't be sure."

"If they are, they shouldn't be surprised to see the boat. I've fished all around this point ever since it was put in two years ago. Building it did something to the water that fish seem to like. It's twice as good an area as it used to be."

Merrie's explanation to Oakes of his reason for wanting to visit the unfinished palace had been straightforward and almost entirely true. He had said he worked for British intelligence and that a rumor had been picked up in Bahrain indicating that one of the contractors working on the palace had sabotaged it in some way. His assignment was to check out the rumor without causing an international incident or embarrassing the otherwise respected contractor.

He had never before intimated to any of his business acquaintances that he had a foot in the world of intelligence gathering, but it went with being a freelance in the field that he was free to do so. He owed secrecy to no one. Besides he had correctly sized up Sarge Oakes as the sort of conservative American who would be awestruck by contact with a genuine spy after growing up in what Merrie understood to be a culture thronging with fictional superagents.

An afternoon off from the Investment Authority had been no problem. Precious little work was done during Ramadan anyway with all government employees on short hours and starvation temperaments.

At Merrie's command, Sarge killed the motor and let the anchor into the water. There was room in the boat for Sarge to lay his fishing gear out in its ritual pattern while Merrie donned flippers and snorkel. Then Merrie was gone, over the side away from the palace without a splash. Sarge made a cast in his direction to have an excuse for checking how visible he was in the clear water. What he saw was not encouraging. Only the most inept lookout would mistake the Englishman's white skin and bathing suit for a shark cruising just below the surface. Sarge hoped for Merrie's sake that no one was guarding against unscheduled visitors.

The swim to shore in the warm water left Merrie slightly

winded as he pulled up on the beach, his lank brown hair in wet strings before his eyes. There was still no sign that anyone was around. From here on in his only hope if stopped would be to bluff his way out: a pompous English skindiver just indulging a passing whim to see what the emir's new palace was going to be like.

Steeling himself for whatever might come, Merrie pulled off his swim fins and stood up. The east wing of the palace was only thirty meters from the shore, but though its back was designed to offer an attractive view to boaters, it did not appear to contain an entrance to the building.

Merrie swore under his breath. He certainly did not intend to let himself be seen on the front side of the palace. Then he spied a steel railing in the distance behind the west wing, apparently marking the location of a staircase to a basement door. Merrie swore again. His preference had been to enter through the east wing. If Pakistani soldiers were at work, he wouldn't find them in the completed section of the structure.

Every step through the soft sand toward the far wing seemed to grind away a tiny fragment of Merrie's determination. If his hunch proved wrong, his trip would have served no purpose and done nothing to restore honor to the Orchard name. But if it was right, the probability of his intrusion being detected was high and the plausibility of his excuse for being there low.

The door to the basement had not yet been installed. The inside was dark and smelled of curing concrete. Cautiously he stepped inside. Straining every sense to its utmost he could detect no indication of life. As his eyes became accustomed to the gloom, he could see that the room he was in was empty except for odds and ends of lumber and iron reinforcing rods. He crossed it as silently as possible and looked into the next room. It too was empty, but beyond it was a lighter doorway and a staircase going up.

By the time he reached the main floor Merrie's heart was

pounding. There was still no sound except the whisper of his bare feet on the cool tile floors. Peeking around the empty door frame at the top of the stairs he saw a wide, empty corridor that appeared to run the length of the wing. Door openings at regular intervals suggested that in time its entire length would be lined with the offices of bureaucrats. Merrie stepped boldly into the corridor and began to walk rapidly down it. After the first three doors it became apparent that the palace's interior was still unfinished. The rooms were vacant, the floors covered with plaster dust.

At its end, the corridor intersected the main axis of the center of the palace. The high echoing space revealed the vast scale of the building, which had not been evident from a distance. Merrie rapidly calculated that even at a run it would take him an hour or more to look into every empty room. Moreover, if no workmen were around, he did not know exactly what else to look for. He opted for an examination of the east-wing corridor at the palace's front. If nothing turned up, he would return to the boat and give up his quest.

Ten minutes later he gave up and headed back to the basement stairs. The unfinished administrative palace had proven to be exactly what it appeared to be. Merrie skipped rapidly down the stairs and then pulled up short with his heart in his throat. Voices were rapidly coming toward him from the dark room on his left. Straight ahead through two rooms was the outside door, but he knew there was no place to conceal himself between where he was standing and the shore.

Instantly he darted to his right through a room he had not yet been in and quickly into the room beyond. Then suddenly he stopped in his tracks. Scarcely visible in the dark before him bulked an enormous mass of boxes and in front of them stood machine guns, recoilless rifles, mortars, and other weapons with less distinctive shapes. Behind him the voices were still approaching. Frantically he scanned the room for a place to hide.

The boxes were carefully stacked flush against the wall leaving no room for him to squeeze behind them. He glanced up and noticed a bare lightbulb hanging from a temporary fixture. His heart pounding, he reached up and unscrewed the bulb. Then, with the voices almost at the door, he dove into an amorphous pile of something rough and abrasive in the corner to the left of the doorway.

Five men in Pakistani costume suddenly entered the room. Immediately they began to gesture at the munitions and speak in a language Merrie didn't understand. He could feel that he was resting on a pile of moderately fine netting. Covered by the noise of their conversation, he insinuated his body behind and then underneath the top part of the pile. His last sight of the men was of one of them trying the switch on the hanging light socket. After that, all he could do was listen.

Working in Bahrain he had acquired a good command of colloquial Arabic and Persian, but neither came close to whatever language the men were using. Single repeated words like Ramadan he recognized along with a sizable number of English terms relating to weaponry, but nothing enabled him to catch the drift of the conversation. Only by the accompanying sounds could he tell that a physical inspection of the armaments was underway.

Then once again panic seized him as he felt one of the nets being lifted from the pile on his back. Helplessly he felt a second one go and then a third. There could only be one or two more before he was uncovered. More conversation by someone almost at his elbow brought a moment's pause. This time he caught two words he had not previously heard. One was the English word June and the other something that sounded like the Persian word for five. But anything further was cut off by the feel again of another net being taken away. Merrie tensed himself for exposure and clutched his snorkel, swim fins, and light bulb tightly to him as if they were protective talismans. A hand grabbed the final net, and he felt it start to pull across his back and legs. There was a spurt of renewed conversation, and the movement of the net ceased. Whether the words spoken had marked his discovery or not he could not tell. Then after a further exchange, the tension on the net was released.

As suddenly as they had come, the unknown men left. Merrie heard the slip-slap of their sandaled feet recede in the distance. He waited ten minutes more and then cautiously lifted the one remaining net from on top of him. Looking at his last veil more carefully, he could not suppress a smile. It was a camouflage net.

Running through the sand and swimming as fast as he could back to the boat completed Merrie's physical exhaustion, but it drove way entirely the unbearable tension he had felt while hidden in the basement of the palace.

In the meantime, Sarge had caught an enormous fish and was excited beyond measure. It had been an adventurous day for him, one worth remembering: he had skipped work, braved the sun, and caught a granddaddy fish. But he was not oblivious to the Englishman's exhausted state. He offered the opinion that Merrie was in need of more regular exercise. As an afterthought, he asked: "By the way, did you find any of your saboteurs?"

"No," said Merrie between heaving gasps for air, "false alarm."

21
WASHINGTON:
THE THIRD WEEK IN MAY

Watching his darkly photogenic boss grill the chairman of the Carl Webster inquiry board, Skip Mittelman could not help regretting that the security aspects of the congressional hearing had dictated closing all sessions to the press. He would personally make good some of the loss of publicity, of course, by passing on a few of the more colorful exchanges with Representative Castrodigiovanni to discreet friends in the trade, but the borderline between being politically useful and leaking something important would be hard to judge. Clearly the David Storm issue would have to be handled with utmost tact.

The California representative known to his earliest and most ardent supporters as "Mickie Cazz, Fighting State's Attorney," fixed cold, penetrating eyes on Colonel Edward Seymour from the intimidating height of the long arc of polished mahogany desk behind which he and his colleagues on the Joint Committee on Intelligence were seated. Secure in the chairman's promise to let him lead the charge, he had already wrung from the colonel some damaging admissions: that Professor Morris Gratz had been privy to all board proceedings despite the fact that as director of the Strategic Research Group he was formally responsible for its lapses in security; that the board of inquiry had knowingly issued a premature report understating the seriousness of Webster's defection; and that the work of the interagency task force assembled to investigate the matter further had been guided by the same Professor Morris Gratz and his associate, Dr. Theodore Bonny.

Colonel Seymour appeared unruffled by the insinuations of incompetence that peppered the congressman's interrogation, but his initially wooden manner of responding became increasingly petrified until even the recurrent litany of his citation of the strong personal recommendation of Professor Gratz by Lincoln Hoskins, first in his position as CIA adviser to the board and then as a full member of the interagency task force, was reduced to a few stony syllables. Sitting behind the congressman's chair, Skip Mittelman accumulated four check marks next to Hoskins's name in his notes.

"Colonel Seymour, I would like to turn now to some testimony adverted to in your report, that of one David Storm, described as a special agent of the FBI. Are you now or were you then aware, Colonel Seymour, that the FBI has no agent, of any rank, named David Storm?" The gasps around the room were music for a former prosecutor's ears. Mickie Cazz had struck again!

The colonel looked frozen in concrete. His lips barely moved as he replied, "I'm not aware that that is the case."

"I have before me a written statement to that effect from the Bureau's director if you wish to see it." Mickie lifted a single piece of paper into the air for all to see and replaced it on the desktop before him. "Could you tell me, Colonel Seymour, how this person named David Storm came to be a witness before your board?"

"He was the author of a preliminary report on the investigation in Cambridge of Carl Webster's disappearance," responded the colonel. "The report was forwarded to me with other pertinent papers when I was assigned the duty of chairing the board. I might add, Congressman, that I have seen hundreds of FBI reports in my day, and this one was no different from the others. It was normal procedure to call Mr. Storm as a witness to allow him to expand upon the report and answer the questions of board members."

"When you say the papers were forwarded to you, what precisely do you mean? Were they handed to you by the director of the Defense Intelligence Agency? Did they come in the mail? Were they stuck in a cubbyhole with your name on it for anyone to look at?"

"If my recollection serves, Congressman, they were hand-delivered by Mr. Lincoln Hoskins when he first came to see me to suggest that Professor Gratz be appointed as a technical adviser to the board."

"Mr. Hoskins again. Tell me, Colonel, how did you locate Mr. Storm to invite him to appear?"

"I telephoned the FBI."

The witness was Lieutenant Thomas O'Malley of the Harvard University police force looking like a pink-cheeked inflatable replica of a professional football player.

"Lieutenant O'Malley, how would you describe the so-called FBI investigation conducted by David Storm? Was it different from other FBI activities of which you are professionally aware?"

"Yeah, not enough people. Every time the FBI gets in on something, you got a lot of people involved. Specialists and like that. The only person who ever came to talk to me or to anyone else that I know of was Storm himself. He talked like there was a lot of other people working on leads and things, but I never saw any."

"Was this impression shared by the Cambridge police officer in charge of the local investigation, the late Mr. Pete Grandeville? Did you bring your doubts about Mr. Storm to his attention?"

"Oh yeah. Me and Pete Grandeville was real close. We was in high school together. I remember telling him something was wrong with this Storm character. He talked too slow, for one thing. Pete said to forget about it. So I said to myself, if it's not the business of the President and Fellows of Harvard College, it's not my business. So I forgot about it. Naturally, if Pete had been a better cop, he woulda done something. You know what I mean?"

"Thank you, Lieutenant O'Malley."

In the witnesses' waiting room Ted Bonny and Morris Gratz waited their turns in silence. Bonny had lost weight as the work of the interagency task force had accelerated. Pale and emaciated to begin with, he was now pale and cadaverous; and his deathly look was accompanied by constant manifestations of nervous energy—tapping feet followed by odd jerks of the head leading to brisk spasms of arm swinging—like a wind-up toy skeleton. Feverishly his mind churned out example after example of ways to brief the senators and representatives on the awful truth of GULFSCENE III as he had finally come to visualize it in the last two days. The task force as a whole had rejected his carefully argued projection that June the fifth was the most probable D-day for an Indo-Pak nuclear coup in the Gulf, but no one could prevent him from giving his opinion to the Joint Committee directly. With two weeks' warning, the Navy's Indian Ocean carrier task force would still be able to nip the plan in the bud.

Morris Gratz provided an old and listless counterpoint to Bonny's barely contained excitement. His expectations of the ordeal awaiting him on the other side of the door to the committee room ran in a far different, if more realistic, direction. Experience with the ways of Washington told him that the Joint Committee could not care less about Carl Webster and what he might or might not be doing in Islamabad. They were hunting for security risks and would not stop until they had fixed the blame on someone. Gratz had no doubts about who the someone would be. Rumor had already reached him of telephone calls made by his dean and department chairman canvassing the views of eminent political scientists as to who would be a good replacement for him as director of the Strategic Research Group.

As the door to the committee room swung open, both men looked up, but the call was for Arch Thornton. As if responding to the summons, which he could not possibly have heard from outside the room, the CIA's imposing Director of Field Operations suddenly entered the witness room from the corridor and strode across to the committee room door. Gratz nodded a greeting to the bristly, gray-haired man, whom he had once entertained in Cambridge during happier times, but received no sign of recognition in response. When you're dead, you're dead, he mused.

Allowing the slightest bend in his ramrod-straight back, Arch Thornton inclined attentively toward the assertive congressman from California. He had just been asked whether it was not true that Carl Webster's whereabouts had been ascertained in Islamabad and that an unsuccessful operation had been launched to secure his release.

"I don't know where you acquired that information, Congressman."

"Is it correct or incorrect, Mr. Thornton?"

"It is not Agency policy to discuss operational matters that are not germane to the subject at hand."

Mickie Cazz leaned forward and looked down the long desk toward the presiding member, the senior senator from Washington. "Would the chair instruct the witness to respond to the question? Its pertinence will quickly be seen."

The senator's voice was heavy with dignity and authority. "It is the ruling of the chair, Mr. Thornton, that the question is germane to the inquiry."

Thornton glared at his interrogator. "The answer to your question, Mr. Castrodigiovanni, is affirmative."

Mickie Cazz bored in. "Would you please tell the committee why the rescue mission failed, Mr. Thornton?"

"Mr. Webster was being held under Pakistani military guard. In a manner that we have been unable to determine, they received sufficient advance warning of our raid to prevent its success and capture one of the participants. That agent remains in Pakistani custody and is being held at an unknown location."

"Thank you, Mr. Thornton. I realize that the failure of this operation must be an embarrassment to you, but I would like to ask you just one more question about it. Who made the decision to conduct the mission, and who served as liaison between Washington and Pakistan in planning it?"

"Mr. Lincoln Hoskins. But let me say now, in the strongest possible way, that Lincoln Hoskins's service to the Agency and to this country has been exemplary in every way over a period of many years, and I resent the implication of your question that Mr. Hoskins may have contributed to the failure of the mission."

Out of their own mouths they shall be condemned, thought Mickie Cazz. Close behind him Skip Mittelman drew a picture of a dagger pointing at Lincoln Hoskins's name in his notes. It was still a matter of wonderment to him that he had been supplied the information about the failed rescue attempt without even asking for it, but if what served the career of Michelangelo Castrodigiovanni also served the interest of some bureaucratic faction in the CIA, so be it.

"My time is almost up, Mr. Thornton, but let me ask you one last question. The committee has already learned that yet another serious security breach occurred when a man named David Storm successfully impersonated an FBI agent and penetrated the investigation of Carl Webster's disappearance. Would you have any reason to believe that Mr. Hoskins may have had a connection with someone named David Storm?"

"No, sir."

"Would you have any notion who this David Storm might be?"

Thornton paused long and visibly weighed the question. "Yes."

"You have?" exclaimed Castrodigiovanni in evident surprise.

"Yes. David Storm was recruited by the Agency several years ago under a program I myself instituted to discover whether violent campus radicals could be converted into effective agents. The program was a failure and has been discontinued. Mr. Storm was one of its few promising products, but he was dismissed from the Agency over a year ago because of mental instability."

The entire Joint Committee was leaning forward following every word of the unanticipated revelation with rapt attention. As Thornton finished speaking, several members looked toward the chairman to seek recognition. Mickie Cazz glanced at the senior senator for guidance. The chair nodded. "Before I relinquish the floor, may I ask whether you know the current whereabouts and activities of Mr. Storm?"

"The Agency maintains records on released agents that would contain that information, Congressman, but I have no personal knowledge."

"How could we have been deleted from the witness list, Morrie?" Ted Bonny sounded frantic as he trailed his boss to the elevator hoping against hope that the committee's suddenly called recess was a mistake and that he would be called back to tell what he knew.

"Just be grateful we were," replied Gratz with the weak, hope-tinged voice of a person on his deathbed who has just received the sacrament of baptism.

"Grateful! In two weeks the shit's going to hit the fan and no one's willing to listen to me!"

"So? In two days you'll probably be out of a job."

Their progress stopped at the closed bronze doors, where their eyes automatically ascended to an arrow indicating the elevator's imminent arrival. Bonny was about to resume his plaintive appeal for an understandable universe when a well-known White House official joined them and raised his eyes to the moving arrow.

The door opened, and the three men entered the richly paneled car. The tomblike silence characteristic of strangers subjected to vertical travel in one another's company persisted until the White House official got off on the second floor. Then Bonny rediscovered his voice.

"I could have told him right then about June fifth! I could have told him, and he could have told the president. He was just standing there!"

"So why didn't you?"

"He would have thought I was a nut."

Gratz raised his eyebrows suggestively.

The White House official, code-named "Ghostwriter" by his superiors in Soviet intelligence, entered a friend's office on the second floor and asked the secretary for stationery and a quiet room to jot down a few notes. She was flattered to indulge the great man's request.

Ghostwriter thought for a long time before beginning to write in a highly personalized and thoroughly illegible shorthand.

Webster hearing off track. No substantive discussion of GULFSCENE III. Agency evidently prepared to sacrifice Lincoln Hoskins. Unknown hand being played by former CIA employee David Storm. Is he working for us?

22
ISLAMABAD:
THE THIRD WEEK IN MAY

"Listen to sense, Carl. No one has set foot in this house in a month but the servants, the guards, and us. Today is May twentieth, so we're almost at the end of the period you're expecting to be assassinated in. And you've also predicted that the assassin will be somebody above suspicion. Now I ask you, what do you expect me to think when you tell me that Lal Chatterjee has invited himself over for tea? Either he is coming to kill you, or your theory is for the birds."

Roxanne was carefully pouring small stones and sandy soil from the garden into a long cylinder of thin cloth sewn from part of a nylon scarf. A thorough canvas of the contents of their prison had uncovered astonishingly little in the way of implements for inflicting injury. A try at stealing tableware had quickly revealed that the cook kept a close count of what was put on the table, and a leg removed from a chair in Carl's bedroom had similarly resulted in prompt detection and replacement. Roxanne's answer had been to request sewing materials (no scissors allowed) on the pretense of making alterations in the poorly fitting clothes provided for her use, and to employ them in secret to improvise weapons. The empty sleeves of the earthen clubs had been kept hidden up to this point, and Carl was taking advantage of his first opportunity to heft one of the floppy, sausagelike weapons. "Lal Chatterjee is not the assassin, Roxanne," he said, banging the dining table with a dull, heavy thud. "You can take my word for it. I've known him well for over a year. We're good friends. Besides, a man with a career like his has no reason for getting involved with spy stuff. He's a very famous nuclear physicist. God knows how many international commissions and projects and so forth he's served on."

"Berkeley PhD, right?"

"Just because your friends out there were radical lunatics doesn't mean everybody was. Besides, he must have been at Berkeley in the fifties, before anyone ever heard of radicalism."

"Heart of the Cold War? Young Indian scientist anxious to help his country steer clear of Soviet domination? A natural for CIA recruitment. Face it, Carl. He's coming here to kill you, and you're just defending him because you like him." She finished sewing shut the third red paisley blackjack casing and wedged it between a seat cushion and the back of the couch.

"He said he wanted to talk to me privately because something is going wrong with the plan. Well, something *is* going wrong with the plan. The Paks are getting ready to cheat, and Lal's probably the only Indian who knows. It's natural for him to want my help. He knows I dreamed this whole thing up. So how else can he see me except by coming here?"

Roxanne was surveying the room with a professional eye. "You say he's overweight and around sixty? That probably means he's not going to try anything physical. I doubt he's trained for it anyway. If this is his first time, he won't use a knife either. Amateurs don't know how. So that leaves a bomb, a gun, poison, or something from special effects."

"I wish you'd stop. Next you'll be wanting to brain him the minute he walks through the door."

"I figured you wouldn't go for that."

"I certainly wouldn't! Lal Chatterjee is a world-famous scientist, and he's coming here to talk to me about something vitally important. I don't want you screwing that up." Carl's voice was becoming heated as he limped after Roxanne in her perambulating examination of the room's defensive potential.

"Carl, I don't have to do anything," she replied snappishly without turning to look at him. "You were the one who wanted protection, and if I've decided to give it to you, you're going to get protected whether you like it or not. If there's any possibility that this nitwit scenario of yours can backfire badly enough to cause a nuclear war, I'll be damned if I'll let anyone kill you before you figure out how to stop the entire fiasco. After that, I'll probably kill you myself for having been such a nuisance."

"I'm no longer impressed by your psychopathic-murderer bit."

She turned on him suddenly. "I'll tell you what. Follow my instructions to the letter when Chatterjee gets here, and I'll let you have your little conversation."

"What instructions?" asked Carl dubiously.

"Lifesaving instructions. One, don't eat or drink anything. Say you have an ulcer. Two, if he puts anything on the floor or on a table or anywhere and walks away from it, run into the garden immediately. It's probably going to blow up. Three, stay close to him at all times, preferably in bodily contact. It's very hard for an amateur to maneuver a gun accurately at too close range. Four, if he wants me to leave the two of you alone, make up a reason for me to stay. Five, if I tell you to do anything, do it and don't ask questions. Six . . . what's six? Oh, yes. Don't let him pick up or use anything. I don't want to find a bomb planted in a chess set or a fruit bowl."

"How do you expect him to drink his tea? Should I ask him to open wide and pour it down his throat?"

"He can eat and drink anything he wants," answered Roxanne seriously. "Oh, something else. No embracing. I don't know if Indians are into the kiss-on-both-cheeks routine, but if he has something lethal under his jacket, an embrace is a good time to use it."

"What will you be doing all this time I'm rubbing thighs with him but refusing his kisses? It reminds me of going to the movies with a girl in ninth grade."

"No wonder you're a failure with women."

"Would you like to resume our debate on that subject?" He

experimented with a hand on Roxanne's chest and was rewarded by the firm, rounded feel of a stone-filled club suspended beneath her loose shirt.

She slapped his hand away. "No horsing around until Lal Chatterjee has left this house with us still alive inside it. While he's here, I'll be sticking close to you and keeping a watch on him. Are you sure he'll be acting alone?"

"What I'm sure of is that he is not coming to assassinate me at all. But when somebody does come, he will certainly be acting alone."

Promptly at four, the muffled sound of voices on the other side of the front door and the shadow of a person through its translucent glass prompted them to the arrival positions Roxanne had decided on. There was the familiar sound of the guard's key in the lock, and the door opened. Roxanne tensed herself along the wall beside the door; Carl was stationed across the room by the kitchen door. Neither was prepared for their first sight of Dr. Lal Chatterjee to be his more-than-ample rear end. The Indian was engaged in a rapid-fire monologue directed at someone outside the house and only slowly backed into the room, closing the door behind him.

Abruptly he turned around with his arms outspread. His hands were empty. He looked around for Carl and finding him, spread his arms yet further in greeting. "There you are!"

Carl held his distance. "Welcome. You're right on time. I was just seeing if the tea is ready."

As Carl turned to the kitchen door and knocked for the servant, Roxanne silently approached the slightly crestfallen physicist from behind. "Good afternoon." The physicist reacted with a start. "You must be Carl's friend Dr. Chatterjee. I'm Lily Mason." She held out her thin hand and professionally assayed the strength and proficiency implied by his handshake. "The tea will be right along. Won't you come over and join me on the couch?" She ushered the gray-haired Chatterjee across the room and seated him in the middle of the couch. Then she took a seat beside him and unobtrusively slid her hand behind the cushion until it made contact with the concealed cosh.

Carl joined them and took the seat on Chatterjee's opposite side. "Hi, good to see you! That was a good session this morning. The tea will be here in a minute. Did you meet Lily? She's been sharing my bungalow. One of the perks of ruling the world. Ha, ha, ha." Squeezed between them on the couch, Chatterjee looked physically uncomfortable and confused by Carl's nervous chatter. "Only kidding. Actually, Lily was already staying here when I arrived. She's doing a study of Islamic political activism, focusing on the group that owns this guest-house we're being so comfortably put up in. Lily teaches political science at Columbia University. When I found that out, I wouldn't let them force her to move to a hotel. We worked out an agreement that allows her to stay here and make my confinement a little less irksome in return for which she gets to write GULFSCENE III up in a book after the dust settles."

"I didn't know," said Chatterjee lamely. Roxanne forced a smile as the physicist peered at her at close range.

"No reason why you should. Here comes tea." The servant settled the heavily laden tray on the low table in front of the couch. Chatterjee sat forward and offered to pour. The Americans shook their heads simultaneously. "Ulcer," said Carl placing his hand on his stomach. Roxanne remained tensely silent.

"I suppose it's very trying to be confined," ventured Chatterjee as he put some bread and biscuits on a plate. "By morning we look to you for guidance, and for the remainder of the day, you are a prisoner. I have complained to General Baber myself about the way you're being treated, but he doesn't listen to me."

"He isn't listening to you on much of anything these days, is he, Lal?"

"Ah, so you've noticed!" replied the Indian gloomily. "Then you know why I wanted to come here. Let me tell you, it was not easy to get the general's permission. But back to why I came." He held out a piece of buttered bread to Carl, who turned it down with one hand raised and the other on his stomach. "Things the general has said in the last few days have raised the suspicion in me that he is not playing straight with us. In particular, he intimated just today that everything might be postponed a brief time because the plans for military occupation of crucial points have come along too slowly, particularly in Saudi Arabia. Of course, this is what he has said to me privately. Ostensibly we are all still planning on June the fifth. Now, what I suspect he may be intending is a postponement at the last minute to freeze India's preparations while secretly he proceeds on his own and attempts a grand coup. Possibly, he might even reveal our nuclear deployment to the Muslim states so that they will call upon him as a savior and actually invite him into the Gulf."

"Not a bad idea," said Carl with professional interest.

"India finds itself in a particularly awkward position, of course, if this happens, precisely because we have been faithful to the scenario thus far. Our nuclear force has been sent to the Gulf and cannot be recalled rapidly to defend us. In addition, we cannot publicly denounce Pakistan's plans before the world without implicating ourselves. Moreover, if we should try to preempt a coup of the sort I've described, General Baber might even be able to seize a part of our nuclear arsenal and use it against us. Obviously, we can't safely detonate the weapons to avoid their capture because of where they are located. So you see, if my suspicions are right, then our adherence to your plan may prove to be a disastrous mistake for India."

"Lal, you're absolutely right to be suspicious. But is it really as bad as it looks? Let's think it through. Obviously, we hope Baber is playing it right, but I must admit I share some of your doubts. Since you're the man on the spot, I know it's your responsibility to warn your government of anything going wrong.

On the other hand, if Baber isn't intending to cheat, a last-minute Indian pullout could well provoke the same consequences you just mentioned. You could lose either way."

"Then in your view we should stay the course and hope for the best?" he asked dubiously.

"In a word, yes. I say this primarily because of one consideration that you didn't mention. If Baber cheats, you will have the Russians on your side. There isn't a chance in the world that they will tolerate a single-handed Pakistani coup that gains them both oil money and operational nuclear weapons. I'm not saying that Baber doesn't have it in mind to sell you out, because I think he may. But whether he knows it or not, it would be a suicidal act. The Russians would destroy him."

"Unless the Americans step in." The physicist's gloom seemed unrelieved.

"Which the new administration won't do. The old crowd might have taken the risk of facing up to the Soviets, but they're gone. A new president isn't going to let himself be dragged into a war by a second-class country like Pakistan. That would be Vietnam all over again."

"Perhaps you are right. I hope so." The Indian suddenly raised his left arm and held it before him. In an almost simultaneous movement behind his back Roxanne raised her foot-long paisley blackjack and poised it over his head. "How long have I been here?" The physicist's examination of the watch on his raised wrist saved him the sight of Carl's horrified look in response to Roxanne's action. "I told the guard when I came in that if I did not knock for him within twenty minutes, he should come in and get me. I had best leave now." The blackjack disappeared again behind the cushion. "You've reassured me somewhat, Carl. I wish you could have done more. But as you say, I have to take the responsibility for informing my government or not." He stood up. Roxanne and Carl stood up with him. "I'll not do anything rash. You can trust me on that."

At the door he shook hands first with Roxanne. "You must write a good book, Miss Mason. Perhaps when everything is over, we will have an opportunity to get to know one another." Tensely poised on the balls of her feet, Roxanne could do nothing but nod. "Carl, it's always a pleasure." He grasped Webster's right hand in both of his own. "I regret that your scenario has proved so much more complicated in reality than it seemed on paper. But we shall persevere." He knocked three times on the door and it opened.

As the heavy glass door closed behind Chatterjee's back, Carl turned to face Roxanne as he said, "You see, he wasn't—" The handsewn club swung down on his forehead with stunning force. Unconscious before he hit the floor, he was unaware of Roxanne's body landing on top of him or a split second later of the sound of gunshots and shattering glass as the magazine of an automatic weapon was emptied through the front door at precisely the point where they had been standing.

Roxanne held her breath for several seconds before the sound of running footfalls signalled the would-be assassin's flight. A pain over her right kidney told her that a piece of flying glass had found its mark. She reached behind her and felt blood soaking through her shirt.

"Carl." She shook the shoulder of the inert body beneath her. "Come on. I didn't hit you that hard." More footsteps, this time coming closer. Roxanne got to her feet just as two Pakistani soldiers armed with automatic rifles arrived at the front door and peered through the iron grill, now devoid of its frosted-glass backing.

"He's dead!" Roxanne pointed a finger at the prostrate body. "The Indian shot him! Don't let him escape!" The astonished guards promptly spun around and ran from the door. "So far, so good," said Roxanne aloud to herself. She pulled her sewing needle from the place on her belt where she had secreted it and, bending down, gave Carl a firm jab in the buttock.

"Ow!" came a muffled cry.

"Get up. Now. We're leaving."

Carl stirred and rolled over. He put a hand to the large swelling on his forehead. "What in the hell happened?"

"Get up. We've got to get out of here before any more guards show up. I'll tell you what happened later. Can you run?"

Carl stood up on shaky legs. "Not very well."

"Then we'll walk and hope that the entire guard force is chasing your friend Chatterjee." From an indeterminate distance came the sound of automatic weapons fire. Roxanne pulled the front door open and pointed to a strip of tape holding back the lock. Then she pointed to the dead body of one of the Pakistani guards on the grass to the side of the door. "Your kindly old physicist took out the guard on the way in. He must have used a silencer. When he appeared to be talking to someone as he entered, he was actually taping the lock. He probably left the machine gun on the ground right in front of the door so he could pick it up as soon as he went out again. Typical overelaborate Tony Zwemer operation. He must have guessed I might be planning to protect you."

"Did Lal try to kill me?" asked Carl as Roxanne tugged him by the arm down the front walk.

"He shot through the door. If you hadn't gone with him to see him out, he would have lured you there. Let's cross over into the woods." A few steps took them into sparse woods strewn with underbrush. "Which direction to a street?"

Carl held his hand to his head and looked about. Then he pointed. "That way." As he said the words, more automatic weapons fire came from the exact direction. He swung his arm ninety degrees. "There's another street over there."

Roxanne led the way through the brush at a rate that Carl could barely manage. "I remember you hitting me on the head," he called softly from several paces behind.

"It was to get you to look dead," she replied over her shoulder. "Our best chance of getting away was to get the guards to chase Chatterjee, and the best way to do that was to get him to think he had succeeded in killing us."

"You could have told me to duck."

"You wouldn't have done it right." Roxanne slowed as a two-lane asphalt road came suddenly into view only ten meters away.

Carl came up behind her. "You're hurt," he said in her ear. "There's a big bloody area on your shirt."

"Glass fell on me," she whispered. "Lucky thing. It must have made me look like I'd been shot. You'll have to patch it up as soon as we get clear."

They crept closer to the edge of the woods. No one was in sight. "Where are we going?" whispered Carl.

As if materializing from nothingness, four huge, turbaned men, with raised rifles trained on Carl, stepped silently from the thick brush on either side. A paralyzing jolt of fear slammed through Carl's body.

"Qorban Ali!" cried Roxanne joyously. "I'm all right," she said in Pushtu. "This man is Carl Webster, the one we were supposed to get." Slowly the rifles lowered.

"What are you saying?" whispered Carl in a shaking voice.

"These are my Afghan brothers. The tallest one is Qorban Ali, the leader of the Khaledzai, one of the Pathan tribes. The others are Aslam, Hasan, and Zalmay."

"What are they doing here?"

"What's going on?" asked Roxanne in Pushtu.

"Mr. Zwemer ordered us to hold this position and give covering fire to an Indian in a white Ford if he was chased in this direction."

"As I told you before, Qorban Ali, Mr. Zwemer is a donkey prick." The Afghans laughed. "His Indian just tried to kill both of us. I've got a bad cut on my back." She half-turned to display the blood stain.

"What are you talking about?" interjected Carl.

"Shut up," snapped Roxanne. "I'm trying to save your god-damn life, and I don't have time to answer your goddamn questions."

Carl shrank back and said nothing.

"Qorban Ali, we have to leave right away."

"Our car is over there, Lady." The tall tribesman pointed down the road to the same van that had been used the night Roxanne was captured.

Three minutes later they were speeding away from the guest-house. A voluble five-way discussion in Pushtu filled the vehicle as they departed Islamabad on the road to its twin city of Rawalpindi. Carl sat in silence at the end of a hard bench by the rear door. The kaleidoscope of strong emotions conveyed by the foreign voices deepened the isolation caused by the unin-telligibility of the language.

After fifteen minutes he said meekly, "Can you tell me what's going on?"

Roxanne was receiving an expert bandaging beneath her raised shirt. "Sure. We're heading for Afghanistan. With the CIA out for your head and the Paks trying to recapture you, it's the only safe place to be."

"What do we do after we get to Afghanistan?"

"That's up to you. Where do you have to go to stop this madness you've started? Or do you *want* to stop it? If you don't, we might as well deliver you to Tony Zwemer."

Carl thought for a moment. "Are you sure it was Chatterjee who tried to kill us?"

"You mean could someone else have been waiting outside the door for him to leave? Negative. It was Chatterjee. When he came in I thought he was doing something to the door, and when he left I saw him ease the door open with his own foot after he knocked on it. If you weren't looking for it, you would have thought it was being opened from outside. But there was no question that he was doing it himself. What difference does it make?"

"A lot. If Chatterjee was the CIA's assassin, then GULF-SCENE III should definitely be stopped. Only I don't think there's any way to do it short of going to Abu Dhabi."

"Abu Dhabi?"

"That's the operations center for the coup. But we're going to be in Afghanistan, and there's no way we're going to get from Kabul to the Gulf in sixteen days with the CIA and the Pakistani army gunning for us."

Finishing his bandaging job, Hasan gave it a final look before lowering Roxanne's shirt. Then he grinned at Carl and made a remark in Pushtu that stirred chuckles from the other Afghans.

"What did he say?" asked Carl.

"Uhhh, he said something to the effect that you look more like a eunuch than a homosexual."

"What!?"

"Calm down. Smile at the brothers. I told them you were homosexual so they wouldn't kill you when they found out we'd been living together alone in that guesthouse for a month. They wouldn't even have bandaged me in front of you otherwise. It's just something you'll have to put up with."

23
WASHINGTON:
THE FOURTH WEEK IN MAY

The stately hearing room filled with murmurs as Lincoln Hoskins took his seat behind the witness table. He started speaking immediately.

"With the chairman's permission, I would like to read a statement before answering questions." The senior senator from Washington nodded augustly. Hoskins extracted a glasses case from his breast pocket and affixed gold-rimmed, aviator-style spectacles before his eyes. "Reports in the press over the past five days concerning prior and confidential testimony before this committee have placed my name before the American public in a fashion that is incorrect, inappropriate, and contrary to the interest both of the United States and of the Central Intelligence Agency. Though I am unaware of either the source of these reports or of their accuracy as reflections of committee testimony, I feel that it is incumbent upon me to speak to them insofar as they represent a personal attack upon myself.

"Mr. Chairman, I would like to state categorically that I have never been personally acquainted with, or heard speak of, any current or former employee of the Central Intelligence Agency named David Storm, nor, to the best of my knowledge, have I ever been acquainted with, or heard speak of any current or former employee engaged in impersonating an agent of the Federal Bureau of Investigation or improperly using Bureau credentials.

"I myself have worked for the Central Intelligence Agency for twenty-two years. My record is completely open to the examination of this committee. It contains no allegation of professional impropriety of any kind. I am, gentlemen, and always have been and shall be a loyal American.

"In the affair of Carl Webster, I believe that the United States is confronted by a serious and proximate threat to its national security. With all due respect for the mandate of this committee to oversee the intelligence operations of our government, I submit that the prolonged nature of the present hearings, and the unprecedented and improper publicity attendant upon them, are hindering the investigation of Carl Webster's activities. It cannot be expected that those of us charged with carrying out that investigation should work effectively when each morning's newspaper presents new and unsubstantiated allegations of disloyalty or impropriety against one or another member of our task force.

"Mr. Chairman, although I recognize that it is not my right to do so, I must nevertheless urge, in the interest of national security, that the committee move as rapidly as possible to bring these hearings to a conclusion." Hoskins looked up from his reading and removed his glasses.

The committee chairman looked gravely down at him. "Thank you, Mr. Hoskins. The chair will recognize Representative Castrodigiovanni."

Mickie Cazz braced his forearms on the top of the desk and leaned forward upon them like an experienced truck driver settling in for the long haul.

"Thank you, Mr. Chairman. Mr. Hoskins, your concern for our nation's security is something that I am sure we all share. I would submit, however, that the danger we face in the present instance arises more from the inadequate security measures and possibly willful abuses by those agencies of government charged with safeguarding that security than from the activities of a single defector who has already accomplished whatever damage he is capable of.

"Impatience with the oversight function of this committee

has been expressed before, but I submit that were it not for these hearings, the new and genuine FBI investigation into last winter's events in Cambridge, which has been underway now for five days, would not have come about. In light of that investigation, Mr. Hoskins, through which we have just now, for the first time, become aware of the likelihood that the man called David Storm was responsible for the murders of Roseanne Webster, Selma Dorfman, Peter Grandeville, and Margaret Inman, I cannot comprehend your assertion that the investigative duty of this committee lies elsewhere. Indeed, it strikes me that only a friend of David Storm could hold such an opinion.

"I would like to start, Mr. Hoskins, by asking you how a false FBI report on an investigation in Cambridge that never took place came into your possession?"

24
HERAT:
THE FIRST WEEK IN JUNE

The shadow of a turbaned giant with upraised arms stalked the wide, desolate, thoroughfare that led into the heart of the ancient city of Herat, looming over its shell-holed, gutted shops; over a menacing Soviet tank parked athwart it; and over a solitary beggar seated in its dust. The morning shadow was thrown by the rear wall of the Herat mosque, the most exquisitely ornamented building in western Afghanistan. Tall corner minarets and a pointed dome at its center gave it its ominous anthropomorphic character.

The hot, straight thoroughfare, the widest within the city's walls, was a failed attempt to attract rich merchants to the mosque area from the congested bazaar, but its devastated appearance bespoke its newfound and unanticipated success as a route for Soviet armor to shoot its way into the repeatedly rebellious city's center.

The lone beggar at the foot of the mosque's wall was Carl Webster. With a promise to return shortly, Roxanne and the brothers had left him alone to wait. Two hours had already passed. The tank had taken up its station fifteen minutes previously.

He was dressed in a dirty white turban, and a torn, ankle-length, cotton coat over ragged *shalwar* pants and shirt. His face was red with sunburn and a two-week growth of russet beard. A homemade crutch lay on the ground beside him; a filthy bandage covered his right foot and ankle.

As a disguise, his downcast head, upraised palm and memorized, all-purpose Arabic blessing were scarcely adequate; but they had thus far served him well. Despite the holiness of the month, mosque-goers were few. Coins had twice been pressed into his hand, but no one had attempted to speak to him. Once a patrol of soldiers in Soviet uniforms had walked past and stopped to confer with the crew of the tank parked with its cannon trained down the street, but they, too, had ignored him.

Neither droning flies nor rising morning temperature disturbed the lame beggar's pose. The previous two weeks had accustomed Carl to fear and enured him to physical discomfort, but more than anything they had forced upon him a psychological isolation in comparison with which his present temporary abandonment was easy to endure.

The first leg of their escape from Pakistan had been simple. The black Chevrolet van covered the hundred and twenty miles to the Khyber Pass, on the border between Pakistan and Afghanistan, in less than three hours. Either the failure of Lal Chatterjee's assassination attempt had not yet been realized, or Anthony Zwemer was proving as incompetent as Roxanne claimed he was.

The pleasure drive turned into hardship at the border. At first the van was able to manage the dirt track winding into the mountains that the Afghans used to smuggle weapons into their occupied country, but eventually they left it at a Pathan village and proceeded on foot. Several times Carl was aware of Roxanne making pleas to the brothers on his behalf to walk slower or take rests, but other than that she ignored him, leaving him to limp along the rough paths as best he could.

Four days of trekking, some in the grueling sun and some at night, when stones on the path were almost invisible, had taken them to the brothers' home village near the city of Jalalabad. Roxanne told him that they had covered fifty miles. To Carl, it seemed like a thousand. Pain shot up his right leg with every step, and on the final day it began to swell ominously.

Bandaging and rest in the village alleviated the pain, but only to make room for a fresh infirmity to take its place: a feeling of total disorientation. Among the mud-brick houses, the wandering goats, and the alien turbaned tribesmen on the barren mountainside, the guesthouse in Islamabad seemed impossibly remote. Cambridge, Massachusetts, belonged to another, half-forgotten, lifetime.

A single room with a woven mat covering part of the dirt floor had been provided to house him. Its only light was a small window set high on an end wall. As his leg became better, he occasionally walked about the village, but mostly he remained indoors. It seemed not to occur to anyone that as a Christian he need not abstain from food and drink during Ramadan, and Carl was afraid to mention the subject. Instead, he sat alone indoors each day and pondered his strange fate while waiting for the brutal sun to finally set.

Roxanne came to see him once at the start of the stay in the village. Aslam, the handsome, strong-featured driver of the van, accompanied her. She was dressed in a gaudy full skirt, long-sleeved blouse, and embroidered vest with a yellow and red scarf around her head. Her manner was more relaxed, even, than after she had made love; but she evinced no interest in Carl's situation beyond a few perfunctory questions about his leg. Her sole concern was what could be done to abort GULFSCENE III. It was the first time since escaping that Carl had been prompted to recall the details of the complex operation inexorably grinding to a conclusion far away in the Gulf, an operation that only days earlier had occupied most of his thoughts. His answer to her inquiry sounded to his own ears like something read from a textbook.

"The principal weakness of any complex operation working in secrecy at a remote location is command and control. GULFSCENE III has two command nodes. One is in Islamabad with General Baber and is essentially invulnerable. The other is the operations center in Abu Dhabi. General Baber's brother-in-law, Brigadier Faiz, is in command there, but his position is vulnerable because he must maintain total secrecy."

"Then we'll go to Abu Dhabi," replied Roxanne.

"How?" asked Carl in the same remote voice.

"That's my problem," she said curtly. Carl looked at the date indicator on his watch as Roxanne and Aslam left his empty room. It read 5.26 FR.

He next saw her late in the day the following Thursday. This time she was accompanied by Qorban Ali. They both looked tired. "It's not promising. We've been to Kabul. The plan is to work through Khaledzai tribesmen in the air force, but it's proving difficult. There are Khaledzai pilots both at Kabul air base and at Begram who would defect and fly us to Abu Dhabi if Qorban Ali ordered it, but the aircraft they are assigned to don't have the range, even one way."

"There aren't many Soviet planes in Afghanistan that do," Carl responded. "Offhand, I'd recommend a MiG-23U. NATO calls it a Flogger-C. It's a two-seat training version of the Flogger-B fighter. Operational range 560–745 miles. Double that for a one-way trip with an external fuel tank and it'll make Abu Dhabi. Intelligence reports Flogger-Cs at Begram, Shindan, and Herat."

"Your knowledge is very impressive, Carl," said Roxanne wearily, "as usual. However, we already got all that information, and we've even found out about a Khaledzai pilot who trains other fliers on MiG-23Us. Our problem is that he's in Herat."

"But Herat's over seven hundred miles from here!"

"When it gets dark, we'll eat and then leave."

Carl felt a gentle wave of interest lap against his apathy. "Roxanne, think a minute. With Russian patrols on the roads, we can only travel at night, right? At this time of year at this latitude, that means eight travel hours a night at the very most.

I'm assuming your friends know how to work around check-points and roadblocks or they wouldn't still be alive, but even with a good vehicle, we're still not going to average more than thirty miles an hour. That makes three nights just to get to Herat." Carl counted the days on his fingers. "Today's June first so tonight takes us to the second, tomorrow night to the third, and the next night to the fourth. And that's just to get to Herat, which must be about twelve hundred miles or so from Abu Dhabi. We still have to get onto a heavily guarded Soviet air-base, steal a plane, fly to the Gulf without being shot down, land somewhere without being arrested, get into Brigadier Faiz's headquarters, and do God-knows-what to stop him before ten AM on the fifth. Let's be realistic. We're not going to get all that done in twenty-four hours."

Roxanne stared at Carl coldly. "You're a real chickenshit, Carl. What does your precious onboard computer say is the probability of one or more atomic bombs going off on or after the fifth with a loss of life of over, say, fifty thousand?"

"Maybe ninety percent," replied Carl testily. "Now ask me the probability of our being able to stop it—that's zero—or of our being killed trying—that's about a hundred. You're being as stupid, Roxanne, as when you thought you could overthrow the American government by putting a bomb in a Bank of America building. That's what makes you radicals so goddamn fatuous: you can't add two and two and get four. Look, you want to feel bad because thousands of people are going to get killed? So feel bad. I'll probably feel bad, too, when it happens. But it's no reason to commit suicide!"

Roxanne turned her face from Carl and exchanged a few words of Pushtu with Qorban Ali, then she turned back to Carl. "I've told Qorban Ali that the eunuch is unwilling to go. He suggests that we tie you up and take you along anyway. Is that what you want, Carl?"

Carl stared angrily at the mat on the floor. "You don't need to do that. I'll come along. I only wanted to tell you what I thought."

Roxanne seemed slightly appeased. "Being a coward doesn't make you altogether wrong, Carl. You're right about the available time. That's why we're going to make part of the trip in daylight and try to save a day."

"Roxanne! The Russians control the Kabul–Herat highway completely during the day! It'll be suicide!"

"Oh shut up, Carl! If one of your atom bombs goes off in the Gulf and kills people, I'm personally going to murder you anyway! You might be happier to get it from the Russians!" With that she rose to her feet and stormed from the room followed by a glowering Qorban Ali.

"Big talk," muttered Carl.

They departed two hours later: Roxanne, now entirely covered in the black tent of an Afghan *chador*; Carl; the four brothers; and five other tribesmen in two stolen Soviet jeeps. Driving without headlights under a half moon, the Pathans' familiarity with their local surroundings seemed to give them extra eyes. After speeding for long stretches on excellent asphalt highway, they would suddenly veer, without apparent provocation, onto a dirt path and wander for miles from one unlit village to another before rejoining the main road. The effect on Carl, wedged on a hard bench seat between two unspeaking tribesmen, was one of continuing isolation and disorientation. The precipitous foreslopes of the colossal Hindu Kush mountain range loomed continually to the north and west, but nothing else was intelligible to his eyes except, occasionally, a distant glimpse of bright lights signaling an army outpost or checkpoint.

Dawn found them completing their last meal until evening in a village quite different from the one in the mountains near Jalalabad. A flat irrigated plain, green with new crops, spread out on all sides. The jeeps had been driven into mud-walled garden enclosures where brushy greens were piled on their canvas roofs for concealment.

From a distance, Carl observed what appeared to be a council of war taking place among a dozen figures squatting beneath some young willow trees along a water course. His participation was not invited. Eventually, Roxanne informed him that they would be moving on promptly and asked him if he could ride a bicycle with his sore leg. To a question regarding where they were now and where they were going, he received a curt answer that they were near the city of Qandahar and would attempt to get through it and beyond during the daylight hours.

Hitherto, Carl's garb had been the Pakistani clothes he had left Islamabad in. But now an old man of the village came to him, surveyed his stature, and then left and returned with dark gray farmer's clothes and sandals. A turban was tied around his head and the bandage removed from his foot and ankle.

The journey into Qandahar took two hours. Carl and the oldest of the brothers, a rugged, bearded man named Zalmay, rode a meandering path through five villages with cages of live chickens tied to the rear fenders of their bicycles. How the others traveled Carl did not know, but when all had gathered safely within a walled courtyard in the city of Qandahar, he noticed that the five tribesmen were no longer escorting them. Garishly painted trucks, junked in various stages of cannibalization, were parked in a disorderly fashion around the dirt lot. Incredibly, by the time the sun reached its glaring zenith, one of the hulks—a scarred veteran from International Harvester with a scene of panther hunting painted on the one remaining cab door—had been fitted by two mechanics too young to shave with four wheels, a radiator and water pump, a gas tank, and what looked like a new gearbox. Then it had been goaded complainingly to life and pronounced fit for carrying them on the next leg of their futile journey.

Aslam drove, with Qorban Ali and Roxanne sharing the cab.

Carl, Hasan, and Zalmay, accompanied by the small arsenal of
weapons they had brought with them from their home village,
bedded down in stifling, almost airless, concealment under
sacks of unginned cotton in the truck's high-sided bed.

Between heat, hunger, thirst, and the painful throbbing the
bicycling had rekindled in his leg, Carl passed hour after hour
in a semistupor, aware only of passages of smooth road being
interrupted frequently by jolts and bumpy detours. Occasionally
the truck stopped and muffled voices could be heard through
the sacks of cotton. Each time Hasan and Zalmay cautiously
eased their guns into position for quick use, but each time the
truck started again without incident.

After what seemed like years, Carl was suddenly jolted alert
by the truck's roaring acceleration on a rough road they had
been traveling for some time. In seemingly instant response
Hasan and Zalmay began worming their way upward through
the cargo with their weapons. Then slowly Carl became aware
of an unfamiliar roar imposing itself over the deafening grind of
the truck's engine. A moment later the shooting began.

The truck lurched violently back and forth as it weaved over
what felt like plowed land, threatening to overturn with every
zag. Frighteningly loud explosions sounded nearby followed by
machine gun bursts almost in his ear as Hasan and Zalmay
returned fire. Then it dawned on Carl that they were under
attack from a helicopter.

Suddenly his heart was racing; he was suffocating. Struggling
with weak arms to find a path through the sacks of cotton to
reach the open air was like being unable to wake from a night-
mare. At last, a blast of hot wind hit his face as his head
reached the surface. The now louder chop of the helicopter's
rotor made it sound closer than it was. Carl turned his head and
located the craft two hundred meters away. A picture flashed
into his mind, the picture in *Jane's All the World's Aircraft* of a
Soviet Mi-24 attack helicopter, and with the image came com-

plete recall of the deadly machine's range, speed, armor, crew size, and weapons array. Then Carl felt tears in his eyes and a jumbled feeling of not wanting to die and of the pathetic inadequacy of Hasan and Zalmay's continuing counterfire against the helicopter's rockets and rapid-fire twenty millimeter cannon.

Lifting his gaze higher, he spied at medium altitude above the Mi-24 the distinctive air intake and pitot boom configuration of a circling MiG-21 fighter. The sight of it wheeling against the cloudless blue sky was oddly calming. Even new rocket explosions bracketing the truck's careening course and puffs of dust from the helicopter's cannon fire marching alongside did not renew his momentary panic. He had mentally accepted the end of the fight as a foregone conclusion. The slightly hilly, barren terrain offered no place to run to. The thought occurred to him that with their deaths he would win his final argument with Roxanne.

Suddenly, at an inestimable distance a thin trail of white vapor spurted rapidly upward in the direction of the MiG. Abruptly the fighter plane shot almost straight up at a prodigious speed, leaving the trail of the missile to pass beneath it and arc back toward the ground. The sound of its harmless detonation out of sight over the hills reached Carl's ears a minute later, but by then his attention had been seized by the sight of the attack helicopter leaning on its side in a sharp U-turn in the direction of the distant hillside whence the missile had come.

As suddenly as it had begun, the attack had ended. The truck continued down the rough track at destructive speed as every eye on board scanned the sky for the helicopter's return. Five minutes passed, then ten. They had topped a low hill and entered a region of villages and green fields. Fifteen minutes. Ahead of them was the low, dust-brown profile of a sizable town.

The truck's arrival in Girishk was celebrated as a major victory. The town near the foothills of the mountains had been under complete guerrilla control for two weeks. Everyone knew that sooner or later the Soviet planes and tanks would come to take it back because of its strategic proximity to the Qandahar–Herat highway and the immense Shindan airbase to the northwest; and when they came, the guerrillas would go back into the hills. But until that day, every successful engagement was a triumph. Though they had missed the MiG with their stolen Russian antiaircraft missile, the attack had saved the truck without loss to Girishk's defenders, who had fled to a cave after firing the SAM; and when it was discovered that the truck contained so prominent a leader as Qorban Ali, the local commander ordered a feast to begin at sundown.

For Carl, the feast was a source of amazement. In over five years of digesting intelligence reports on the Afghan resistance, he had never found mention of the fighting tribesmen's ability to relax and celebrate between battles. Although an assortment of leers led Carl to guess that the story of his alleged homosexuality was steadily making its way through the large gathering of men squatting on low platforms in the open-air teahouse, no one actually attempted to speak to him. Happy to be alive, and satisfied to be alone in the joyous crowd, he concentrated on eating the rice and stew with his fingers and tried not to think of Roxanne.

But Roxanne and her quixotic dream of flying to Abu Dhabi could not be forgotten. In the midst of the feast her *chador*-clad form entered at the heels of Qorban Ali, the commander Mohammed, and a young, dark man with black hair, an uncommonly low hairline, and a disheveled Soviet uniform. Mounted on one of the platforms, Mohammed and then Qorban Ali made speeches to the guerrillas, gesturing frequently toward the dark man, who presently began to smile. The crowd responded with enthusiastic cries of *"Allahu akbar."* Carl could understand nothing.

The feasting was still continuing at midnight when Hasan

came up and tugged at his arm. Carl rose and followed him to the town's main street, where an old American schoolbus bearing the clasped-hands motif of a defunct foreign-aid program was parked by the water-filled earthen gutter. Inside he could see the other brothers and Roxanne divested of her black shroud and back in tribal clothing. He took a deep breath and clambered aboard.

Surprisingly, Roxanne seemed friendly and willing to talk to him once Girishk and the celebrating guerrillas had been left behind and the bus had found its way onto the broad concrete highway leading to Herat. Their talk was brief and without reference to their earlier disagreement. Implicit in the news that Roxanne had to impart, however, was the message that the stop in Girishk had brought her own goal of flying to Abu Dhabi a giant step closer.

The dark soldier at the feast, it turned out, had been a captured Soviet airman; not a Russian, but a Muslim Tatar from the region of the lower Volga River. He had been taken by the guerrillas during an ambush of a truck leaving Shindan airbase, but his posting was to Herat. He had been their prisoner for a week, and Mohammed had been working industriously, but without success, to convert him to the cause of the resistance on the ground of their common faith.

Roxanne's unforeseen arrival had changed the situation. She had gone with Qorban Ali to view and admire the great store of arms captured by the Girishk guerrillas, and the airman had been shown off to them as a special prize. When Mohammed had boasted of his goal of converting the Tatar to the Afghan cause, Roxanne had started at the word Tatar. As she related the story to Carl, her mere mention to the prisoner in his native language that she was the granddaughter of Yunus Asefoglu, the greatest modern master of the Tatar language and the intellectual conscience of the Bashkir nationalist movement, had been enough to totally reverse his attitude.

At this point, the story became confused because of Carl's problems understanding the exact relationship between Tatars, Bashkirs, and other Turkic peoples of the USSR, about which Roxanne herself was not altogether clear, and then cut short by a bone-rattling detour onto a rough dirt road, which the bus had not been designed for even when new.

When she took it up again back on the highway two hours later, fatigue was rapidly setting in. Roxanne's interest in detailing the airman's miraculous conversion had dissipated, and she satisfied herself with its relevant outcome: a plan devised with the prisoner's help for entering the Herat airbase—or more precisely, a plan for Carl to enter the Herat airbase.

Carl listened numbly to his fate and didn't bother to argue. They had been steadily on the move for most of the previous twenty-eight hours, which made argument over anything, including a death sentence, seem pointless. The plan would either work, or it wouldn't. Sleep was more important.

The drive through the night into Herat passed without incident. The bus was abandoned on the southern outskirts of the city within sight of its immense, eroded, mud-brick rampart composed of hundreds of years of fortifications built upon the ruins of previous walls, the current dilapidated wall being well on its way to becoming the most recent layer of decay. Higher than the wall in the far distance rose the giant artificial hill of the ancient citadel, equally eroded but still, Carl knew, a usable fortress for resisting the Russians.

Following the advice of the Girishk guerrillas, they split into pairs and made their way by foot around the southeast corner of the rampart and northward through residential areas until they reached the road to the mosque's main portal. There they rendezvoused and considered an unforeseen problem.

Carl's abandonment in the dust at the mosque's rear had not been part of the plan. But his sore leg could hobble no further. Together they helped him to the mosque and waited against a blue mosaic wall in its huge courtyard, schooling Carl on proper beggars' behavior while Aslam went in search of suitable rags. On Aslam's return, the transformation from fugitive to object of charity was quickly performed. Effectively disguised in her *chador*, Roxanne accompanied the pathetic cripple on his wooden crutch to the point at the shady but seldom-frequented rear of the building that they had chosen for his pleading. Then they left him.

Now it was well after ten, and Roxanne and the brothers had still not returned. A second patrol of soldiers walked up the broad thoroughfare behind the mosque and stopped at the tank, where they exchanged words with its commander, standing with his head and shoulders out of the low, streamlined turret. A little girl in colorful clothes and carrying a cloth bundle walked by and pressed a coin into Carl's hand.

"*Al-hamdu li'llah*," he mumbled as she walked on. Then he realized that a small piece of paper was with the coin in his hand. As inconspicuously as possible, he lowered his dirty claw to the level of his downcast eyes and read its message. At the same time he heard the jingle of a horse harness and looked up quickly to see a two-wheeled passenger cart slowly approaching him with a driver at the reins and an enormously fat passenger sitting on the backward-facing seat behind him.

"*Ay Baba!*" shouted the fat man as the chariotlike *ghadi* slowed. He was patting the bench beside him gesturing to Carl with his other hand.

The beggar responded, "*Al-hamdu li'llah*." Slowly and with unfeigned pain and stiffness, he clambered to his feet using the crutch for support. The note had simply said "Look up." He hobbled to the cart and tried to figure out how to get in. With the fat man pulling and the driver at pains to keep the horse from reacting to the vehicle's sway, Carl finally got on board. The Russian patrol was looking their way with amusement, which increased markedly with the horse's evident difficulty in getting the cart going again with the new addition to the load.

The trip was not far. The fat man motioned for Carl to dismount in front of a gate in a whitewashed wall in the same residential sector he had walked through earlier in the day. As soon as Carl reached the ground, the vehicle pulled away with no further word from either occupant. Carl turned and knocked on the gate.

Roxanne and the brothers were within the fruit tree-shaded courtyard. Within it as well was an open-fronted house. He asked Roxanne what was happening, and she told him to go inside and sleep. He did not have to be told twice.

The straw-filled mattress was wet with perspiration when he awoke. The air was hot and still. His watch read 3:14 P.M. A push of a tiny button changed it to 6.03 SA. Roxanne's gesture had less than forty-three hours to run. He rolled onto his side and noticed a basin of water and an old Schick safety razor on a brass tray on the floor. Next to them was a piece of paper bearing the word SHAVE.

The courtyard was filled with bright sunshine and the loud, high-pitched buzzing of insects. Zalmay and Aslam were lying on their backs in the shade of the house. Qorban Ali was sitting cross-legged with his back to a shiny-leaved apricot tree, sewing. Carl looked about for Roxanne and did a double take on seeing her emerge from the outhouse in the corner of the courtyard carrying a ewer of water but otherwise looking exactly like a short, thin Soviet soldier.

"How do you like the fit?" she said as she came up to him and put the latrine ewer down on the brick threshold. "I've worn so many Russian uniforms over the last three years that Qorban Ali knows my size perfectly. I hope he does as well with yours. The closest we could get to your size from the local resistance people was a little small, but Qorban Ali is letting it out. You're going to be a captain. Congratulations."

"What I'm going to be is dead."

Roxanne was studying his face. "Your chin and cheeks are whiter than the rest of your face."

"How is your plan shaping up? Have some more patriotic Mongolians shown up and offered you air cover for your journey to Abu Dhabi?"

"Tatars aren't Mongolians, and the plan is doing fine. I have a map for you." She squatted down and pulled a piece of paper out of her tunic. Putting it on the ground, she began tracing her finger from a small square with an X in it. "Here we are at this house. You follow this street down to its end, then turn east. That'll be a major road. You go on that past a huge old British colonial-style hotel on your left, about half a mile, and at the next main street you turn right. Maybe a mile down that road you'll see a modern-looking concrete building coming up on the left. That's the airport hotel. The Russians built it twenty years ago and now they're using it as an officers' billet. Just before you get to it, there's a dirt road on the left that takes you to a service gate."

"With a guardhouse."

"With a guardhouse. The military police are Afghan army men with Russian officers. You'll be alone, and you look like a Russian, so they'll just look at your pass and let you through. They'll assume you don't speak their language."

Carl had heard the plan before. "And if one of their officers is present in the guardhouse?"

"Then he will come out to talk with you, and you'll either be arrested or killed," said Roxanne matter-of-factly.

"That's the way I remembered it. Do you still think the chances are about fifty-fifty there will be an officer there?"

"That's what my Tatar hero said, and that's what the local guerrillas say, too."

"What about my carrying a machine gun and mowing them all down if they catch on?"

"Don't be silly." She pointed again at the map. "After you get inside, you drive this way, and then take a left. When you get to the far end of that road, stop. We come through the fence here." She drew an X with her pencil. "These buildings are low-priority storage, so with luck no one will see me join you. Then we get going again, heading for the end of this runway. We have to leave the road and cross this open area to get to it, but the brothers will stage a diversion back in that storage area when they see we're about to do it. The plane should be right here. We just hop in, and off we go."

Carl shook his head. "You're out of your mind."

"Maybe, but here's a final piece of insurance. Don't let anyone see it." Roxanne reached again into her tunic and extracted a flat package wrapped in newspaper.

Carl took it and peeked inside. "It looks like bread."

"It is bread. I want you to be eating it when you reach that guardhouse. The Afghan guards will assume you're making fun of their religion. If they're angry, they'll be less likely to take a close look at you."

Carl put the package into his shirt. "At least I won't die hungry," he said gloomily.

An hour later, the guardhouse was in sight. Carl put a sweaty palm on the big black knob of the Russian jeep's floor shift and eased the heavy vehicle into a lower gear to slow down. On the seat beside him was what he hoped was a valid pass. His passport photograph had been artfully cut apart, the face framed by the uniform hat and uniform of a genuine identification photo, and reshot during the time he had been begging at the rear of the mosque. The quality of the forgery was excellent. Also beside him was a ridged piece of Afghan bread studded with sesame seeds.

As two guards stepped forth from the iron-roofed shed, he

grabbed the bread and nervously took a large bite, and then another. By the time he brought the jeep to a halt and looked out the window at the dark man holding out his hand, Carl's cheeks were bulging with a massive cud of bread. Holding the remaining chunk in his left hand, he retrieved the pass with his right. As he handed it to the soldier, a tall, blond, square-faced officer carrying a pistol stepped out of the shed and began walking toward the jeep.

Instantly, Carl's entire body was seized by a jolt of adrenaline. Every joint went weak. The bread in his throat was choking him. Reflexively, he emitted a violent cough propelling the sodden wad of bread directly into the face of the Afghan soldier. The guard leaped back with a shout, raising his machine gun as he did so. Carl uttered a strangled scream, and as he did, he heard a second voice chiming in with almost the same sound. He looked and saw that the Russian officer was bent double with laughter, while the entire contingent of Afghan guards glowered at Carl.

Still laughing, the officer casually picked up the pass from the ground where it had been dropped and tossed it back through the jeep's window. With a loud pleasantry in Russian, the officer waved Carl toward the gate and stared sternly at the Afghan standing at the counterweight until he lifted it.

Carl waved weakly back and drove through. His hands were shaking so badly that it was difficult for him to steer, but no one noticed. By the time he reached the rendezvous point where the road passed behind a fenced-in dump full of wooden crates, he had recovered slightly. Where Roxanne had been hidden, he could not determine. Suddenly she was beside him on the seat, and he had not even seen her before the door opened.

"Piece of cake, wasn't it?" said Roxanne with a grin on her face.

Carl couldn't speak.

The brothers' diversion came precisely on time. Carl had just left the road and was bulling the jeep between two sections of a temporary jet exhaust baffle when a series of explosions went off at their rear. Carl stepped on the gas as Roxanne looked around.

"Wow! What a fire!" she said with almost childish excitement.

Carl was oblivious to her words. They were now on a runway with their destination in view. He scanned his field of vision for sight of the plane. Finally, he saw it: a high-winged, needle-tipped, fifty-five-foot-long fighter with a distinctively angled tail. Its taxi path was from his left-rear quadrant. The point of intercept was perfectly calculated.

In moments they were climbing from the jeep's hood onto the airplane's wing. The canopy of the rear seat was raised and waiting. Carl couldn't believe there had been no alarm. He stepped inside and was barely seated when Roxanne dropped onto his lap. The canopy whirred shut, barely clearing her ducked head, and a sudden surge of acceleration pressed her heavily against him. In seconds they were airborne and climbing fast.

Roxanne craned her head in the impossibly cramped seat and looked Carl in the eye from five inches away. "What did I tell you? A piece of cake!" she said gleefully.

25
ARAMCO E-6:
THE FIRST WEEK IN JUNE

"Christ on a crutch," said Virgil Foltz to the hot desert wind as the jet warplane passed overhead at an ominously low altitude. A deformed lump of plasticized TNT he had been shaping to fit against the leg of a water tank dangled at the end of his long arm. The jet swept a clean arc in the cloudless sky and headed back toward the landing strip at an even lower altitude. It waggled its wings. "The mother's gonna land." Virgil ran three steps forward through the powder-fine sand and abruptly stopped. From a holster under his arm he withdrew a chrome-plated flask and tipped his head back for a long pull. "Never die sober," he said, smacking his lips.

The jet touched down through a cloud of black smoke blowing across the runway from burning drums of oil ignited by one of Virgil's earlier explosive charges. "There's someone here!" exclaimed Roxanne. Carl could see nothing but an expanse of Russian uniform tunic. "Imran was right when he said there was a helicopter! I see it, too! We're going to do it, Carl!"

The two-hour, supersonic, low-altitude flight from Herat had been mostly through Iranian airspace over salt deserts and denuded mountains. Imran, the Khaledzai pilot, had stated, and from his earlier study of Iranian air capabilities Carl had concurred, that the threat of interception was negligible once out of Afghanistan.

Hence, the flight had been relaxed, if physically uncomfortable in the cramped cockpit, and largely consumed by a bilingual debate over where to land. Imran had recommended—in Pushtu—a landing strip in Saudi territory, just over the Abu Dhabi border, marked on his Soviet flying chart as being three thousand feet long and out of use. Carl had argued for some stretch of highway between Abu Dhabi city and the Oman border on the grounds that landing on an abandoned airstrip in the middle of the wrong country's desert, with no likelihood of finding ongoing transportation, was patently stupid. Roxanne had weighed the two positions and decided that it was better to risk being stranded in the desert than to take a chance on a head-on collision with a sheikh's Cadillac. The pilot's glimpse of a helicopter parked by the smoke-swept runway had confirmed her judgment.

Outside in the heat, the lanky, potbellied Oklahoman, whose helicopter it was, was loping through the sand toward the end of the runway with one hand on his broad-brimmed straw hat as the MiG rolled to a stop and its drag parachute deflated. The Afghan insignia blazoned on the tail was unfamiliar, but the two large Cyrillic letters preceding the number 121 on the nose below the cockpit brought him up short. Virgil had dropped out of college Russian after one semester, but even half drunk he still remembered the alphabet.

"Oh my God, it's the Russians," he said aloud. He looked around for his helicopter pilot but saw nothing but black smoke and reddish sand. "Looks like ol' Prince Talal was right about these airstrips." Fingers of fear were gripping his muzzy mind, where they encountered tendrils of alcoholic bemusement. He resumed his advance toward the plane at a walk. Simultaneously, the two cockpit canopies opened. He slowed his pace. Three figures in Russian uniforms climbed out onto the wing and jumped to the ground; the shortest, thinnest one was holding a pistol. Virgil struggled to recall the little Russian he had once known.

"*Droog*," he called out loudly. "Friend. Peace. *Meer*." He pointed at himself. "*Amerikansky*. Aramco." Two of the three were walking purposefully toward him; the other lagged behind limping badly. "*Rabotnik. Nyet kapitalist*." The fingers of fear were beginning to strangle him. Remembering that he was still carrying the TNT, he instantly dropped it and raised his hands over his head.

"We need your helicopter," shouted the gun wielder.

Virgil was taken aback both by the gender of the voice and the excellence of its American accent. "You speak English?" he asked, enunciating as carefully as he could. "I'm Virgil Foltz. I work for Aramco. Oil." He thought of the Russian word. "*Kerosene.*"

"Look, buddy," said Roxanne sternly, stopping ten feet away, "all we want is your helicopter. Either you give it to us, or I kill you. It's as simple as that."

"Are you defecting?" asked Virgil incredulously.

"No, goddamn it. We're Americans."

"Americans?"

"We're going to Abu Dhabi. You're not here alone, are you?"

Virgil craned his neck to look around his raised arms. "Hell no. I've got a pilot around here somewhere. If he's got any wits, he's probably in the helicopter radioing Dhahran. You sure you fellas are American?" The tendrils of bemusement were counterattacking. "How come you're in a Russian plane? And those are Russian uniforms, too, aren't they?"

Carl had finally hobbled up to join Roxanne and Imran. "We're American spies, Mr. . . . Foltz? Was that your name? I couldn't quite get it. We've just escaped from Afghanistan." He pointed at the pilot. "This man's in the Afghan air force. He wants political asylum here. But the two of us," he indicated himself and Roxanne, "have to get to Abu Dhabi immediately with an important message for the American ambassador. That's why we need to borrow your helicopter." Carl sounded like he was saying he had just gotten off the bus and wanted to know which way was north.

Virgil tipped up the right side of his hat brim and scratched his head. "Mind if I have a drink?" he said, reaching for the flask in his armpit. Roxanne's gun clicked menacingly. "Hold on, hold on. I'm just reaching for the booze. See? It's in here." He lifted his arm and gestured widely beneath it. Roxanne watched closely as he unscrewed the top of the flask and tipped it into his mouth. "Thank you. I didn't use to drink so much, but all this religious teetotaling in Saudi kinda gets to you. You end up taking a drink just for patriotic purposes, if you know what I mean. Now then, you say you're American spies from Afghanistan. Is that it?"

"Shut up," ordered Roxanne sharply. "We're going to start walking toward the helicopter. When you see your pilot, tell him to stand away from it with his hands up. I'm an excellent shot, and I won't mind killing you the slightest bit."

"Whatever you say, ma'am," said Virgil. He turned toward the helicopter, which was partially obscured by the blowing black smoke on the far side of the MiG. The Russian-uniformed trio stood aside to let him pass. Leading the way against the hot wind with his hands up, Virgil called back over his shoulder, "You know, if you'd wanted to go to Abu Dhabi to deliver a message, you coulda just landed at the airport. They'd of let you. But maybe you just overflew it a little. Is that it?"

"Keep walking," replied Roxanne.

"You folks ain't fixin' to overthrow the king, are you? 'Cause if you are, I'm with you a hundred percent. Nothing personal against the king, mind, but it'd sure be nice to shake this place up a bit. I'm pretty damn sick of Saudi."

"How big's your helicopter?"

"Four seats, but two of them are full of supplies and TNT. You aren't smugglers, are you? Coals to Newcastle if you are. I got enough home brew with me to set up in business."

"What's the TNT for?"

"Blowin' up airstrips. You won't believe this, but what I'm doin' here is destroying this place. If you fellas had landed two hours later, there'd of been holes all over that runway. The Saudi Ministry of the Interior wants all these old strips destroyed to keep people from landing on 'em. Kinda funny, ain't it?"

A short distance away a reed-thin man in snow white gown and red-checked headdress stepped down from the bubble of the helicopter. "Better get out of the way, Ahmad, and put your hands up," called Virgil. "I don't know who these folks are, but the one right behind me is a little lady with a gun and a bad temper." To his captors he added, "Ahmad works for the Ministry. Prince Talal sends him along to keep an eye on me."

They stopped and waited for the Arab to walk clear of the machine. Roxanne had a rapid exchange of questions and answers in Pushtu with the pilot Imran.

"Mr. Foltz," began Carl, who had just caught up with the group, "I'd like to explain—"

"Keep quiet, Carl. When you said the Ministry, buddy, did you mean the Ministry of the Interior?"

"That's right. Counterespionage division. Prince Talal bin Talal is the man in charge."

"Our pilot wants political asylum. He would like to stay here with your man from the Ministry and wait for the authorities to come, but that would leave us without anyone to fly the helicopter. You don't, by any chance, know how, do you?"

"Yes, ma'am," answered Virgil with a grin. "I used to fly all over these parts."

"Good. You'll take us to Abu Dhabi then."

"Course, that was before I took up serious drinkin'. You don't mind if I have another snort, do you?" He reached for his flask and drained it without objection. "Whew! That's rough." In a subdued voice he added, "You know, I'm really only doing this for ol' Ahmad's benefit. This Prince Talal sort of blackmailed me over my drinking into wrecking all these nice airstrips. So I like to show off a bit for Ahmad, it bein' Ramadan and all, because he can't do nothing about it till we get back. Then I'll probably get my ass kicked out of the country. But I can fly a helicopter with no problem. Never you mind about that."

Roxanne and Carl glanced at each other and read similar mixed looks of hope and despair in one another's face.

"Now then, if we're fixin' to go to Abu Dhabi," continued Virgil in a slightly slurred managerial tone, "I gotta know where to land, and I gotta know what you're planning to say when we're all arrested. I'd also suggest that you do something about those uniforms. Somebody might just start shooting when they see you and ask questions later."

"You're a funny man, Mr. Foltz," said Roxanne in a quizzical voice. "I have half a mind to tell you what's going on and ask you to join us so I don't have to keep this gun on you all the time. How much TNT have you got?"

"Call me Virgil. Well now, this is runway E-6; and I've got enough to do E-4, D-2, and maybe D-1 before heading back to Dhahran. That's if I don't waste any. But oil prospecting gives you a good feel for how to use the stuff."

Roxanne looked at the rangy, red-faced engineer and pondered. Then she said, "What would you say if I told you that the day after tomorrow there's going to be a coup in all the countries in the Gulf and probably an atomic bomb explosion, too, possibly killing tens of thousands of people?"

Virgil looked bemused. "If I was home, I'd ask my wife Billie to pray for us. But as I'm not, I guess I'd say that that sounds bad."

"I'd like to explain in a little more detail, Virgil," ventured Carl.

"In the air," said Roxanne decisively. "Virgil, go get your friend Ahmad's clothes. They should be all right for me. Carl, you just wear your undershirt and Virgil's hat, and trade your shoes for his boots. Maybe you can pass for a Texan." Carl shuddered at the additional torture being prescribed for his aching leg and ankle.

Twenty minutes later they were aloft, leaving behind in the featureless desert waste the rapidly dwindling figures of the Afghan pilot and a stripped, enraged, and humiliated Ahmad.

"Pray for us, Billie!" shouted Virgil over the engine's roar. In an alcoholic fog he consulted his instruments, put the setting sun on his left, and set a course for Abu Dhabi.

26
ABU DHABI:
THE FIRST WEEK IN JUNE

Two pairs of eyes took special note in the growing dusk of the descent of a helicopter toward the square concrete landing pad on the lawn of the Abu Dhabi Hilton. One pair was large and brown with a piercing quality like that of a certain sixteenth-century drawing by Angelo Bronzino. The other was the light but intense color of faded blueberry stains on a white tablecloth.

Merrie Orchard, the owner of the first, was sitting in a rented Datsun in front of the nearby headquarters of the Abu Dhabi National Oil Company, a serpentine building designed on the pattern of the Watergate complex in Washington, D.C., as an architectural showpiece on the elegant beach road. Excitedly, he started the car as the chopper sank below his line of sight behind the palm trees on the median strip. For three weeks he had been waiting for fate to reward his ingenuity in uncovering the lineaments of a Pakistani conspiracy with an opportunity to achieve worldwide fame. With hope in his heart he sensed that the moment was at hand.

The owner of the other pair of eyes was standing outside the lobby door on the drive-through entranceway that pierced the hotel. He watched with interest the disembarking of the helicopter's three occupants: a short, thin Arab with a Saudi-style headdress; a fleshy man of medium height, who walked with a limp and looked decidedly tacky in a white undershirt vest and straw hat; and a tall, gangly man carrying a wooden crate the size of a microwave oven. As they approached the lobby entrance, the blue-eyed watcher stepped into the travel agency across the driveway and out of sight.

"My name is Virgil Foltz," Virgil said with forced sobriety to the Pakistani room clerk as he lowered his box of TNT carefully to the ground and fished in a hip pocket for his passport. "You should have received a telephone call from Dhahran reserving a room for three."

The well-trained clerk kept his eyes from wandering to the too large hat and indecently long gown of Virgil's disreputable-looking companions. "Yes, Mr. Foltz. Dhahran called, but we could not fill their request because we had no vacancies. However, we then received a call from ADNOC requesting that you be allowed to use one of their courtesy suites. So you will be in suite 1216–1218. Do you have any luggage?"

"No, just this box; but it contains a delicate instrument, and I want to carry it myself."

The clerk was pushing registration cards toward the three guests. "As you wish, sir. Please fill out these. I will need your passports. You can collect them tomorrow morning. If you need them before then, we can make a special arrangement."

"Tomorrow will be fine," said Virgil grandly. "Incidentally, our helicopter was registering an oil leak as we were landing. I've radioed for a mechanic to come and fix it, but it will have to stay where it is until he's had a look if that's all right."

The room clerk dipped his head in respectful consent.

"You're incredible, Virgil," said Roxanne admiringly as the automatic elevator door whispered shut.

The oilman favored her with an inebriated grin. "Maybe it's a trade-off for ruining my liver. It helps to have a prince behind you, though. Old Talal bin Talal gave orders for no one to interfere with me doing what he asked me to do or to ask any questions. So you said you wanted the Hilton; I radioed Dhahran and said I wanted the Hilton; and I just figured it was a sure thing that we'd got the Hilton."

"But for how long?" said Carl wearily. "Are we going to be able to get a little sleep before the police come?"

In the lobby, the young, blond man with lavender-blue eyes

approached the reception desk and displayed an identification card bearing the seal of the U.S. Department of State to the careful scrutiny of the clerk. "I would like to see the passports of the two Americans that just went upstairs," he said with abnormal slowness.

"All three were Americans, sir," replied the clerk primly as he reached beneath the desk for the passports.

David Storm looked carefully through the small blue booklets. "This one is invalid. It has had the photograph removed. I will have to take it with me to our embassy. Would you please tell me what room Mr. Webster is in?"

"Suite 1216–1218. Would you like me to ring him up?"

"That won't be necessary," said Storm.

A minute later, Meredith Orchard entered the lobby and walked up to the registration desk. "May I help you, sir?" asked the clerk.

Merrie pulled a neat leather card case out of the breast pocket of his tropical suit and opened it to reveal official-looking credentials. "Yes. Would you kindly tell me which room the individuals who just arrived in the helicopter are in?"

The Pakistani examined the card and looked up dubiously. "You're with the *British* embassy, sir?"

"That is correct."

The clerk frowned. "Would you like me to ring them up for you?"

"No, the room number will do."

"As you wish, sir. They are in suite 1216–1218."

"Thank you very much indeed."

As the Englishman strode off toward the elevators, the clerk picked up a telephone and punched the number of the twelfth-floor suite.

Burning from mouth to gut with a huge libation of Seven Heaven he had concocted from the Seven-Up in the suite's lavishly stocked minibar and his own replenished flask to celebrate their safe arrival, Virgil scarcely felt his feet touch the floor as he padded in his socks to the foyer to answer a timid knock on the door. He opened the door wide and gazed with drunken detachment upon a trim blond man with striking blue eyes and a gun pointed at his stomach.

"Oh shit," he said resignedly, raising his hands over his head. "You shoot me, and it's gonna spoil the whole week."

"Where's Carl Webster?" The blond man drew out the question in agonizing fashion. Virgil jerked his head back toward his left shoulder to indicate the sitting room behind him. "Turn around and walk inside slowly." Virgil did as instructed. David Storm stepped into the foyer and reached for the open door to close it.

Suddenly, a telephone rang inside the sitting room. For an instant both men froze. Then Storm agilely darted around the oilman and into the two-story room, where he pulled up short, poised on spread, flexed legs with both hands holding the gun before him. "Don't!" he ordered sharply. Roxanne's hand halted an inch from the ringing instrument. She looked at the intruder in astonishment.

"David!? What are you doing here?"

"Where's Webster?" The gun's aim remained steadily on Roxanne's midsection as his eyes carefully swept the room. He beckoned Virgil toward the phone table with his head. "Over with her." The Oklahoman complied. Storm lifted his gaze to the mezzanine level of the suite, where a heavily mirrored bed area overlooked the sitting room. Bathroom noises were audible coming from the short, dark hall at the top of the free-standing staircase. "Up there?" The telephone stopped ringing.

"What are you doing, David?," said Roxanne desperately. "We're here to stop GULFSCENE III! You don't know what's going to happen!"

The muffled flush of a toilet was heard, drawing all eyes upward. There was the sound of a door opening, and a triangle of wall in the hallway lit up. Storm swung his gun toward it.

"Carl, stop!"

The loud crack of a gunshot punctuated Roxanne's scream. David Storm spun in a half circle, dropping his weapon, and collapsed on the floor.

In from the foyer walked Merrie Orchard with a smoking revolver gripped tightly in his hand. "The door was open. I hope you don't mind." He looked at his fallen victim. A bloodstain was spreading rapidly on the back of his thigh. "I'm afraid I hit an artery," he observed with concern.

"Who are you?" asked Roxanne. Carl was gaping over the mezzanine railing.

"Meredith Orchard, chartered accountant. I hope I've shot the right person." There was worry in his voice. "You are here about the Paks in the palace, aren't you?"

David Storm writhed in pain and reached for his wounded leg. In a lightning quick burst of movement, Roxanne dove across the room to a couch, rolled along it in a lithe, twisting motion as she grabbed for her gun, and came to rest sitting on the floor firing. Three shots smashed into David Storm's body just as he raised the pistol he had pulled from his ankle holster to firing position. By the time Merrie spun around, the life was gone from the lavender-blue eyes.

"I forgot for a moment about his ankle holster," said Roxanne, trembling. The red-checked *ghutra* had slid from her long black hair. Everyone looked at the dead body. "He was the only man I ever wanted to marry," she added in a choking voice.

"You folks ain't fixin' to stay here now, are you?" slurred Virgil, who had sagged into a chair, flask in hand.

"Best not," said Merrie officiously. "Let's be off. I have a car. I do hope this is about the Paks. It doesn't do to shoot the wrong people."

Roxanne kept staring at the body with a stunned look on her face.

"It's the Paks," confirmed Carl.

"You're CIA?" queried Merrie doubtfully.

"No. You shot the CIA. They don't know about the Paks. We're the only ones who know what's happening, and they're trying to stop us by mistake."

"You foze ain' fizzin' ta stay," interrupted Virgil from a semi-stupor.

"He's right. Let's go." Merrie started for the door.

"Grab the TNT," called Carl, descending the stairs. "I don't think Virge is up to carrying it." Merrie stopped and looked around. Carl pointed. "That crate over there: full of TNT. It's the only equipment we've got." He pulled Roxanne to her feet from the couch without resistance. Virgil miraculously made it up on his own.

The parade through the plush lobby drew an audience of stares, the onlookers' expressions ranging from amusement to disgust. The impeccably attired Englishman incongruously carrying a wooden crate on his shoulder was immediately followed by a tall, reeling drunk; three steps behind came a woman, wearing a disgracefully long man's *thob*, on the arm of a badly limping man in his undershirt.

At the reception desk the Pakistani clerk picked up the telephone and punched the number of the American consulate. His eyes followed the motley procession contemptuously as the instrument buzzed in his ear.

"Hello? Is this the American Consulate? This is the reception desk at the Abu Dhabi Hilton. An American guest is just leaving the hotel. He checked in with a mutilated passport, which your Mr. Storm said was invalid when he picked it up. I thought I should inform you that he is leaving. What's that? Storm. He works for you. He took the passport up with him in the elevator and has not come down." The clerk consulted the register. "The guest's name is Carl Webster. Yes, I can wait." The mismatched quartet was still visible through the lobby window crowding themselves awkwardly into a small, Japanese car. "Hello? Yes, the Hilton. This is Mr. Khan at reception. No, Mr. Webster is just now driving off. Would you wait one second, please?" A porter had sprinted out of an elevator and was chattering breathlessly in Urdu in the clerk's face. An ashen look came over Mr. Khan's features. "Hello, Consulate? It seems that your Mr. Storm has been shot to death. That's correct. Storm. In Mr. Webster's suite. Yes, I'll hold."

Carol Oakes's mother's philosophy was that a house full of company is a house full of friendship. Removing the fresh sheets from the linen cupboard for the Filipino houseboy to make up the two guest rooms, Carol caustically reappraised the homily in her mind. Merrie Orchard was an absolute sweetie and a terrifically attractive flirt at a cocktail party, but asking Sarge to put him up with three friends on the spur of the moment at ten at night was outrageous.

She herself would not have stayed in an old hotel like the Khalidiya Palace, and she was surprised that Merrie had chosen the place himself; but regardless of the shortage of hotel space in Abu Dhabi, it was simply scandalous for a first-class establishment to be unable to find other places for people to sleep. It was just like Merrie, of course, to volunteer to impose on friends as a favor to the hotel management, but Carol didn't see why, if it was the hotel's faulty plumbing that had forced their guests out of their rooms, the management itself didn't put the poor souls up in their own homes.

She had expressed her opinion in blunt terms to Sarge and instructed him to raise a complaint with the emir. Life was hard enough in Abu Dhabi without this. They had had to shut off the tape of *The Last Tango in Paris* before they got to the X-rated parts.

"Have they eaten?" she shouted.

Her spouse's voice came back faintly from the living room where he was tidying up. "Merrie didn't say. But it's ten o'clock. They must have."

The door chime announced the uninvited guests' arrival. Carol palpated her fresh hairdo in a mirror before going to the door.

"Merrie!" she exclaimed delightedly, accepting his very un-English embrace and enthusiastic kiss on the cheek. "Come in. These are your friends. You poor dears. How awful to be flooded out of your rooms. I'm Carol Oakes. We're delighted to have you."

The visitors ate everything the houseboy could find in the kitchen. The tall one named Virgil single-handedly downed two bottles of white wine. During intermissions between rounds of small talk, Carol looked daggers at her perplexed husband. The light-haired man from Cambridge was really very engaging, despite the fact that the shirt he had had to borrow from Merrie was too small for him and pulled open at the buttons. He even knew people at Harvard whom Carol and Sarge knew. But the man with the pot-belly was an obvious lush, and Mrs. Webster looked as though her best friend had just died and was barely civil.

On the other side of the table, ravenously toothpicking Vienna sausages into her mouth one after another, Roxanne was struck by the unparalleled vapidness and altogether otherworldly character of the conversation.

The enigmatic Merrie Orchard was continuing to prove himself a person of amazing resource. Burdened with three unpresentable and exhausted strangers, he had managed, in scarcely half an hour, to ditch the Datsun, steal a roomy Pontiac, check out of his hotel room in the Khalidiya Palace, and make sleeping arrangements that were sure to keep them all safe until the next day. All in the enthusiastic hope that they were here "to see about the Paks." And now he was cooly chattering away about West Indian banking laws and their notorious loopholes as if he really were a chartered accountant.

Carl, on the other hand, had continued to be a taciturn, negative, dispirited drag on the entire operation until the moment he stepped into the Oakes's house, at which point he brightened like a morning glory in sunshine and began to spout an unending stream of tedious Cambridge and Harvard anecdotes, to the obvious delight of the banker's horse-faced spouse.

At least Virgil had run true to form and fallen asleep in his chair after two bottles of wine.

Roxanne listened to the conversation as if it were in an unknown tongue while complex memories of Qorban Ali and David Storm passed feverishly through her mind. She felt herself beginning to seethe with anger. Less than thirty-six hours to disarm a hidden army and stop an atomic bomb, she thought, and the only people who can do it are talking about sailboat racing.

Sober, or comparatively so, Virgil looked at the morning sunshine and his three strange companions with equal pain. Carol Oakes, after a husbandly twist of the arm, had cordially insisted that they all stay and enjoy the swimming pool while they waited for the hotel to call them about their rooms and their luggage. Then she had departed to lay before her friends her tale of Sarge's spineless submission to Meredith Orchard's outrageous requests. The houseboy was left to service the needs of the guests.

What Virgil heard, as the bright light reflecting from the blue pool penetrated directly into what he thought of as his hangover-headache—gland hidden just behind his eyes, was unbelievable. It reminded him of his uncle Chester, who had lived out his last years as a demented paranoid in a nuthouse. In a quiet, overrefined British voice, the man who had walked in from the hotel corridor and shot the other man without asking questions explained that he was an accountant and also a freelance spy working for several governments, but of late devoting all his intentions to tracing what he surmised was a Pakistani conspiracy to seize control of the Gulf.

Then, instead of laughing in his face, the guy with the bad foot claimed that the Pakistani conspiracy was actually something that he himself had invented, and that he had been *kidnapped* to Islamabad to *help*—Virgil wasn't sure he heard right—carry it out. But the plan had gone wrong and had to be stopped. And that was what he had escaped in a Russian MiG from Afghanistan to do.

And finally, the thin woman, who looked a hell of a lot more fetching in Carol Oakes's lavender bikini than in a Russian uniform or an Arab nightgown, claimed that she was really a professional killer trained by the CIA, but that she was actually working *against* the CIA right at the moment because the CIA didn't know what was going on.

Virgil skipped his own turn at show-and-tell in favor of swigging a second Bloody Mary delivered by the Filipino houseboy. He shut his eyes and felt his body bake. Half his attention paid to the lunatics was more than their due.

Merrie was drawing a sketch map with a felt-tip pen on the white enamel surface of a round metal patio table. "This is the palace on the north side of the spit aligned east and west. I've been inside twice in the last three weeks, but I haven't found any trace of the operations center you're talking about. But it must be there because the Pakistani Special Services Group guard contingent is there. When you watch them, they look as busy as fieldmice planting their trees; but after a bit you catch on to what they're really doing. My guess is that this entire fence line is lined with mines and booby traps, and probably the roadsides, as well. That means that if we're going to get in, it's got to be from the water. At least, that's how I've done it myself.

The guard is spread thin. I think they don't have more than twenty men altogether. It's not hard to time their patrol through a starlight scope and swim in."

"So who has a starlight scope?" asked Carl.

"I do," replied the Englishman. "The problem, actually, isn't so much getting into the palace as doing something once you're there. It must have two hundred rooms."

"But they must have transmitting and receiving equipment someplace if they're going to broadcast their ultimatum throughout the Gulf and coordinate the commando teams," observed Roxanne, examining the sketch. "Don't you know the plan, Carl?"

"Not the minor details. My guess, though, would be that you should be able to spot the right part of the palace by looking for an aerial antenna. They have to have one if they expect to be heard from Kuwait to Masqat and receive replies from the operations groups."

"There isn't one," responded Merrie decisively. "I've scanned the roofline a hundred times. There's nothing there. And there's no place else on the spit for one to be."

Carl looked at his watch. "They're on the air in twenty-three hours. They'd better build one quick."

The three fell silent as each surveyed the sketch for an answer to the problem. Virgil downed the last of the Bloody Mary and felt a familiar buzz in the head begin to quell its ache. "I think I'll mosey on over to ADNOC this afternoon and telephone Dhahran. Would that be disrupting you fellas' spy stuff too much? I just been thinkin' that tomorrow's a holiday for the end of Ramadan, and I might get Billie to fly over here and join me. Have a toot before I get fired. Nobody's gonna do nothing back in ol' Dhahran except go to the mosque. Can't say as I care whether I ever see a minaret again for the rest of my life."

Carl sat bolt upright in his chair looking as though an ice cube had been slipped into his bathing suit.

"Incredible!" The other two looked at him quizzically. "Merrie, have you left something out of your sketch?"

The Englishman looked at the tabletop and shook his head slowly.

"Where will the emir and the palace workers pray?"

He looked at the tabletop again. "My God, you're right. I forgot a little mosque right here beyond the west wing. It's finished already."

"Does it have a minaret?"

"Of course . . . Aha! I think I see what you mean. The aerial could be run up inside the minaret—"

"—and only extended the last few feet to become visible when they're ready to go," said Carl finishing the thought.

The three scrutinized the tabletop again. The silence of the passing seconds betrayed a rising feeling of excitement.

Virgil broke the tension from his lounger several feet away. "Why dontcha blow the fuckin' minaret up?" he said laconically. There was no response. He leaned his buzzing head to one side and looked toward the table. The three plotters were staring at him pointedly.

"Can you do it with what you've got in that crate?" asked Carl.

"Beats me. Show me what the minaret looks like, and I'll tell you."

27
ABU DHABI:
THE FIRST WEEK IN JUNE

A plan finally in mind, the necessary looting of the Oakes home was accomplished in minutes. Roxanne and Carl selected the darkest shirts and trousers from Carol and Sarge's bulging closets. Virgil filled the holstered flask under his shirt with cognac. And Merrie uncovered the spare keys to his friend's car and boat in a dresser drawer. Meanwhile, oblivious to the ransacking of the bedrooms, the houseboy scowled bad-temperedly at his sandwich makings as he prepared a picnic hamper to Merrie's order.

At three they drove to the parking lot of the Abu Dhabi Investment Authority and exchanged the Pontiac for the banker's Mercedes. Then it was on to the deserted dhow building yard by the water. Rocking gently on the light waves next to Sarge's modest motorboat was a thirty-foot sailing vessel with a low, rakish cabin. There was no one about under the hundred-degree-plus afternoon sun to see a dinghy heavily loaded with four people, a large wooden crate, a picnic hamper, and a black suitcase row out to the sailboat and not row back.

Carl's and Roxanne's heads almost touched at the point where the bunks in the sweltering forward compartment of the cabin angled together to fit the curvature of the bow.

"Roxanne?" said Carl.

"Hmm?"

"I want to apologize."

"Okay."

"I mean for not believing we could do this. I still don't think we can, but I wanted to tell you that I admire you for persevering." There was no response. "Are you mad at me?"

Roxanne sighed. "No. It's just that you're hard to be with. Every time you do something right or come up with a good idea, you want a medal; and the rest of the time you either sulk or play games. You're not really very grown up, Carl."

Carl listened to the water lapping at the hull and thought. "None of us is very grown up, Roxanne. Virge thinks getting drunk is patriotic. You kill people during tantrums. This guy Merrie seems to imagine he's a real-live James Bond. And I have my games." He looked along the opposite bunk at Roxanne's thin body and thought that the bikini gave her a look of preadolescence. "I don't think real adults would ever get mixed up in this kind of business."

Roxanne thought of Qorban Ali and the brothers. "Only by necessity; not by choice."

"Will you go back to Afghanistan if you get out of this?"

There was a silence; then an answer. "No."

Carl smiled. Enough for now, he thought. He shut his eyes and gave himself up to the humid heat and the gentle movement of the boat. He tried to visualize the three men he expected to find waiting for them in the mosque across the water.

Silence reigned in the main cabin. Merrie lovingly cleaned and caressed the five handguns he had brought with him in a custom-built suitcase from Bahrain, at great expense in the form of a bribe to customs. Binoculars, a starlight scope, two cameras, and a metal kit filled with assorted spy equipment were neatly laid out on the table next to a tomato and cucumber sandwich. He had hoped that as a man with technical training, Virgil Foltz might be interested in the various features of the expensive weapons; but the oil engineer had turned surly and uncommunicative immediately upon agreeing to accompany the expedition.

Drenched with perspiration, Virgil tried to concentrate on calibrating radio detonators and attaching them to twelve amorphous lumps of TNT, but his mind kept turning to thoughts of his wife and son. He cursed the sobriety that he blamed for his incomprehensible acceptance of the three lunatics' scheme. If they were right, they were all going to get killed; and if they were wrong, he couldn't imagine a more heinous crime in Abu Dhabi than blowing up the emir's personal minaret.

"I've got a son in college," he said. "I hope my insurance covers this and leaves him with something besides a stainless-steel still to remember his dad by."

Merrie stifled an old, familiar feeling of emptiness inside and buffed vigorously at a fingerprint smudge on his Walther. Then he opened a small plastic cosmetic jar and carefully began to smear the shiny parts of the guns with a matte black pigment.

By ten-thirty it was dark. Overhead lights came on in the boatyard, and workers began to clamber over the wooden skeletons of dhow hulls. Hammering and sawing sounds carried over the water of the inlet to the sailboat.

Through a small porthole Merrie scanned the sandy access road beyond Sarge's conspicuous Mercedes, which he had parked in its usual place.

"Nothing."

"Let's go do it, then," said Roxanne grimly.

The motorboat bobbed on the dark water a hundred meters off the beach behind the administrative palace while Merrie struggled to keep his starlight scope steady enough to observe the patrol route of the guards. To his amazement he saw that a barrier of what looked like either concertina wire or razor ribbon had been unrolled since nightfall along the beach edge behind the west wing and the mosque. A two-man patrol passed behind it and repassed twenty minutes later. The square concrete minaret, set a slight distance apart from the small, domed mosque, presented a black silhouette against a lambent, moon-lit sky.

Whispering in the dark, almost invisible to one another in

black clothing and makeup, they reconsidered the plan. Originally Virgil was to have made directly for the base of the minaret while Roxanne fanned diagonally right to cover the eastern approach and Merrie left to cover the western extremity of the promontory. With his limited mobility, Carl was to have protected the boat and stayed ready for an emergency retreat. But now it was apparent that even getting onto the beach would be a challenge.

"I don't think there's any way to cross the wire without tripping an alarm," hissed Roxanne. "That means instead of twenty minutes between patrols, we only have as long as we can hold them off while Virgil does the job. When we cross the wire, Virgil runs like hell and tries to make the minaret before they can get lights on us. We draw fire as long as we can and hope it's long enough." No one spoke. "Any of you see any other way to do it?"

The implicit elimination of the possibility of escaping passed simultaneously through the three men's minds. Nothing could be heard but the lapping of the water and the distant cry of a night-fishing bird.

"How shall we cross the wire?" Merrie Orchard's refined voice was a model of composure.

"Tip the boat over on top of it sideways," replied Roxanne with authority. "Virgil runs over, and the three of us stay on the sand behind it and use it for cover."

Sober as a judge, Virgil hefted Merrie's custom-fitted suitcase, now full of primed explosive charges. He had studied the minaret from a distance through binoculars and estimated that he could plant the devices in less than ten minutes. He wondered now if he would even have five.

Carl and Merrie quietly dipped their paddles into the water and set the boat in motion. There was nothing more for anyone to say.

Minutes later, with a sandy scrape, the boat's keel fixed itself in shallow water five meters from the wire barrier. As the four shadowy figures slid out into the water on either side, it floated free, and they guided it forward until it scraped again. They paused momentarily to get a firm grip on the gunwales and then surged forward together, skidding it through the shallows with them.

At the coil of barbed wire they stopped. The recurrent cry of the distant bird seeking its prey was all they could hear. The four gathered on the water side of the boat and readied themselves. Everything expendable had been discarded in the water, but the boat was still heavy with the outboard motor, their last thin thread of hope for escape, which no one had dared to cut. They heaved together, and the boat went up and over.

In two steps Virgil's long legs carried him over the makeshift bridge and away into the dark. Somewhere they could hear a bell ringing. Then from the west wing to their right, the yellow beam of a searchlight flashed on and began to pick its way along the line of the wire.

"It's out of range," whispered Merrie, crouched behind the boat. The light crept silently closer. Roxanne nudged the Englishman and pointed toward the gap between the palace and the mosque on the side opposite the minaret. Shadowy figures were moving in the spot indicated. She held up four fingers.

Suddenly Merrie leaped to his feet. He hurtled across the boat and dashed to his right along the inside of the wire toward the oncoming stream of light. For a moment he was visible, a dark running figure against the yellow, and then he was through it and into the dark beyond.

A single shot rang out from between the buildings that Roxanne had pointed to, quickly followed by a short burst of machine gun fire. The beam of the searchlight reversed its direction and tracked back rapidly in an effort to find the target.

Roxanne had kept her eyes away from the mesmerizing light and retained enough night vision to see three running figures silhouetted against the light marble of the palace's west wing. She tracked them in her aim. There was another gunshot, and a glance to the side showed the search beam halted on a distant spot of sand with a black human shape horizontal in its center. Then she opened fire and at the same time heard a series of shots from Merrie. The searchlight blinked out, and the darkness seemed deeper than before.

"Virgil's planted two," whispered Carl in Roxanne's ear, the starlight scope held to his eyes. "It should take another five minutes."

Roxanne's first shots had halted the movement toward Merrie's position. For a long interval no shots were fired. Then movement began again. She counted the shadows on the beach before her. There were six in a widely dispersed pattern moving toward her. She heard the report of Merrie's gun. It sounded nearer than before. Carl swung the starlight scope down the beach.

"He's coming back."

The Pakistanis had seen the running form as well, and fresh machine-gun firing erupted from the gap between the buildings. Roxanne squeezed off two more rounds at the nearest human targets. With a resounding clatter Merrie collided with the boat and slid across it and onto the sand behind.

"You okay?" asked Roxanne between two more shots.

"Cut my leg on that bloody wire, but otherwise all right. How are we doing?"

With hollow-sounding thuds two bullets struck the fiberglass side of the boat. Roxanne and Merrie fired back simultaneously.

"They're being cautious," said Roxanne softly. "They've figured out we're a small group so they won't use flares or grenades. They don't want to get the U.A.E. army down here."

"The Paks on service with the army should be able to keep that from happening," whispered Carl. He put the scope to his eyes and looked toward the minaret. "Virgil's halfway around. He's between the minaret and the mosque now."

The oil engineer was perspiring heavily, his long frame wedged into the three-foot space separating the minaret from the mosque. He was feeling about in a rough, square hole in the concrete for a place to affix the TNT. His fingers came in contact with a thick cable, and then another. Suddenly it dawned on him in the pitch blackness that he had stumbled upon the connection point between the aerial in the minaret and the transmitter in the mosque.

"Hot damn!" he whispered excitedly. "After this one we can call it a day." It took only seconds for him to wedge the malleable explosive firmly among the cables. He gave a thought to the six charges still in the suitcase at his feet. The hell with it, he said to himself. He picked up the case and pushed it as far as he could into the hole. It went over an edge and dropped. Virgil's heart stopped, waiting for an explosion. Instead, after a moment's delay, there was the dull thud of a landing on soft sand. His heart started again.

The occasional gunshots that had reached his ears while he was feverishly concentrating on mining the base of the tall structure had sounded remote and irrelevant. But as he peered from his narrow passage in the direction of his only escape route, a massive wave of fear hit him. He could see a semicircle of widely spaced shadows slowly advancing on the large dark shadow of the motorboat. A dash through the closing net to the boat was the only way. If he could just get that far, he could trip the detonator and blow the minaret, and they could hope to escape in its aftermath. But his legs refused to take the first step.

He unbuttoned his shirt and reached inside for the flask of cognac. Never die sober, he thought. He unscrewed the top and lifted the chrome-plated container to his lips.

"What's that!?" said Roxanne, startled, as a bright glint of moonlight winked from the base of the minaret.

"He's taking a drink," replied Carl softly.

"But that flask can be seen!"

A single shot rang out from somewhere on the left. The metallic moonglint disappeared. Virgil felt a painful slap on the back as a rifle bullet severed his spine. Then he felt nothing at all.

"They got him," said Carl. Two of the shadows were running toward the minaret.

"But we still have the detonator," said Merrie, taking a shot at one of the shadows.

"We do?" said Roxanne.

"Don't we?" responded the Englishman.

A minute passed. None of them spoke. The shadows were creeping nearer.

"To think we came this close," said Carl dejectedly.

From the dark a clear voice spoke out with a Pakistani intonation. "Would you please surrender. Your friend is dead. You cannot escape. This is Major Hamza Rahim speaking. If you surrender, you will be treated in accordance with military regulations."

28
ABU DHABI:
THE FIRST WEEK IN JUNE

The open space under the modern concrete dome of the mosque was brilliantly lit. Communications consoles and generators were spotted about in a rough circle crisscrossed by sinews of electrical cable. The several Pakistani technicians busily at work paid no attention to the black-clad trio ushered into the room by a four-man guard.

Major Hamza Rahim, still clad in his laborer's garb, prodded the three toward a screened-off corner of the room. On the far side of the partition was a conference table covered with maps and charts. The three men sitting around it stood as the prisoners entered.

"Good evening," said Arch Thornton with the warm cordiality usually reserved for close friends. The CIA official was wearing Pakistani army fatigues without insignia. To either side stood a leathery-faced army officer with waxed mustaches and a trim, slightly younger-looking man in civilian clothes with sunken gray eyes and etched lips. "We've been expecting you. May I introduce my colleagues. This gentleman on my right is Brigadier Faiz of the Army of Pakistan, field commander of Operation Tanzim." He looked at Carl's blacked face. "I'm afraid, Mr. Webster, we couldn't preserve your GULFSCENE III as a code name. And this gentleman on my left is Mr. Andras Kovacs, the man who deserves the credit for devising our little scenario."

"Are you all right, Carl?" asked the man with the gray eyes concernedly.

"The three of us are okay, Uncle Andras, but they killed our friend."

"Your friend was burying dynamite around our antenna. It was a clever idea, but Major Rahim's men have disarmed the charges," said Thornton. He shifted his attention to Roxanne and Merrie, who wore similar looks of dejection and bewilderment. "Miss Samsun, it's a pleasure to meet you at last. I'm Arch Thornton. Since I was responsible for your original entry into the Agency, I want to apologize to you personally for using you as we have. And you must be the remarkable Mr. Orchard. It took us a while to track down who you were after we heard about the unfortunate killing of David Storm. But your friend Captain Aubrey in Manama set us straight. I think you are to be congratulated for carrying out a very daring and almost successful operation. Had it not been for your intervention, Storm would have nipped this party in the bud at the Hilton."

"David . . .?" began Roxanne.

"Security chief for Operation Tanzim. I understand he was a friend of yours. We're all sorry to lose him. He did a splendid job. Without him the details of GULFSCENE III would have surfaced months ago and ruined our entire plan."

"I don't understand," said Roxanne in a weak voice, reflecting a sudden feeling of intense fatigue.

"I think perhaps Mr. Webster does." Thornton lifted a shaggy white eyebrow in Carl's direction. "But let me ask Andras to explain it to you. We have plenty of time. It's still almost ten hours before the ultimatum goes out."

Andras cleared his throat as if beginning a public address. "Carl, I want you to listen to this closely because I'm going to tell you something you don't know about your father." Age had not lessened the vocal resonance that had once enthralled the teenage nephew. "During the war, your father and I belonged to a resistance group in Hungary. I was still in school, and the group was made up of factory workers; but Anton was the leader and he let me in. In 1943 the group made contact with the OSS, and we began to receive American supplies. Arch was liaison with us. For almost a year we were quite effective at industrial sabotage, but then the Nazis discovered us. Everyone was arrested, except for Anton. Even though the war was coming to an end then, we were all condemned to be hanged; and we would have been if there hadn't been a successful raid on the prison by a Communist resistance group.

"After we were freed, we found out that your father had betrayed us to the Nazis in return for a guarantee of safety for himself, and also for you. It was something none of us questioned. There was written evidence to support it. From that day on, until two years after your stepmother and I left Indiana for California, I had no reason whatsoever to believe that your father had not betrayed us. Nothing he said during those years I was living with you carried the slightest weight against the evidence I had seen with my own eyes. When I heard that he had killed himself, I didn't weep a single tear, even though I knew I was largely responsible.

"I want to be very clear and frank about this, Carl, because I have since that time found out that your father was innocent, and that I was wrong. In California, I was located and recruited for the CIA by Arch, who was then organizing an Eastern European network. It was from him that I found out the truth. Anton had been framed by the same Communists who freed us from the Nazi jail because they were already preparing for the war's end and were afraid of his anti-communist leadership potential. The written evidence had been concocted by a Communist who had spent four years posing as a Nazi collaborator for just this kind of purpose.

"Obviously, this isn't the time to tell you how I felt on learning all this and how I feel today about what I did to your father, but maybe after Operation Tanzim is over we can talk it over more comfortably. The point of the story is that that experience taught me a lesson about the effectiveness of moles and of disinformation that I can never forget. And it was the inspiration for thinking up Operation Tanzim."

"Let me interrupt," interjected Thornton. "Our guests may not be interested in all of this family history. What you, Carl, and indeed all three of you, have been doing, from the day this all started until this very moment, is playing a carefully planned role as sources of disinformation for Soviet intelligence. For several years we have suffered from the existence, somewhere in the executive branch of the government—I suspect even in the White House—of a KGB mole who is so highly placed that every major operation planned during my period as Director of Field Operations has been tipped in advance. Whoever this mole is, he works so skillfully that many of my colleagues don't even believe he exists."

"So the only way to deceive him," resumed Andras, "was actually to deceive our own intelligence community. If the Russians could be made to think we regarded GULFSCENE III as a genuine security threat because we actually did regard it as one, and their always trustworthy mole reported as much to them, then it would become impossible for them to penetrate beneath it to discover Operation Tanzim. Arch and I discussed the idea in principle, but it was just a vague speculation until I hit upon the idea of using you, Carl, as our vehicle. You were perfectly placed, and I was confident I understood how you thought and how you would react to suggestions."

"So, Mr. Thornton, when you fed me that suggestion about the Pakistanis and the Indians jointly taking over the Gulf at Morrie Gratz's cocktail party in Cambridge, that was the first step of Operation Tanzim?" The look of professional fascination on Carl's face contrasted sharply with the looks of fatigue and bafflement on Roxanne's and Merrie's.

"Yes, and you played your role perfectly, with a bit of nudging from time to time by Lal Chatterjee and our Pakistani friends," answered Thornton. "In fact, Andras's scenario has worked right down to the letter. There've been some bad moments, of course; and I regret to say that your friend outside is not the only person who has lost his life. But no great project succeeds without some difficulties, and this one is going to succeed, I assure you. By noon tomorrow General Baber will rule the Gulf, the United States will immediately recognize him, and the energy supplies of the Free World will be permanently secure."

"Won't there be an atomic bomb?" asked Roxanne forlornly.

"Oh yes. Part of the Agency's contribution is what I call a minidemonstrator. It's planned to shoot just the way GULF-SCENE III has it. It goes up on a little rocket over the water, where everyone can see it, and pop! Neat and clean, no fall-out."

"Then we've been doing everything for nothing?" she asked in a trembling voice.

"Not at all, my dear. For heaven's sake, there's no need to cry about it. Your escapade from Islamabad to here has put the crowning touch on our Gulf scenario. Whatever the Russians think by this time—and they have to be pretty damn confused—they can't possibly believe that the CIA is actually involved because it wouldn't make any sense for one of its teams operating in Afghanistan to steal a plane and fly to Abu Dhabi if it were. It's thanks to that kind of improvisation that the Russians are going to face a fait accompli tomorrow that they are completely unprepared for. And it's not facetious of me to add that the three of you are going to be regarded as heros when this is all finished." Thornton was smiling like a nursery school teacher explaining to her charges that naptime is more fun than playtime. "You all need rest, though. This will make much more sense in the morning. Major Rahim?" The SSG officer stamped his sandaled feet to attention. "Would you take our guests to the palace?" He turned his face to address Roxanne. "I hope it will be all right if you all spend the night in the same room. I'm afraid we'll still have to keep you under guard, and we can't afford to tie up too many men."

"Before we go, may I ask one question, Mr. Thornton?" said Carl.

"Of course."

"You were right when you guessed that I had figured out what was happening. As soon as you surfaced the only Indian in Islamabad as one of your agents, I knew that the Pakistanis had to be working with the CIA rather than with India. But one point escapes me because what you said about the mole in the White House comes as new information. If the mole is as highly placed as you think he is, it must be a risk even to tell your plans to the president. Does the president, in fact, know what is going to happen tomorrow?"

Thornton looked aloof and stern. "I'll be frank with you, Mr. Webster. The answer is no. I'm afraid the president cannot be trusted. Only ten key individuals in Washington, men whom I have known for many years, were needed to implement the plan, because our Pakistani friends have done most of the real work. As aggravating as it may seem, our new president is going to get credit he doesn't deserve for a brilliant coup that he doesn't even know about. But that's part of the burden those of us who truly care about the security of our country learn to put up with."

An expression of angry astonishment had exploded like a thunderclap on Roxanne's face. "Only ten people!? You and nine of your male cronies have decided to rearrange the world because you think it's better for America!?"

"Would you take them away, Major," said Thornton coldly.

Strong hands gripped the backs of Roxanne's elbows and steered her around. The four guards herded the prisoners before them like sheep, out of the screened alcove and across the mosque's marble floor with its veins of electrical cable. At the door to the building Andras Kovacs caught up with them and put his hand on Carl's shoulder.

"I want to tell you I'm sorry about your father, Carl." His voice sounded choked.

"Why do you call him my father instead of your brother?" said Carl. "Do you think I can absolve you?" Then he turned to the door being held open by a guard and followed Roxanne and Merrie into the dark.

"I'm so angry at those bloody sods I could kill them with my own hands!" exclaimed Merrie vehemently to his half-awake fellow prisoners. The outburst was his first conversational offering in over three hours.

"A little late for that, isn't it," said Roxanne dully.

"Exactly my point!"

"You didn't make any point." She yawned widely. The wash basin in their basement cell had been put to good use in removing the black from her face.

"The point is," he said orotundly, "that we were brazenly manipulated in that interview in the mosque, and we didn't even realize it. There's a term for the technique that I can't quite remember. It's something like cognitive dissonance, but that's not precisely it. What it is is a technique used to break and subdue prisoners. I learned about it from my wife's lover in Bahrain. After you capture someone, you present him with a version of reality that is so utterly different from what he thought it was, and so utterly convincing, that he becomes psychologically immobilized. He no longer believes he's living in the same world he was living in before he was captured. That's what Thornton did to us, and I've only just now realized it. One moment we were all expecting to die and willing to take as many of them with us as we could, and the next moment, when we were actually within reach of the people we had been trying to stop, we just stood there like zombies because Thornton explained to us that we had been living in the wrong world. So now here we are sitting around doing nothing as if the game were over. I ask you, is there any reason in the world why we should not still be trying to do what we set out to do?"

"Too tired?" ventured Carl from his seat on the edge of a folding cot.

"Seriously."

"Seriously, I suppose not. Aside from the details, nothing is very different from what I had guessed it to be. I scoped out a dozen scenarios like this back in Cambridge, and every one of them produced a better than even chance of a war with Russia. That's why I asked if the president knew. No American president would agree to Thornton's plan. Rationalizing world energy reserves and preventing the Gulf countries from eating each other up or collapsing internally are reasonable national goals, but no one is going to risk a nuclear exchange or a war in Europe over them."

"Why didn't you say that in the mosque?" asked Roxanne angrily. "You both made me feel like a fool for complaining about ten megalomaniacs trying to change the world."

Carl shrugged. "What was the point?"

Merrie consulted his watch. "The sun will be up in about three hours. The chances are that the guards will bring us breakfast before then so we won't profane Ramadan. It seems to me that gives us our only chance. We attack, and if one of us makes it, he or she goes for the mosque."

"Let me lead the way with the guards," said Roxanne with a set jaw. "Men never expect a woman to kill them."

The three lay tensely on their bunks staring at the bare concrete-block walls and listening for footsteps beyond the heavy, locked door. Every few minutes one or another consulted their watch.

"If one of you makes it and I don't," said Merrie softly, "tell my wife that I want her to give fifty thousand dollars to Virgil Foltz's son. Gwendolyn doesn't much care for me, but she'll understand why, and she'll do it. And one more thing. See to it that the newspapers know who I am."

Neither Carl nor Roxanne spoke.

Time passed. Breakfast didn't come.

Outside the palace a bright morning sun rose in a cloudless sky. No light penetrated to the basement room, but each of the prisoners knew the time and privately contemplated the start of the last day of the Ramadan fast.

Carl's watch read 9:32. He looked over at Roxanne gazing fixedly at the ceiling.

"If we had gotten out of this, I was going to ask you to marry me, Roxanne." There was no reply. "They'll have to shoot us eventually, you know. We know too much. The reason they haven't done it already, I suspect, is that they don't want to offend Brigadier Faiz. He's too good a soldier to agree to it."

"Be quiet, Carl," said Roxanne gently.

After a brief silence, Carl spoke again. "Would you have said yes? It may sound a little trite, but I thought maybe we could go someplace together and sort of start over. Lead a nice, nonlethal life."

"Yes, Carl, I would have. Now for Christ's sake shut up!"

In the silence they all heard what sounded like distant footsteps. Like a synchronized team of performers, they raised their wrists and looked at their watches.

Minutes passed. Voices and sounds of activity filtered through the door. More minutes.

At 9:55 they jumped to their feet at the sound of a key in the lock. "This is Major Hamza," came a loud voice from the other side. "We have your breakfast. Would you please stand together on the far side of the room."

In the mosque, Brigadier Faiz took his seat before a microphone attached to a dial-covered communication console. Around the room, operators seated at other consoles prepared to open contact with their assigned commando groups poised for action in the six target countries. The brigadier pressed a button. A small electric motor pushed a cluster of aerial antennae from a metal housing inside the minaret into the bright morning air above.

The door to the cell opened slowly. Facing the three captives was Major Hamza Rahim. Two soldiers were close behind him with automatic rifles raised and pointing into the room. The major stepped through the door and stood beside it. A servant followed him in and placed a large round aluminum tray of food on the floor.

Roxanne gathered her breath and tensed her body to spring. The tiny electronic chime on Carl's watch beeped twice to toll the hour.

In the suddenly quiet mosque Brigadier Faiz switched on the powerful transmitter and spoke into the microphone: "*Allahu akbar!* God is great!"

As if answering to the snap of a hypnotist's fingers, six radio detonators in Virgil Foltz's black suitcase resting on the sandy floor of an inaccessible foundation pit beneath the winding staircase of the minaret awoke at the first pulse of the transmission and ignited a shuddering blast of TNT. The shock wave pulverized the interior walls of the nearly enclosed chamber, while the debris-laden gases exploded through the rough hole that had been made to admit the antenna cables, tearing out the side of the tower.

The muffled, floor-shaking boom and the winking out of the console lights halted Brigadier Faiz in mid-word. In the basement of the palace, the heavy thud of the subsurface concussion froze Roxanne at the point of springing. Major Hamza's watchful eyes flickered but did not look away from his charges.

For seconds the heavy minaret stood still with its base half blown away. Then, slowly, it leaned toward the mosque and fell. The delicately engineered concrete shell of the dome cracked at the first hit, and the minaret continued inexorably through the building to the ground, cutting the small mosque in half through its middle.

The screeching, tearing, crunching sound of the minaret's fall brought a look of awe to the faces of everyone in the basement room of the palace. Through the aftershocks of falling masonry and the patter of small debris a bond of silence united prisoners and guards.

Finally, a woman's voice spoke. "Major Hamza," it said in a subdued tone, "let us help you look for survivors."

29

MOSCOW:
THE FOURTH WEEK IN JUNE

In the bowels of KGB headquarters, a round-shouldered, long-faced man in wire spectacles studied two brief documents on the desk before him. General Maxim Tejirian had ordered one of them and was dissatisfied with it. It was a report on the mysterious incident in Abu Dhabi and the ensuing rumors involving a reputed English superspy named Meredith Orchard.

A chartered accountant, thought the general wearily, how absurd. And we don't know a thing about him. What's this rot about him single-handedly destroying Arch Thornton? Another of Thornton's tricks, I suppose.

The other document was a fresh and startling communication from Ghostwriter. General Tejirian read it for the fiftieth time and still shook his head in amazement.

PRESIDENT DESIRES NEW CIA CHIEF IN WAKE OF DISASTER. HE HAS OFFERED ME THE JOB. SHOULD I ACCEPT?